WITHDRAWN FROM STOCK
DUBLIN CITY PUBLIC LIBRARIES

Remainder

Remainder

Tom McCarthy

W F HOWES LTD

This large print edition published in 2006 by
W F Howes Ltd
Unit 4, Rearsby Business Park, Gaddesby Lane,
Rearsby, Leicester LE7 4YH

1 3 5 7 9 10 8 6 4 2

First published in the United Kingdom in 2006
by Alma Books Limited

Copyright © Tom McCarthy, 2005

The right of Tom McCarthy to be identified as
the author of this work has been asserted by him
in accordance with the Copyright, Designs and
Patents Act, 1988.

All rights reserved

A CIP catalogue record for this book is available
from the British Library

ISBN 1 84632 836 5

Typeset by Palimpsest Book Production Limited,
Grangemouth, Stirlingshire
Printed and bound in Great Britain
by Antony Rowe Ltd, Chippenham, Wilts.

FOR MY PARENTS

CHAPTER 1

About the accident itself I can say very little. Almost nothing. It involved something falling from the sky. Technology. Parts, bits. That's it, really: all I can divulge. Not much, I know.

It's not that I'm being shy. It's just that – well, for one, I don't even remember the event. It's a blank: a white slate, a black hole. I have vague images, half-impressions: of being, or having been – or, more precisely, being *about* to be – hit; blue light; railings; lights of other colours; being held above some kind of tray or bed. But who's to say that these are genuine memories? Who's to say my traumatized mind didn't just make them up, or pull them out from somewhere else, some other slot, and stick them there to plug the gap – the crater – that the accident had blown? Minds are versatile and wily things. Real chancers.

And then there's the Requirement. The Clause. The terms of the Settlement drawn up between my lawyer and the parties, institutions, organizations – let's call them the *bodies* – responsible for what happened to me prohibit me from discussing, in any public or recordable format (I know this bit

1

by heart), the nature and/or details of the incident, on pain of forfeiting all financial reparations made to me, plus any surplus these might have accrued (a good word that, 'accrued') while in my custody – and forfeiting quite possibly, my lawyer told me in a solemn voice, a whole lot more besides. Closing the loop, so to speak.

The Settlement. That word: *Settlement. Set-l-ment.* As I lay abject, supine, tractioned and trussed up, all sorts of tubes and wires pumping one thing into my body and sucking another out, electronic metronomes and bellows making this speed up and that slow down, their beeping and rasping playing me, running through my useless flesh and organs like sea water through a sponge – during the months I spent in hospital, this word planted itself in me and grew. *Settlement.* It wormed its way into my coma: Greg must have talked about it to me when he came round to gawk at what the accident had left. As the no-space of complete oblivion stretched and contracted itself into gritty shapes and scenes in my unconscious head – sports stadiums mainly, running tracks and cricket pitches – over which a commentator's voice was playing, inviting me to commentate along with him, the word entered the commentary: we'd discuss the Settlement, though neither of us knew what it entailed. Weeks later, after I'd emerged from coma, come off the drip-feed and been put onto mushy solids, I'd think of the word's middle bit, the *-l-*, each time

I tried to swallow. The Settlement made me gag before it gagged me: that's for sure.

Later still, during the weeks I sat in bed able to think and talk but not yet to remember anything about myself, the Settlement was held up to me as a future strong enough to counterbalance my no-past, a moment that would make me better, whole, complete. When most of my past had eventually returned, in instalments, like back episodes of some mundane soap opera, but I still couldn't walk, the nurses said the Settlement would put me back on my feet. Marc Daubenay would visit and brief me about our progress towards Settlement while I sat in plaster waiting for my bones to set. After he'd left I'd sit and think of sets – six games in tennis or however many matching cups and plates, the scenery in theatres, patterns. I'd think of remote settlements in ancient times, village outposts crouching beneath hostile skies. I'd think of people – dancers, maybe, or soldiers – crouching, set, waiting for some event to start.

Later, much later, the Settlement came through. I'd been out of hospital for four months, out of physiotherapy for one. I was living on my own on the edge of Brixton, in a one-bedroom flat. I wasn't working. The company I'd been with up until the accident, a market-research outfit, had said they'd give me paid sick leave until May. It was April. I didn't feel like going back to work. I didn't feel like doing anything. I wasn't doing anything. I passed my days in the most routine of activities: getting up and washing, walking to the shops and back again, reading the papers, sitting in my flat. Sometimes I watched TV, but not much; even that seemed too proactive. Occasionally I'd take the tube up to Angel, to Marc Daubenay's office. Mostly I just sat in my flat, doing nothing. I was thirty years old.

On the day the Settlement came through, I did have something to do: I had to go and meet a friend at Heathrow Airport. An old friend. She was flying in from Africa. I was just about to leave my flat when the phone rang. It was Daubenay's secretary. I picked the phone up and her voice said:

'Olanger and Daubenay. Marc Daubenay's office. Putting you through.'

'Sorry?' I said.

'Putting you through,' she said again.

I remember feeling dizzy. Things I don't understand make me feel dizzy. I've learnt to do things slowly since the accident, understanding every move, each part of what I'm doing. I didn't choose to do things like this: it's the only way I can do them. If I don't understand words, I have one of my staff look them up. That day back in April when Daubenay's secretary phoned, I didn't have staff, and anyway they wouldn't have helped in that instance. I didn't know who the *you* was she was putting through – Daubenay or me. A trivial distinction, you might say, but the uncertainty still

4

made me dizzy. I placed my hand against my living-room wall.

Daubenay's voice came on the line after a few seconds:

'Hello?' it said.

'Hello,' I said back.

'It's come through,' said Daubenay.

'Yes, it's me,' I answered. 'That was just your secretary putting us through. Now it's me.'

'Listen,' said Daubenay. His voice was excited; he hadn't taken in what I'd just said. 'Listen: they've capitulated.'

'Who?' I asked.

'Who? Them! The other side. They've caved in.'

'Oh,' I said. I stood there with my hand against the wall. The wall was yellow, I remember.

'They've approached us,' Daubenay continued, 'with a deal whose terms are very strong each way.'

'What are the terms?' I asked.

'For your part,' he told me, 'you can't discuss the accident in any public arena or in any recordable format. To all intents and purposes, you must forget it ever happened.'

'I've already forgotten,' I said. 'I never had any memory of it in the first place.'

This was true, as I mentioned earlier. The last clear memory I have is of being buffeted by wind twenty or so minutes before I was hit.

'They don't care about that,' Daubenay said. 'That's not what they mean. What they mean is that you must accept that, in law, it ceases to be actionable.'

I thought about that for a while until I understood it. Then I asked him:

'How much are they paying me?'

'Eight and a half million,' Daubenay said.

'Pounds?' I asked.

'Pounds,' Daubenay repeated. 'Eight and a half million pounds.'

It took another second or so for me to take in just how much money that was. When I had, I took my hand off the wall and turned suddenly around, towards the window. The movement was so forceful that it pulled the phone wire with it, yanked it right out of the wall. The whole connection came out: the wire, the flat-headed bit that you plug in and the casing of the hole that that plugs into too. It even brought some of the internal wiring that runs through the wall out with it, all dotted and flecked with crumbly, fleshy bits of plaster.

'Hello?' I said.

It was no good: the connection had been cut. I stood there for some time, I don't know how long, holding the dead receiver in my hand and looking down at what the wall had spilt. It looked kind of disgusting, like something that's come out of something.

The horn of a passing car made me snap to. I left my flat and hurried down to a phone box to call Marc Daubenay back. The nearest one was just round the corner, on Coldharbour Lane. As

I crossed my road and walked down the one lying perpendicular to it, I thought about the sum: eight and a half million. I pictured it in my mind, its shape. The eight was perfect, neat: a curved figure infinitely turning back into itself. But then the half. Why had they added the half? It seemed to me so messy, this half: a leftover fragment, a shard of detritus. When my knee-cap had set after being shattered in the accident, one tiny splinter had stayed loose. The doctors hadn't managed to fish it out, so it just floated around beside the ball, redundant, surplus to requirements; sometimes it got jammed between the ball and its socket and messed up the whole joint, locking it, inflaming nerves and muscles. I remember picturing the sum's leftover fraction, the half, as I walked down the street that day, picturing it as the splinter in my knee, and frowning, thinking: *Eight alone would have been better.*

Other than that, I felt neutral. I'd been told the Settlement would put me back together, kick-start my new life, but I didn't feel any different, fundamentally, from when before Marc Daubenay's secretary had phoned. I looked around me at the sky: it was neutral too – a neutral spring day, sunny but not bright, neither cold nor warm. I passed my Fiesta, which was parked half-way down the street, and looked at its dented left rear side. Someone had crashed into me in Peckham and then driven off, a month or so before the accident. I'd meant to get it fixed, but since coming

7

out of hospital it had seemed irrelevant, like most other things, so the bodywork behind its left rear wheel had stayed dented and crinkled.

At the end of the road perpendicular to mine I turned right, crossing the street. Beside me was a house that, ten or so months previously, two months before the accident, the police had swooped on with a firearms team. They'd been looking for someone and had got a tip-off, I suppose. They'd laid siege to this house, cordoning off the road on either side while marksmen stood in bullet-proof vests behind vans and lampposts, pointing rifles at the windows. It was as I passed across the stretch of road they'd made into a no man's land for that short while that I realized that I didn't have Marc Daubenay's number on me.

I stopped right in the middle of the road. There was no traffic. Before heading back towards my flat to get the number I paused for a while, I don't know how long, and stood in what had been the marksmen's sightlines. I turned the palms of my hands outwards, closed my eyes and thought about that memory of just before the accident, being buffeted by wind. Remembering it sent a tingling from the top of my legs to my shoulders and right up into my neck. It lasted for just a moment – but while it did I felt not-neutral. I felt different, intense: both intense and serene at the same time. I remember feeling this way very well: standing there, passive, with my palms turned outwards, feeling intense and serene.

I walked back to my flat, not down the road I'd come up but down one that ran parallel to it. I found the number, then set out again down the first road, the one perpendicular to mine. I passed my car again, its dent. The man who'd crashed into me had gone over Give Way markings, then driven off. Just like the accident itself: the other party's fault each time. I passed through the siege zone again. The man who the police had been looking for hadn't been in the house. When they'd realized this, the marksmen had wandered out from behind their cover and the regular officers had untied and gathered up the yellow-and-black tape they'd tied across the road to demarcate the restricted area. If you'd arrived there minutes later you wouldn't have known anything had happened. But it had. There must have been some kind of record – even if just in the memories of the forty, fifty, sixty passers-by who'd stopped to watch. Everything must leave some kind of mark.

Daubenay and I had been cut off in mid-conversation. When I stuck my fifty pence in the phone in the box and called back, the receptionist answered. I'd met her before, several times. She was smart and formal, in her early thirties, slightly horsey.

'Olanger and Daubenay,' she said. 'Good afternoon.'

I could see in my mind the desk she sat behind, the leather seats that faced it, the glass coffee table.

9

The reception area looked out over a cobbled courtyard, through a low window to her right.

'Could I have Marc Daubenay's office please?' I said.

'Putting you through.'

A silence followed, not the quietness of the office but the type of silence you get when no input's coming down the line. My picture of Olanger and Daubenay faded, ousted by the caged façade of a cab office just beside the phone box. *Movement Cars*, it said; *Airports, Stations, Light, Removals, Any Distance*. A man was wheeling a large Coke vending machine into the doorway, tilting it slowly, taking its weight on his shoulders. I wondered what *Light* meant in this context, and felt a slight wave of that dizziness again. *Airports*, read the writing on the window. My friend Catherine would be arriving at Heathrow in just over an hour. There was a click on the line, then Marc Daubenay's secretary picked up.

'Marc Daubenay's office,' she said.

This woman was older, forty-plus. I'd come across her too, each time I'd visited Marc Daubenay. It was she who'd called me minutes ago. She always looked stern, austere, slightly chastising even. She never smiled. I gave her my name and asked to speak to Daubenay.

'Trying his line now,' she said. 'No, I'm afraid it's busy. He's talking to someone.'

'Yes, he's talking to me,' I said. 'We were talking,

10

and we got cut off. I think he's trying to phone me back.'

'If you hang up I'll tell him to try again.'

'No,' I said, 'that's no good. My phone's come out of the wall. It's broken. We were talking and it broke. I'm sure he's trying to phone me now. Perhaps you could break in and tell him.'

'I'll have to go through,' she said.

I heard her setting the receiver on its side, then footsteps, voices, hers and Daubenay's, in the next room. *He's on your line?* Daubenay was saying. *But his phone's gone dead. I've been trying it for the last ten minutes.* She said something to him that I couldn't make out, then I heard his footsteps coming to the phone in her room, then a rustle as he picked it off the desk.

'You there again?' he said.

'We got cut off,' I told him.

The phone's display window was counting my money down and had already got to thirty-two. Peak rates. I dug into my pockets for more coins but only pulled out two-pence pieces.

'How much did you hear?' Daubenay asked.

'The figure. Could you say it again?'

'Eight and a half million pounds,' Daubenay repeated. 'You understand the terms governing your acceptance of this sum?'

'I can't tell anyone?'

'You can't discuss, in any public or recordable format, the nature and/or details of the incident.'

'I remember you telling me that,' I said.

'You'll lose the whole lot if you do, plus any surplus this might have accrued while in your custody.'

'Accrued, yes,' I said. 'I remember that bit too. And is it legally enforceable?'

'It most certainly is,' he answered. 'Given the status of these parties, these, uh, institutions, these, uh . . .'

'Bodies,' I said.

'. . . bodies,' he continued, 'almost anything's enforceable. I strongly suggest we accept. We'd be crazy not to.'

'What do I have to do?' I asked him.

'Come in tomorrow. They're biking over documents for you to sign. Come at around eleven: they should be here by then.'

The Coke-machine man was wheeling his empty trolley back out of Movement Cars. It was *Light Removals*, not *Light* then *Removals*. It just looked like that, the way they'd laid the words out. The phone's display window was in the teens now. Daubenay was congratulating me.

'What for?' I asked him.

'It's an unprecedented sum,' he said. 'Well done.'

'I didn't earn it,' I said.

'You've suffered,' he replied.

'That's not really the right . . .' I said. 'I mean, I didn't choose to – and in any . . .'

And the phone cut right there, in mid-conversation again.

I walked back to my flat to get more coins. I walked back down the same street parallel to the one perpendicular to mine, then out again along the perpendicular one, as before: past the Fiesta, the ex-siege zone. I put two pound coins in this time. Daubenay seemed surprised to hear me.

'I think we've just about got it wrapped up,' he said. 'Go and have a glass of champagne. See you at eleven tomorrow.'

He hung up. I felt foolish. It hadn't been necessary to call him again. Besides, I needed to get to the airport fast now, eight and a half million or not. As I left the phone box I pictured Catherine's plane somewhere over Europe, bearing down towards the Channel, towards England. I walked back for a third time to my flat, still using the same route, picked up my coat and wallet, and had made it to beside a tyre shop halfway between the siege zone and the phone box when I realized I'd left the piece of paper with the flight number on it in my kitchen.

I turned back again, but stopped immediately as it occurred to me that perhaps I didn't need the information: I could just look at the arrivals board and see which flight was coming from Harare. There wouldn't be more than one at any given time. I turned back out and was about to start walking onwards when it struck me that I didn't know which terminal to go to. I would have to go and get the details after all. But then before I'd taken a single step towards my flat I remembered that they have lists posted up in tube compartments on the Piccadilly Line, telling you which terminal to go to for each airline. I turned round yet again. Two men who'd walked out of a café next to the tyre shop were looking at me. I realized that I was jerking back and forth like paused video images do on low-quality machines. It must have looked strange. I felt self-conscious, embarrassed. I made a decision to go and pick the flight details up after all, but remained standing on the pavement for a few more seconds while I pretended to weigh up several options and then come to an informed decision. I even brought my finger into it, the index finger of my right hand. It was a performance for the two men watching me, to make my movements come across as more authentic.

When I finally broke out of the circuit I'd now covered four or five times, following the same route each time, perpendicular road out and parallel road back, even crossing each road at the same spot, beside the same skip or just after the same manhole cover – when I finally turned left down Coldharbour Lane towards Brixton Tube, it occurred to me that from now on I didn't need to move along the ground at all. I was so rich that I could have ordered up a helicopter, told it to come and land in Ruskin Park, or if it couldn't land then hover just above the rooftops, lower a rope and winch me up into its stomach, like they do when rescuing people from the sea. And yet I kept to the ground, ran my eyes along it like a blind man's fingers reading Braille, concentrating on my passage over it: each footstep, how the knees bend, how to swing my arms. That's the way I've had to do things since the accident: understand them first, then do them.

Later, as I sat inside the tube, I felt the need, like I'd done every time I'd taken the tube up to Angel, to picture the terrain the hurtling car was covering. Not the tunnels and the platforms, but the space, the overground space, London. I remembered being transferred from the first hospital to the second one two months or so after the accident, how awful it had been. I'd been laid flat, and all I'd been able to see was the ambulance's interior, its bars and tubes, a glimpse of sky. I'd felt that I was missing the entire experience: the sight of the ambulance weaving through traffic, cutting onto the wrong side of the road, shooting past lights and islands, that kind of thing. More than that: my failure to get a grip on the space we were traversing had made me nauseous. I'd even thrown up in the ambulance. Riding to Heathrow on the tube, I experienced echoes of the same uneasiness, the same nausea. I kept them at bay by thinking that the rails were linked to wires that linked to boxes and to other wires above the ground that ran along the streets, connecting us to them and my flat to the airport and the phone box to Daubenay's office. I concentrated on these thoughts all the way to Heathrow.

Almost all the way. One strange thing happened. It might seem trivial to you, but not to me. I remember it very clearly. At Green Park I had to change lines. To do this at Green Park you have to ride the escalator almost to street level and then take another escalator down again. Up in the lobby area, beyond the automatic gates, there were some payphones and a large street map. I was so drawn to these – their overview, their promise of connection – that I'd put my ticket into the gates and walked through towards them before I'd realized that I should have gone back down again instead. To make things worse, my ticket didn't come back out. I called a guard over and told him what had happened, and that I needed my ticket back.

'It'll be inside the gate,' he said. 'I'll open it for you.'

He took a key out of his pocket, opened the gate's ticket-collecting flap and picked up the top ticket. He inspected it.

'This ticket's only for as far as this station,' he said.

'That's not mine, then,' I said. 'I bought one for Heathrow.'

'If you were the last person to pass through, your ticket should be the top one.'

'I was the last one through,' I told him. 'No one came past after me. But that's not my ticket.'

'If you were the last one through, then this must be your ticket,' he repeated.

It wasn't my ticket. I started to feel dizzy again.

'Hold on,' the guard said. He reached up into the feeding system on the flap's top half and pulled another ticket out from where it was wedged between two cogs. 'This yours?' he asked.

It was. He gave it back to me, but it had picked up black grease from the cogs when he'd opened the flap, and the grease got on my fingers.

I walked back towards the down escalator, but before I got there I noticed all these escalator steps that were being overhauled. You think of an escalator as one object, a looped, moving bracelet, but in fact it's made of loads of individual, separate steps woven together into one smooth system. Articulated. These ones had been dis-articulated, and were lying messily around a closed-off area of the upper concourse. They looked helpless, like beached fish. I stared at them as I passed them. I was staring at them so intently that I stepped onto the wrong escalator, the up one, and was jolted onto the concourse again. As my hand slipped over the handrail the black grease got onto my sleeve and stained it.

I have, right to this day, a photographically clear memory of standing on the concourse looking at my stained sleeve, at the grease – this messy, irksome matter that had no respect for millions, didn't know its place. My undoing: matter.

CHAPTER 2

After the accident – some time after the accident, after I'd come out of my coma and my memory had come back and my broken bones had set – I had to learn how to move. The part of my brain that controls the motor functions of the right side of my body had been damaged. It had been damaged pretty irreparably, so the physiotherapist had to do something called 'rerouting'.

Rerouting is exactly what it sounds like: finding a new route through the brain for commands to run along. It's sort of like a government compulsorily purchasing land from farmers to run train tracks over after the terrain the old tracks ran through has been flooded or landslid away. The physiotherapist had to route the circuit that transmits commands to limbs and muscles through another patch of brain – an unused, fallow patch, the part that makes you able to play tiddly-winks, listen to chart music, whatever.

To cut and lay the new circuits, what they do is make you visualize things. Simple things, like lifting a carrot to your mouth. For the first week or so they don't give you a carrot, or even make you try to move your hand at all: they just ask you to visualize taking a carrot in your right hand, wrapping your fingers round it and then levering your whole forearm upwards from the elbow until the carrot reaches your mouth. They make you understand how it all works: which tendon does what, how each joint rotates, how angles, upward force and gravity contend with and counter-balance one another. Understanding this, and picturing yourself lifting the carrot to your mouth, again and again and again, cuts circuits through your brain that will eventually allow you to perform the act itself. That's the idea.

But the act itself, when you actually come to try it, turns out to be more complicated than you thought. There are twenty-seven separate manoeuvres involved. You've learnt them, one by one, in the right order, understood how they all work, run through them in your mind, again and again and again, for a whole week – lifted more than a thousand imaginary carrots to your mouth, or one imaginary carrot more than a thousand times, which amounts to the same thing. But then you take a carrot – they bring you a fucking carrot, gnarled, dirty and irregular in ways your imaginary carrot never was, and they stick it in your hands – and you know, you just know as soon as you see the bastard thing that it's not going to work.

'Go for it,' said the physiotherapist. He laid the carrot on my lap, then moved back from me slowly, as though I were a house of cards, and sat down facing me.

Before I could lift it I had to get my hand to it. I swung my palm and fingers upwards from the wrist, but then to bring the whole hand towards where the carrot was I'd have to slide the elbow forwards, pushing from the shoulder, something I hadn't learnt or practised yet. I had no idea how to do it. In the end I grabbed my forearm with my left hand and just yanked it forwards.

'That's cheating,' said the physio, 'but okay. Try to lift the carrot now.'

I closed my fingers round the carrot. It felt – well, it *felt*: that was enough to start short-circuiting the operation. It had texture; it had mass. The whole week I'd been gearing up to lift it, I'd thought of my hand, my fingers, my rerouted brain as active agents, and the carrot as a no-thing – a hollow, a carved space for me to grasp and move. This carrot, though, was more active than me: the way it bumped and wrinkled, how it crawled with grit. It was cold. I grasped it and went into Phase Two, the hoist, but even as I did I felt the surge of active carrot input scrambling the communication between brain and arm, firing off false contractions, locking muscles at the very moment it was vital they relax and expand, twisting fulcral joints the wrong directions. As the carrot rolled, slipped and plummeted away I understood how air traffic controllers must feel in the instant when they know a plane is just about to crash, and that they can do nothing to prevent it.

'First try,' said my physio.

'At least it didn't fall on anyone,' I said.

'Let's go for it again.'

It took another week to get it right. We went back to the blackboard, factoring in the surplus signals we'd not factored in before, then back through visualization, then back to a real carrot again. I hate carrots now. I still can't eat them to this day.

Everything was like this. Everything, each movement: I had to learn them all. I had to understand how they work first, break them down into each constituent part, then execute them. Walking, for example: now that's very complicated. There are seventy-five manoeuvres involved in taking a single step forward, and each manoeuvre has its own command. I had to learn them all, all seventy-five. And if you think *That's not so bad: we all have to learn to walk once; you just had to learn it twice,* you're wrong. Completely wrong. That's just it, see: in the normal run of things you never *learn* to walk like you learn swimming, French or tennis. You just do it without thinking how you do it: you stumble into it, literally. I had to take walking lessons. For three whole weeks my physio wouldn't let me walk without his supervision, in case I picked up bad habits – holding my head wrong, moving my foot before I'd bent my knee, who knows what else. He was like an obsessive trainer, one of those ballet or ice-skating coaches from behind the old iron curtain.

'Toes forward! Forward, damn it!' he'd shout. 'More knee! Lift!' He'd bang his fist against the board, against his diagrams.

Every action is a complex operation, a system, and I had to learn them all. I'd understand them, then I'd emulate them. At first, for the first few months, I did everything very slowly.

'You're learning,' my physio said; 'and besides, your muscles are still plastic.'

'Plastic?'

'Plastic. Rigid. It's the opposite of flaccid. With time they'll go flaccid: malleable, relaxed. Flaccid, good; plastic, bad.'

Eventually I not only learnt to execute most actions but also came up to speed. Almost up to speed – I never got back to one hundred per cent. Maybe ninety. By April I was already almost up to speed, up to my ninety. But I still had to think about each movement I made, had to understand it. No Doing without Understanding: the accident bequeathed me that for ever, an eternal detour.

After I'd been out of hospital for a week or so, I went to the cinema with my friend Greg. We went to the Ritzy to see *Mean Streets* with Robert De Niro. Two things were strange about this. One was watching moving images. My memory had come back to me in moving images, as I mentioned earlier – like a film run in instalments, a soap opera, one five-year episode each week or so. It hadn't been particularly exciting; in fact, it had been quite mundane. I'd lain in bed and watched the episodes as they arrived. I'd had no control over what happened. It could have been another history, another set of actions and events, like when there's been a mix-up and you get the wrong holiday photos back from the chemist's. I wouldn't have known or cared differently, and would have accepted them the same. As I watched *Mean Streets* with Greg I felt no lesser a degree of detachment and indifference, but no greater one either, even though the actions and events had nothing to do with me.

The other thing that struck me as we watched the film was how perfect De Niro was. Every move he made, each gesture was perfect, seamless. Whether it was lighting up a cigarette or opening a fridge door or just walking down the street: he seemed to execute the action perfectly, to live it, to merge with it until he was it and it was him and there was nothing in between. I commented on this to Greg as we walked back to mine.

'But the character's a loser,' Greg said. 'And he messes everything up for all the other characters.'

'That doesn't matter,' I answered. 'He's natural when he does things. Not artificial, like me. He's flaccid. I'm plastic.'

'He's the plastic one, I think you'll find,' said Greg, 'being stamped onto a piece of film and that. I mean, you've got the bit above your eye, but . . .'

'That's not what I mean,' I said. I'd had a small amount of plastic surgery on a scar above my right eye. 'I mean that he's relaxed, malleable. He flows into his movements, even the most basic ones. Opening fridge doors, lighting cigarettes. He doesn't have to think about them, or understand them first. He doesn't have to think about them because he and they are one. Perfect. Real. My movements are all fake. Second-hand.'

'You mean he's cool. All film stars are cool,' said Greg. 'That's what films do to them.'

'It's not about being cool,' I told him. 'It's about just being. De Niro was just being; I can never do that now.'

Greg stopped in the middle of the pavement and turned to face me.

'Do you think you could before?' he asked. 'Do you think I can? Do you think that anyone outside of films lights cigarettes or opens fridge doors like that? Think about it: the lighter doesn't spark first time you flip it, the first wisp of smoke gets in your eye and makes you wince; the fridge door catches and then rattles, milk slops over. It happens to everyone. It's universal: everything fucks up! You're not unusual. You know what you are?'

'No,' I said. 'What?'

'You're just more usual than everyone else.'

I thought about that for a long time afterwards, that conversation. I decided Greg was right. I'd always been inauthentic. Even before the accident, if I'd been walking down the street just like De Niro, smoking a cigarette like him, and even if it had lit first try, I'd still be thinking: *Here I am, walking down the street, smoking a cigarette, like someone in a film.* See? Second-hand. The people in the films aren't thinking that. They're just doing their thing, real, not thinking anything. Recovering from the accident, learning to move and walk, understanding before I could act – all this just made me become even more what I'd always been anyway, added another layer of distance between me and things I did, Greg was right, absolutely right. I wasn't unusual: I was more usual than most.

I set about wondering when in my life I'd been the least artificial, the least second-hand. Not as a child, certainly: that's the worst time. You're always performing, copying other people, things you've seen them do – and copying them badly too. No, I decided it had been in Paris, a year before the accident. That's where I'd met Catherine. She was American, from somewhere outside of Chicago. She worked for a large humanitarian organization, some kind of lobbying outfit. They'd sent her on the same intensive language course my company had sent me on. It strikes me as odd, thinking about it now, that she couldn't have learnt French back in Illinois. Considering they'd lose me in a year, my company were making a bad investment – but they didn't claim to be making it on behalf of starving children.

Anyway, I met Catherine while on that course. We hit it off together straight away. We'd get giggling fits in classes. We'd go out and get drunk in the evenings instead of doing homework. One time we found a rowing boat tied up on the Quai Malaquais embankment, climbed inside, untied it from its moorings and were just about to paddle it away using our hands when some men came along and turfed us out. Another time – well, there were lots of other times. The point is, though, that in Paris hanging out with Catherine I felt less self-conscious than I had at any other period of my life – more natural, more in-the-moment. Inside, not outside – as though we'd penetrated something's skin: the city, perhaps, or maybe life itself. I really felt as though we'd got away with something.

We'd corresponded pretty regularly since then. It had dropped off on my part after the accident, of course, but as soon as I'd got my memory back I'd written to her and brought her up to date. In February, just as I was coming out of hospital, she'd written to tell me that she was being sent to Zimbabwe and would pass through London on the way back. We wrote more frequently after that. Our letters acquired a sexual undertone, something our in-person friendship had never had. I started imagining having sex with her. I developed various fantasy scenarios in which our first seduction might take place, which I'd play, refine, edit and play again.

In one of these scenarios, we were in my flat. We were standing in the hallway between the kitchen and the bedroom, although flashes of Paris and a Chicago which I'd never seen broke in, brasserie windows flanked with skyscrapers and windy canals jostling with the yellow walls. I'd say something witty and suggestive, and Catherine would reply *You'll have to show me* or *Why don't you show me?* or *You're really going to have to show me that,* and then we'd kiss, floating towards my bedroom. In another version, we were somewhere in the country. I'd driven her out in my Fiesta, then drawn up and parked beside a field or wood. I'd have her standing in profile, because she looked better this way, with curly hair half-hiding her cheek. I'd move up close beside her, she'd turn to me, we'd kiss and then we'd end up making love in the Fiesta while treetops full of birds chirped and shrieked in ecstasy.

I never got this second sequence quite down, though, due to the difficulty of manoeuvring us both into the car without bumping our heads or tripping on the belts that always hung out from the doors. And then I'd worry about where I'd parked it, and whether someone might speed round a bend and crash into it like the drive-off guy from Peckham. The other scenario too, the corridor one: as we floated to the bedroom I'd remember there were loads of mouldy coffee cups beside the bed, and that the sheets were old and dirty. If it wasn't that then it was that the neighbours were right outside and I hadn't drawn the curtains and they'd start up a conversation through the windows, or – well, *something* always came along and short-circuited these imaginary seductions, fucked them up. Even my fantasies were plastic, imperfect, unreal.

When Catherine flew into London on the day the Settlement came through, I arrived at the airport just after her flight was due in. I saw from the Arrivals screens that it had landed and I hurried over to the area where the sliding screen doors separate the customs and immigration area from the public terminal. I leant against a rail and watched passengers emerge from these doors. It was interesting. Some of the arriving passengers scanned the waiting faces for relatives, but most weren't being met. These ones came out carrying some kind of regard to show to the assembled crowd, some facial disposition they'd struck up just before the doors slid open for them. They might be trying to look hurried, as though they were urgently needed because they were very important and their businesses couldn't run without them. Or they might look carefree, innocent and happy, as though unaware that fifty or sixty pairs of eyes were focused on them, just on them, if only for two seconds. Which of course they weren't – unaware, I mean. How could you be? The strip between the railings and the doors was like a fashion catwalk, with models acting out different roles, different identities. I leant against the rail, watching this parade: one character after another, all so self-conscious, stylized, false. Other people really were like me; they just didn't know they were. And they didn't have eight and a half million pounds.

After a while I tired of watching all these amateur performances and decided to buy a coffee from a small concession a few feet away. It was a themed Seattle coffee bar where you buy caps, lattes and mochas, not coffees. When you order they say *Heyy!* to you, then they repeat your order aloud, correcting the word *large* into *tall*, *small* into *short*. I ordered a small cappuccino.

'Heyy! Short cap,' the man said. 'Coming up! You have a loyalty card?'

'Loyalty card?' I said.

'Each time you visit us, you get a cup stamped,' he said, handing me a card. It had ten small pictures of coffee cups on it. 'When you've stamped all ten, you get an extra cup for free. And a new card.'

'But I'm not here that often,' I said.

'Oh, we have branches everywhere,' he told me. 'It's the same deal.'

He stamped the first cup and handed me the cappuccino. Just then someone called my name and I turned round. It was Catherine. She'd cleared customs already and had been standing in the coffee bar all the time I'd been watching the sliding doors.

'Heyy!' I said. I went over and hugged her.

'I tried calling you,' said Catherine as we disentangled, 'but your phone's not working.'

'I've just become rich!' I said.

'Well heyy!'

'No, really. Just now, today.'

'How come?' she asked.

'Compensation for my accident.'

'My God! Of course!' She peered into my face. 'You don't look like – oh yes, you've got a scar right there.' She ran the first two fingers of her left hand down the scar above my right eye, the one I'd had plastic surgery on. When they got to the end of the scar's track, they stayed there. She took them away just before they'd been there too long for the gesture to be ambiguous. 'So they've paid up?' she said.

'An enormous amount.'

'How much?'

I hadn't prepared myself for this question. I stuttered for an instant, then said: 'Several – well, after tax and fees and things, a few hundred thousand.'

Maybe a kind of barrier came down between us right then. I felt bad about lying, but I couldn't bring myself to say the whole amount. It just seemed so big, too much to even talk about.

We took the tube back to my flat. We sat beside each other, but her profile wasn't quite as sexy as I'd made it by the field and the parked Fiesta in my fantasy. She had a couple of spots on her cheek. Her dirty and enormous purple backpack kept falling over from between her legs. When we

30

arrived, the phone unit was still lying untwitching on the carpet.

'Wow! Did it get hit by lightning?' she said – then, with a gasp, added: 'Oh! I'm sorry. I mean, I didn't . . . I know it wasn't lightning, but . . .'

'Don't worry,' I said. 'It doesn't . . . I mean, I don't think of it like . . .'

My sentence petered out too, and we stood facing one another in silence. Eventually Catherine asked:

'Can I go take a bath?'

'Sure,' I said. 'I'll run it for you. Would you like tea?'

'Tea!' she said. 'That's so English. Yes, I'd like tea.'

I made tea while she took her bath. I considered whether or not to open the door and take it in to her, but decided not to, set the cup down outside the bathroom and told her through the door that it was there.

'Cool,' she said. *'Qu'est-ce qu'on fait ce soir?'*

What are we doing this evening, she meant. I know she said it in French to try to remind us of our time in Paris, but I didn't feel like answering in French. And I felt slightly miffed about the English quip. Of course tea is English: what did she expect?

'We're meeting my friend Greg,' I said back through the door. 'Near here, in Brixton.'

Greg was my best friend. It was he who'd hooked me up with Daubenay, through an uncle of his.

31

He lived in Vauxhall – maybe still does, who knows. We'd arranged to meet in the Dogstar, a pub at the far end of Coldharbour Lane. He was already there when Catherine and I showed up, buying a pint of lager at the bar.

'Greg, Catherine – Catherine, Greg,' I said.

Greg asked us what we'd have. I said a lager. Catherine took one too, but said she wanted to use the toilet first and asked Greg where it was. Greg told her and then watched her as she walked off. Then he turned to me and asked:

'Friend, or "friend"?'

'F . . .' I began, then told him: 'Greg, the Settlement's come through.'

'Marc Daubenay's swung it?'

'Yes. They're settling out of court.'

'How much?' Greg asked.

I looked around, then lowered my voice to a whisper as I told him:

'More than one million pounds!'

By this point we were walking towards a table and Greg had a pint of lager in each hand. He came to a sudden standstill when I told him this – so quickly that some beer from his two glasses sloshed onto the wooden floor. He turned to face me, let out a whoop and made to hug me before realizing that he couldn't while he was still holding the beers. He turned away again and hurried on towards the table, holding the hug, until he'd set the glasses down. Then he hugged me.

'Well done!' he said.

It felt strange – the whole exchange. I felt we hadn't done it *right*. It would have seemed more genuine if he'd thrown the drinks up in the air and we'd danced a jig together while the golden drops rained slowly down on us, or if we'd been young aristocrats from another era, unimaginably wealthy lords and viscounts, and he'd just said quietly *Good show, old chap* before we moved on to discuss grouse shooting or some scandal at the opera. But this was neither-nor. And beer got on my elbow when I leant it on the table.

Catherine came back.

'Have you heard his news?' Greg asked her.

'Sure have,' she said. 'Like wow! It's so much money!'

'Keep the figure quiet,' I told them both. 'I don't want it to, you know . . . I still haven't . . .'

'Sure,' they both said. Greg picked up his glass and toasted:

'Cheers!' he said. 'To . . . well, to money!'

We clinked glasses. As I took the first sip of my lager I remembered Daubenay telling me I should go and drink a glass of champagne. I turned to Greg and Catherine and said:

'Why don't I buy us a bottle of champagne?'

Neither of them answered straight away. Greg held his hands out in an open gesture, making goldfish motions with his mouth. Catherine looked down at the floor.

'Wow, champagne!' she muttered. 'I guess I'm not acclimatized yet culturally. From Africa, I mean.'

Greg suddenly became all boisterous and cheery and said:

'We've got to! What the hell! Do they do it in here?'

We looked around. The pub wasn't that full. There were scruffy, dreadlocked white guys wearing woolly jumpers, plus a few people in suits, plus this one weird guy sitting on his own without a drink, glaring at everybody else.

'They probably do have champagne if the guys in suits are here,' I said. 'I'll go and ask.'

The barmaid didn't know at first if they had any. She disappeared, then came back and said yes. I didn't have enough cash on me and had to write a cheque.

'I'll bring it over,' she said.

When I came back, Greg was checking the call list on his mobile and Catherine was looking at the ceiling. They both focused on me now.

'It's so incredible!' said Catherine.

'Yeah: well done,' said Greg.

'Marc Daubenay said that too,' I told him. 'I didn't do anything. Just got hit by a falling . . . falling stuff, you know. You're the one who achieved something, getting hold of Daubenay. Greg found my lawyer for me,' I explained to Catherine. 'You know, Greg, I'll have to give you some commission on that, some kind of . . .'

'No! No way!' Greg held his hand up and turned his head away. 'It's all yours. Spend it on yourself. Yeah: what are you going to do with all that money?'

'I don't know,' I told him. 'I haven't thought about it yet. What would you do?'

'I'd . . . well, I'd start an account with a coke dealer,' said Greg. 'I'd tell him: here's my bathtub, fill it with cocaine, then come back in a few days' time and top it up until it's full again, then same again a few days after that. And find me a girl with nice, firm tits to snort it off.'

'Hmm,' I said. I turned to Catherine and asked her: 'What would you do?'

'It's totally your call,' she said, 'but if it were me I'd put money towards a resource fund.'

'Like savings?' I asked.

'No,' she said; 'a resource fund. To help people.'

'Like those benevolent philanthropists from former centuries?' I asked.

'Well, sort of,' she said. 'But it's much more modern now. The idea is that instead of just giving people shit, the first world invests so that Africa can become autonomous, which saves the rich countries the cost of paying out in the future. Like, this fieldwork I've been doing in Zimbabwe: it's all about supplying materials for education, health and housing, stuff like that. When they've got that, they can start moving to a phase where they don't need handouts any more. That Victorian model is self-perpetuating.'

'An eternal supply,' said Greg, 'a magic fountain. And I'd tell him to find another girl with a rock-solid ass so I could snort the coke off that when I'd got tired of snorting it off the first girl's tits.'

'You think I should invest in development in Africa, then, rather than here?' I asked Catherine.

'Why not?' she said. 'It's all connected. All part of the same general, you know, caboodle. Markets are all global; why shouldn't our conscience be?'

'Interesting,' I said. I thought of rails and wires and boxes, all connected. 'But what do they, you know, *do* in Africa?'

'What do they do?' she repeated.

'Yeah,' I said. 'Like, when they're just doing their daily thing. Walking around, at home: stuff like that.'

'Strange question,' she said. 'They do a million different things, like here. Right now, building is very big in Zimbabwe. There's loads of people pulling homes together.'

Just then the barmaid arrived with the champagne bottle and three glasses. She asked me if I wanted her to open it.

'I'll do it,' I said. I wrapped my fingers round the top, trying to penetrate the foil cover with my nails. It was difficult: my nails weren't sharp enough, and the foil was thicker than I'd thought.

'Here, use my keys,' said Greg.

I wrapped my fingers round his set of keys. Catherine and Greg watched me. I moved my hand back to the champagne bottle's top, made an incision in the foil, then pinched the broken flap and started pulling it back, slowly peeling the foil off.

'Shall I help?' Catherine asked.

'No,' I said. 'I can do it.'

'Sure,' she said. 'I didn't mean . . . you know, whatever.'

I peeled the foil right off and was about to start untwisting the wire around the cork when I realized we still had our beers.

'We should knock these off first,' I said.

Greg and I started gulping our pints down.

'Whole villages are getting housing kits,' said Catherine. 'These big, semi-assembled homes, delivered on giant trucks. They just pull them up and hammer them together.'

'And they all slot in just like that?' I asked her. 'Without hitch?'

'They're well-designed,' she said.

Greg set down his beer and burped. 'There's a party this Saturday,' he said. 'David Simpson. You know David Simpson, right?'

I nodded. I knew him vaguely.

'Well, he's just bought a flat on Plato Road, off Acre Lane. Just round the corner from here. He's having a house-warming party Saturday, and you're invited. Both of you.'

'Okay,' I said.

I gulped the last of my beer and started on the wire around the cork. It was a pipe-cleaner wire frame, like the frame beneath those dresses eighteenth-century ladies wore. I had to pinch it between my fingers and twist it. I managed this and started working the cork with my thumbs, but it wouldn't go.

'Let me try,' Greg said.

I handed it to him, but he couldn't do it either.

'You have to . . .' Catherine began, but just then the cork flew out with a bang. It only missed my head by half an inch. It hit a metal light clamped to the ceiling and then fell back to the floor.

'Woah!' said Greg. 'You could have had your accident all over again. If that light had fallen on you, I mean.'

'I suppose so,' I said.

'Do the honours, then,' said Greg.

I poured the champagne and we drank. It wasn't very cold, and it had a weird smell, like cordite. Catherine still had two glasses on the go, the champagne and the beer. She alternated, taking sips from each.

'You could do both,' said Greg.

'I'm sorry?' I said.

'Live like a rock star *and* give to these housing projects in Kenya. It's enough money to do both.'

'Zimbabwe,' Catherine said. 'Yeah but it's not just housing. Housing is a vital aspect, but there's education too. And health.'

'Hey,' Greg said, 'did I tell you about the time I took coke with this rock band? I was with this . . .'

He stopped and looked up. Catherine and I looked up too. Greg had stopped because the weird guy who'd been on his own had shuffled over to beside our table and was glaring at us. We looked back at him. He shifted his gaze from one

38

of us to the other, then on to the table and the champagne bottle, then to nowhere in particular. Eventually he spoke:

'Where does it all go?'

Catherine turned away from him. Greg asked him:

'Where does what all go?'

The weird guy gestured vaguely at the table and the bottle.

'That,' he said.

'We drink it,' Greg answered. 'We have digestive systems.'

The weird guy pondered that, then *tssk*-ed.

'No. I don't mean just that,' he said. 'I mean everything. You people don't think about these things. Give me a glass of that stuff.'

'No,' said Greg.

The weird guy *tssked* again, turned round and walked away. Other people were trickling into the bar. Music started playing.

'Does this champagne smell of cordite to you?' I asked.

'What?' said Greg.

'Cordite,' I said, raising my voice above the music.

'Cordite?' Greg said, raising his voice too. 'What does cordite smell like?'

'This,' I answered.

'I don't think so,' Greg said. 'But look: that time, I was with this friend – well, with this guy I knew – and he played in a band, and . . .'

'What time?' Catherine asked. She'd finished her first glass of champagne and had poured herself another.

'When I took coke with this band,' Greg told her. 'We all went in a van, to an after-gig party. It was somewhere up in Kentish Town, Chalk Farm. There were – hang on . . .' He poured himself another glass as well. 'There were . . .'

'Wait,' I said. 'Say I were to give towards this reserve fund . . .'

'Resource,' Catherine corrected me.

'Yeah, right,' I said. 'Well, could I . . . I mean, how would I fit in?'

'Fit in?' she asked.

'Yes,' I said. 'How am I connected to it all? Do I need to go there? Even if I don't, could I go anyway, and watch?'

'Maybe you could take the virgin with the firmest ass as collateral,' said Greg. 'And then another with the firmest tits as interest on your investment. Then, each time you snort a line off her: *bingo!* instant connection.'

'Why do you need to see it?' Catherine said. 'Isn't just knowing it's happening good enough?'

'No,' I said. 'Well, maybe. But I'd need . . .' I felt a kind of vertigo. I knew what I meant but couldn't say it right. I wanted to feel some connection with these Africans. I tried to picture them putting up houses from her housing kits, or sitting around in schools, or generally doing African things, like maybe riding bicycles or singing. I didn't know: I'd never been to Africa, any more than I – or Greg – had ever taken cocaine. I tried to visualize a grid around the earth, a kind of ribbed wire cage like on the champagne bottle, with lines of latitude and longitude that ran all over, linking one place to another, weaving the whole terrain into one smooth, articulated network, but I lost this image among disjoined escalator parts, the ones I'd seen at Green Park earlier. I wanted to feel genuinely warm towards these Africans, but I couldn't. Not that I felt cold or hostile. I just felt neutral.

'Well, anyhow,' said Catherine. 'That's what I'd do. But that's just me. It all depends on what you feel will give you the greatest, you know . . .'

Her voice trailed off. Greg came back in with his cocaine story. Then they went on to talking about Africa, where Greg had been once, on some safari. This led them back after a while to arguing about what I should do with my new fortune; then they truced up and chatted about Africa again. We went on in this vein for quite some time. The whole damn evening, probably. It went round in cycles, over the same ground again and again. I zoned out after a while. I knew already that I had no desire either to build schools in some country I'd never been to or to live like a rock idol. The Dogstar filled up and the music got louder and louder, so that Catherine and Greg had to shout to make themselves heard. And shout they did. We had another bottle of champagne and three

41

more beers. They ended up quite drunk. I felt stone-cold sober the whole night.

Catherine and I left Greg outside the bar and walked back to my flat. I had to pull the sofa in the living room out into a bed for her. It was fiddly, finicky: you had to hook this bit round that bit while keeping a third bit clear. I hadn't done it before we went out – deliberately, in case the extra bed wouldn't be needed. But it was needed. Catherine had already begun to annoy me. I preferred her absence, her spectre.

CHAPTER 3

The next day I went to see Marc Daubenay. His office was up at Angel, as I mentioned earlier. I rode the tube there, concentrating on the overhead terrain, keeping a grip on it.

Daubenay's subordinates must have been told about the Settlement. The first one, the horsey young receptionist, buzzed me straight through, glancing at me nervously, as though I were contagious. The second, Daubenay's secretary, rose from her desk and opened Daubenay's door as soon as I came into her outer office, holding me all the while with her austere gaze. It really was chastising, that gaze – like the school secretary's when you've been sent to the headmaster's office for doing something bad.

Marc Daubenay rose to his feet and shook me warmly by the hand.

'Congratulations once more!' he said. 'It's a stupendous settlement!'

His face was beaming, wrinkling the skin around his eyes and on his forehead. He must have been in his late fifties, early sixties. He was tall and thin, with white hair swept over his thinning pate. He wore a waistcoat beneath his jacket and a thin-striped shirt and tie beneath that. Very proper. He remained behind his desk as he shook my hand. His desk was quite wide, so I had to kind of lean across it for my hand to reach his, and to concentrate on keeping my balance while the desk's edge prodded my leg. Eventually he sat down and gestured for me to do the same.

'Well!' he said. 'Well!' He leant back in his chair and drew his arms out wide. 'We have a very pleasing resolution to our case.'

'Resolution?' I said.

'Resolution,' he repeated. 'End, completion, finish. You sign these papers and it's all done. The funds will be transferred as soon as they're biked back.'

I thought about this for a while, then said:

'Yes, I suppose it is. For you.'

'What's that?' he asked me.

'A resolution,' I said. 'End.'

Daubenay was flicking through a mass of papers. He pulled several out, turned them around to face me and said:

'Sign this one.'

I signed it.

'And this one,' he said. 'And this, and this. And that one too.'

I signed them all. After he'd gathered them back and straightened them into a stack I asked him:

'Where do all the funds go?'

'Yes, good question. I set up a bank account for

them this morning. In your name, of course. It's just to provide a landing pad for them. A holding tank, as it were. You can close it down and take them all out if you like, or you might choose to keep it open. I've also taken the liberty,' he continued, flicking through his documents again, 'of booking you an appointment with a stock-broker.'

He handed me a dossier. It had gilded ornate writing on it, like the lettering on birthday cakes, spelling out the name Younger and Younger.

'They're the best in the business,' said Daubenay. 'Absolutely independent – yet well-connected at the same time. Ear to the ground, as it were. Matthew Younger will deal with you if you choose to go.'

'Which one is he?' I asked.

'He's the son,' Daubenay answered. 'Father's Peter, but he's semi-retired now. It's been running for three generations.'

'Shouldn't it be Younger and Younger and Younger then?' I asked.

Daubenay thought about this for a moment.

'I suppose it should,' he answered.

'Although when the youngest one comes up he can become the second one, and the father who was the second one can become the first one, and the first one can just drop off the end,' I said. 'It's all about what position they're in. They rotate.'

Marc Daubenay looked at me intently for several seconds. Eventually he answered:

'Yes. I suppose you're right.'

Younger and Younger's office was close to Victoria Station. I took the tube there. As I came up to street level, out onto the concourse in front of the station, rush hour was getting underway. Commuters were streaming past me, heading back down the steps into the tube. I stood there for several minutes trying to work out which way Younger and Younger's office was while hurrying men and women dressed in suits streamed past me. It felt strange. After a while I stopped wondering which way the office was and just stood there, feeling them hurrying, streaming. I remembered standing in the ex-siege zone between the perpendicular and parallel streets by my flat two days earlier. I closed my eyes and turned the palms of my hands outwards again and felt the same tingling, the same mixture of serene and intense. I opened my eyes again but kept my palms turned outwards. It struck me that my posture was like the posture of a beggar, holding his hands out, asking passers-by for change.

The feeling of intensity was growing. It felt very good. I stood there static with my hands out, palms turned upwards, while commuters streamed past me. After a while I decided that I *would* ask them for change. I started murmuring:

'Spare change . . . spare change . . . spare change . . .'

I continued this for several minutes. I didn't follow anyone or make eye contact with them – just stood there gazing vaguely ahead murmuring *spare change* again and again and again. Nobody gave me any, which was fine. I didn't need or want their change: I had eight and a half million pounds. I just wanted to be in that particular space, right then, doing that particular action. It made me feel so serene and intense that I felt almost real.

The office turned out to be slightly to the station's north, facing the gardens of Buckingham Palace. The receptionist here made Olanger and Daubenay's sloanette look like a supermarket checkout girl. She wore a silk cravat tucked into a cream shirt and had perfectly held hair. It never once moved as she lowered her mouth towards the intercom to let Matthew Younger know that I was there or walked into a small kitchen area to make me coffee. Above her, also sculpted into frozen waves, mahogany panels rose up towards high, ornately corniced ceilings.

Matthew Younger came in before she'd finished making me the coffee. He was short, really quite short – but when he shook my hand and said hello his voice boomed and filled up the whole room, billowing out to the mahogany panels, up to the corniced ceiling. It struck me as strange that someone who physically filled so little space could project such a rich sense of presence. He shook my hand heartily – not as cheerfully as Daubenay had, but more assertively, with a firm grip, bringing his transverse carpal ligament into play. Most hand-shakes don't involve the transverse carpal ligament:

47

only the really firm ones. He gestured out of the reception room towards a hallway.

'Let's go upstairs,' he said.

I made towards the hall, but hesitated in the doorway because the receptionist was still preparing the coffee for me.

'Oh, I'll bring it up,' she said.

Matthew Younger and I walked up a wide, carpeted staircase above which hung portraits of men looking rich but slightly ill and into a large room that had one of those long, polished oval tables in it which you see in films, in scenes where they have boardroom meetings. He set a dossier on the table top, slipped off the elastic band keeping it closed, slid a piece of paper from it which I recognized from the heading as coming from Marc Daubenay's office, and began:

'So. Marc Daubenay tells me you've come into rather a large sum of money.'

He looked at me, waiting for me to say something in response. I didn't know what to say, so I just kind of pursed my lips. After a while Younger continued:

'Over the last century the stock market has outperformed cash in every decade apart from the thirties. Far outperformed. As a rule of thumb, you can expect your capital to double over five years. In the current market conditions, you can reduce that figure to three, perhaps even two.'

'How does it work?' I asked him. 'I invest in companies and they let me share in their profits?'

'No,' he said. 'Well, yes, that's a small aspect of it. They give you a dividend. But what really propels your investment upwards is speculation.'

'Speculation?' I repeated. 'What's that?'

'Shares are constantly being bought and sold,' he said. 'The prices aren't fixed: they change depending on what people are prepared to pay for them. When people buy shares, they don't value them by what they actually represent in terms of goods or services: they value them by what they *might* be worth, in an imaginary future.'

'But what if that future comes and they're not worth what people thought they would be?' I asked.

'It never does,' said Matthew Younger. 'By the time one future's there, there's another one being imagined. The collective imagination of all the investors keeps projecting futures, keeping the shares buoyant. Of course, sometimes a particular set of shares stop catching people's imagination, so they fall. It's our job to get you out of a particular one before it falls – and, conversely, to get you into another when it's just about to shoot up.'

'What if everyone stops imagining futures for all of them at the same time?' I asked him.

'Ah!' Younger's eyebrows dipped into a frown, and his voice became quieter, withdrawing from the room back to his small mouth and chest. 'That throws the switch on the whole system, and the market crashes. That's what happened in '29. In theory it could happen again.' He looked sombre

for a moment; then his hearty look came back –
and, with it, his booming voice as he resumed:
'But if no one thinks it will, it won't.'

'And do they think it will?'

'No.'

'Cool,' I said. 'Let's buy some shares.'

Matthew Younger pulled a large catalogue from
his dossier and flipped it open. It was full of charts
and tables, like some kind of tidal almanac.

'With the kind of capital you've got earmarked
for investment,' he said, 'I think we can envisage
cultivating quite a large portfolio.'

'What's a portfolio?' I asked him.

'Oh, that's what we call the spread of your invest-
ments,' he explained. 'It's a bit like playing a
roulette table – with the important distinction that
you win here, whereas in roulette you mostly lose.
But with a roulette table, there are sectors, clusters of numbers you can bet on, then rows, then
colours, odds/evens and so on. The wise roulette
player covers the whole board strategically rather
than staking all his chips on just one number.
Similarly, when playing the stock market you
should cover several fields. There's banking,
manufacturing, telecommunications, oil, pharmaceuticals, technology . . .'

'Technology,' I said. 'I like technology.'

'Good,' Younger said. 'That sector's one we're
very well-disposed towards as well. We could . . .'

'What was the one you mentioned just before
that?' I asked.

'Pharmaceuticals. The big drug companies are always an . . .'

'No: before that.'

'Oil?'

'No: signals, messages, connections.'

'Telecommunications?'

'Yes! Exactly.'

'That's a very promising sector. Mobile telephone penetration is increasing at an almost exponential rate year after year. And then as more types of link-up between phones and internet and hi-fi systems and who knows what else become possible, more imaginary futures open up. You see the principle?'

'Yes,' I said. 'Let's go for those two: telecommunications and technology.'

'Well, we could certainly *weight* your portfolio in that direction,' Younger began – but paused when the perfectly-held-hair receptionist walked in. 'Ah, here's your coffee,' he said.

She was carrying it on a small tray, like the ones stewardesses use in aeroplanes. As she set it down on the polished table I noticed that it was a two-part construction: the cup itself, then, slotted into that, a plastic filter section where the coffee grains themselves were. It made me think of those moon landing modules from the Sixties, the way the segments slot together. There was a saucer too, of course: three parts. The receptionist lowered the whole assemblage gently down onto the table's surface, set a small jar of cream, a bowl

51

of rough-hewn blocks of sugar and a spoon beside it, and then blasted away again with the tray.

'We could certainly look at *weighting* it that way,' Younger continued. 'But my point in putting forward the roulette analogy was that it's best to cover several sectors of the . . .'

'Yes, I understand,' I told him. 'But I want to know where I am. To occupy a particular sector, rather than be everywhere and nowhere, all confused. I want to have a . . . a . . .' I searched for the right word for a long time, and eventually found it: 'position.'

'A position?' he repeated.

'Yes,' I said. 'A position. Telecommunications and technology.'

Now Younger looked flustered.

'While I view both these sectors as most promising ones, I feel that this degree of localization, and especially given the great sum we're proposing to invest, does represent an excessive level of exposure to contingencies. I'd much prefer . . .'

'If you won't do it,' I said, 'I'll go to another stockbroker.'

Younger tensed up. He seemed to shrink even more; his voice shrank into silence while he took in what I'd said. Then he struck up that hearty look once more, took a deep breath and boomed out:

'We can do it. Absolutely. It's your money. I merely advise. I'd advise a degree of diversification – but if you don't want that, then that's perfectly . . .'

'Telecommunications and technology,' I said. As soon as he'd explained how it worked, I'd known exactly what I wanted, instantly. It was my money, not his.

Matthew Younger started flicking through the pages of his almanac. I lifted the filter section off my coffee cup and tried to balance it on the saucer's edge, but it fell off onto the table. I noticed that the water hadn't filtered through completely: black goop was still seeping from the gauze bottom, running out across the table's surface. I dabbed at it with my fingers, trying to stop it reaching the table's edge and dribbling onto my trousers. But diverting it just made the stream run faster, and I ended up getting it on my trousers and my fingers too. It was sticky and black, like tar.

'I do apologize,' Matthew Younger said. He reached into his jacket pocket and pulled out a clean silk handkerchief. I rubbed my fingers with it until the wet stuff had gone dry and gritty; then I handed it back to him and he started talking me through the telecommunications and technology sections of his almanac.

Within half an hour we'd chosen a company that made small chips for computers, two of the major mobile telephone network providers and one handset manufacturer, one terrestrial telephone and cable television company, an aerospace researcher and manufacturer, an outfit that did encryption for the internet, another that made software whose function I didn't really understand, a producer of flat audio speakers, some other software people and another micro thing. I can't remember them all: there were plenty of them. There was a games company, an interactive TV pioneer, a business who make those handheld gadgets that let you know exactly where you are at any given time by bouncing signals into space and back again – more, lots more. By the time I'd left we'd sunk more than eighty per cent of my money into shares. A million we kept in cash and placed in a building society account that Younger helped me fill in the forms for right there. We kept one hundred and fifty thousand in the holding tank account that Marc Daubenay had opened for me that morning.

'I might need cash suddenly,' I said to Matthew Younger as he saw me out of Younger and Younger's premises.

'Of course,' he answered. 'Absolutely. And don't forget that we can sell shares at any time too. Call whenever you need me. Goodbye.'

It was still rush hour. I didn't feel like going back into the tube. Instead, I walked down to the river, slowly, through the back streets of Belgravia. When I got there I walked east, crossed Lambeth Bridge, stepped down onto Albert Embankment, found a bench and sat there for a while looking back out across the Thames.

I thought of the time Catherine and I had got into the boat on the embankment in Paris. It had been morning, a fresh blue one, and the sun had been opening these cracks of light up everywhere across the water – dancing, brilliant slits, opening. Now it was dusk. The city had that closing-ranks look, when it gathers itself up into itself but shuts you out. It was glowing, but it wasn't heating me. As I sat there it occurred to me that I could go and stand on almost any street, any row, any sector, and buy it – buy the shops, the cafés, cinemas, whatever. I could possess them, but I'd still be exterior to them, outside, closed out. This feeling of exclusion coloured the whole city as I watched it darken and glow, closing ranks. The landscape I was looking at seemed lost, dead, a dead landscape.

I didn't want to go back home to Brixton. Catherine was out and about looking at the city too: museums, shopping, stuff like that. I didn't feel like seeing her anyway. I walked along the embankment towards Waterloo, passing the back of St Thomas's Hospital. Beside the large doors for supply deliveries and the caged-off refuse area, the staff parking spaces were marked out. Ambulance drivers were lounging beside their vehicles, smoking. Catering staff were wheeling trolleys around. I'd looked forward to that in hospital: the moment when the trolley comes. The conversation the person pushing it makes with you is banal and instantly forgettable, just like the food, but this is good because it means you can have the same conversation again a few hours later, and again the next day, and the next, and still look forward to it. Everything in hospital runs on a loop. I watched the trolleys clatter round their circuits from the kitchens to the wards' back entrances, the bin bags piling up in the rubbish compound, the ambulance drivers and their vehicles, still between marked lines.

Eventually I crossed the river again and walked up to Soho. On the corner where Frith Street cuts across Old Compton Street at an exact ninety-degree angle I noticed one of those Seattle-theme coffee shops I'd bought that cappuccino in while waiting to meet Catherine at Heathrow. I remembered that I had a loyalty card, and that if I got all ten of its cups stamped then I'd get an extra cup – plus a new card with ten more cups on it. The idea excited me: clocking the counter, going right round through the zero, starting again. I went inside and ordered a cappuccino.

'Heyy! Short cap,' the girl said. It was a girl this time. 'Coming up. You have a . . .'

'Right here,' I said, sliding it across the counter.

She stamped the second cup and handed me my cappuccino. I took it over to a stool beside the window. It was one of those long, tall windows that take up a whole wall. I sat up against it and watched people going by. It must have been around eight o'clock. Media types were leaving offices and club types were heading into bars and restaurants. Some people were wheeling a screen along the street – one of those baroque old folding screens with oriental decorations on it. There'd been screens like that in hospital – without the decoration, of course: just white folding screens they pulled around your bed when they wanted to turn you over or undress you. The people pushing the screen along Old Compton Street were maybe two or three years younger than me, in their middle to late twenties. They must have been taking it to or from one of the production company studios that are dotted around Soho. They looked like television people: they had short, dyed hair and Diesel and Evisu clothes and small, colourful mobiles in their spare hands and back pockets. I wondered if their phones were helping to project an imaginary future for one of the stocks I was buying into, to propel it upwards.

I went and bought another cappuccino, got my card stamped a third time and came back to my window seat. The media types pushing the screen had paused in the middle of the street because they'd bumped into another group of media types who were sitting outside one of the other coffee shops. They were all calling over to one another, walking back and forth between the screen and the second coffee shop, waving, laughing. They reminded me of an ad – not a particular one, but just some ad with beautiful young people in it having fun. The people with the screen in the street now had the same ad in mind as me. I could tell. In their gestures and their movements they acted out the roles of the ad's characters: the way they turned around and walked in one direction while still talking in another, how they threw their heads back when they laughed, the way they let their mobiles casually slip back into their low-slung trouser pockets. Their bodies and faces buzzed with glee, exhilaration – a jubilant awareness that for once, just now, at this particular right-angled intersection, they didn't have to sit in a cinema or living room in front of a TV and watch other beautiful young people laughing and hanging out: they could be the beautiful young people them-selves. See? Just like me: completely second-hand.

I bought a third cap, got the fourth cup on my card stamped and came back to the stool by the window. The media types and their screen had gone. A car alarm went off a few streets away and continued beeping intermittently, at intervals of three or four seconds. Beside my bed in hospital there'd been a monitor and a plastic lung that had beeped and rasped at roughly the same interval. During the lightening of my coma – that's their word for it, 'lightening' – when my mind was still asleep but getting restless and inventing spaces and scenes for me to inhabit, I'd found myself in large sports stadiums, either athletics venues with tracks marked out on clay and asphalt running round them, or else cricket grounds with white crease and boundary lines painted on the grass. There'd been a commentary and I'd had to join in with it, commentate as well. I'd had to speak my commentary to the rhythm of these beeps and rasps or else I'd fade out of the scene. I'd known the situation was a strange one, that I was unconscious and imagining it, but I'd also known that I had to keep the commentary up, to fill the format, or I'd die.

As I sat by my window watching people go by, I wondered which of them was the least formatted, the least unreal. Not me – that was for sure. I was an interloper on this whole scene, a voyeur. There were other people sitting behind windows too, in other coffee shops, mirroring me: interlopers too, all of them. Then there were tourists, shuffling awkwardly along and glancing at the people behind windows. Even lower down the pecking order, I decided. Then there were the clubbers. They were mostly gay – scene gay, with tight jeans and gelled hair and lots of piercings. They were like the media types with the screen: performing – to the onlookers, each other, themselves. They crossed from coffee shop to coffee shop, bar to bar, kissing their friends hello and clocking other men exaggeratedly, their gestures all exaggerated, camp. They all had tans, but fake ones, got on sunbeds in expensive gyms or daubed on from a tin. Theatrical, made up, the lot of them.

I must have been on my sixth cappuccino when I noticed a group of homeless people. They'd been there all the time that I'd been watching, camouflaged against the shop fronts and the dustbins, but I started paying attention to them now, observing them. One of them was sitting wrapped up in a polyester sleeping bag with a dog curled up on his lap. His friends had a spot twenty or so yards up the street – three or four of them. They'd move from their spot intermittently to go and visit him, one at a time, sometimes two; then they'd turn around and head back for their own spot. I watched them intently for a long time. The further-up-the-street people would approach the wrapped-up dog guy with a sense of purpose, as though they had messages for him, important information. They'd impart their messages, then go away; but one of them would come back seven or so minutes later with an update. Sometimes they'd take over from him, filling in his spot while he and his dog sauntered up to theirs.

I started seeing a regularity to the pattern of their movements, the circuits they made between the two spots, who replaced whom, when and in what order. It was complicated, though: each time I thought I'd cracked the sequence, one of them would move out of turn or strike out on a new route. I watched them for a very long time, really concentrating on the pattern.

After a while I started thinking that *these* people, finally, were genuine. That they weren't interlopers. That they really did possess the street, themselves, the moment they were in. I watched them with amazement. I wanted to make contact with them. I decided that I *would* make contact with them After the wrapped-up dog guy had sat back inside his sleeping bag for the fourth time and I could more or less safely predict that none of his friends would come over to him for seven or so more minutes, I got up from my stool, left the coffee shop and walked across the street to where he sat.

His dog saw me coming first. It uncurled and perked up, looking at me all alert and sniffing. Then the wrapped-up guy looked up too. He must have been in his late teens. His skin was delicate, very pale with small red dabs on it where veins had burst beneath the surface. I stood in front of him for a while, looking down. Eventually I asked him:

'Can I talk to you?'

He looked up at me in the same way as his dog had: quizzically, excited and defensive at the same time.

'You a Christian then?' he asked.

'No. No, I'm not a Christian,' I said.

'I don't want no nothing from the Christians,' he said. 'Make you pray before they feed you and all that. Big bunch of fucking hypocrites.' His voice was slow and drawn out, but quite nasal. It reminded me of strung-out rock stars from the Sixties – Bill Wyman, someone like that. I wondered if he was strung out too.

'I'm really not a Christian,' I told him. 'I just want to talk to you. I want to ask you something.'

'What?' he said. His mouth stayed open after he'd pronounced the word.

'I . . .' I began – then realized that I didn't know

exactly what it was I wanted to ask him. I said: 'Can I buy you something to eat?'

'Give us a tenner if you like,' he said.

'No,' I said. 'Let me buy you a meal. I'll buy you a big meal, with wine and everything. What do you say?'

He looked up at me with his mouth still hanging open, thinking. I wasn't a Christian soul-hunter, and he could tell I wasn't police. Then his face sharpened and he asked:

'You ain't no nonce, is you?'

'No,' I said. 'You don't have to do anything. I just want to buy you a meal, and talk to you.'

He scrutinized me for quite a bit longer. Then he closed his mouth, sniffed loudly, smiled and said:

'Alright.'

He stepped out of his sleeping bag, whistled to his friends up the street, signalled to one of them to come and take his place, then slapped his thigh and whistled again more quietly, to his dog this time. We headed off together, out of Soho onto Charing Cross Road, heading north. I took him to a Greek place just by Centre Point. The waitress, an old woman with big glasses, didn't want to let his dog in at first. I handed her a twenty-pound note, told her it would behave itself and asked for a bone for it to gnaw on. We sat down and she brought him a big lamb bone which he chewed beneath the table quietly.

'What would you like?' she asked. She was all smiles now, after the twenty pounds.

I ordered a bottle of expensive white wine and mixed starters and asked for a few minutes to decide on our main course. She nodded, still smiling, and walked off to the kitchen.

'Well!' I said. I leant back in my chair and drew my arms out wide. 'Well!'

My homeless person watched me. He picked up his napkin and fidgeted with it. After a while I asked:

'Where are you from?'

'Luton,' he said. 'I came here two years ago. Two and a half.'

'Why did you leave Luton?' I asked him.

'Family,' he said, still picking at the napkin. 'Dad's an alkie. Beat me up.'

The waitress came back with our wine. My homeless person watched her breasts as she leant over the table to pour it. I watched them too. Her shirt was unbuttoned at the top and she had nice, round breasts. She must have been about his age, eighteen, nineteen. We watched her as she turned and walked away. Eventually I raised my glass.

'Cheers!' I said.

He took his glass and drank from it in large gulps. He gulped down half of it, wiped his sleeve across his mouth, set the glass down and, emboldened by the alcohol already, asked me:

'What do you want to know then?'

'Well,' I said. 'I want to know . . . Well, what I want to know is . . . Okay: when you're sitting on your patch of street, sitting there wrapped up in your

sleeping bag, with your dog curled up in your lap . . .
You're sitting there, and there are people going by
– well, do you . . . What I really want to know . . .'

I stopped. It wasn't coming out right. I took a
deep breath and started again:

'Look,' I told him. 'You know in films, when
people do things – characters, the heroes, like
Robert De Niro, say – when they do things, it's
always perfect. Anything at all. It could be opening
a fridge, or lighting up a – no, say picking up a
napkin, for example. The hero would pick it up,
and give it a simple little flick, and tuck it in his
collar or just fold it on his lap, and then it wouldn't
bother him again for the whole scene. And then
his dialogue will be just perfect too. You see what
I mean? If you or I tried that, it would keep slipping out and falling.'

My homeless person picked his napkin up again.
'You want me to tuck it in my shirt?' he asked.

'No,' I told him. 'That's not the point. The point
is that I wonder, I just wonder, whether you're
aware of this. When you sit on your corner.'

'I don't use no napkins when I eat,' he said.

'No! I mean, that's not what I mean. Forget the
napkin. It was an example. What I mean is, are
you . . . When you do things – talking with your
friends, say, or asking passers-by for money – well,
are you . . .'

'I only ask them cos I can't get any,' he said,
putting down his napkin. 'If I had a job I wouldn't,
would I?'

64

'No, look,' I said, reaching my hand out across the table, 'that's . . .' but my hand hit the wine glass. The glass fell over and the wine sloshed out across the tablecloth. The tablecloth was white; the wine stained it deep red. The waiter came back over. He was . . . She was young, with large dark glasses, an Italian woman. Large breasts. Small.

'What do you want to know?' my homeless person asked.

'I want to know . . .' I started, but the waiter leant across me as he took the tablecloth away. She took the table away too. There wasn't any table. The truth is, I've been making all this up – the stuff about the homeless person. He existed all right, sitting camouflaged against the shop fronts and the dustbins – but I didn't go across to him. I watched him and his friends, their circuits down to his spot and back up to theirs again, their sense of purpose, their air of carrying important messages to one another. They swaggered territorially, spitting on the pavement, swinging their shoulders as they changed direction even more exaggeratedly than the media types before them, not even bothering to look round as they crossed the road to see if cars or bikes were coming. They had a point to prove: that they were one with the street; that they and only they spoke its true language; that they really *owned* the space around them. Crap: total crap. They didn't even come from London. Luton, Glasgow, anywhere, but somewhere else, far away, irrelevant. And then their swaggering, their arrogance: a cover. Usurpers. Frauds.

I didn't go and talk to him. I didn't want to, didn't have a thing to learn from him. Besides, I hate dogs, always have.

CHAPTER 4

A couple of days later, on Saturday, I went to David Simpson's party. His new flat on Plato Road was on the second floor of a converted house. It was about a hundred years old, I suppose. Not a bad space. He hadn't done it up yet: there were wires dangling from the ceilings and lines sketched out in pencil on the walls showing where shelves were going to go up, plus little diagrams scrawled beside switches showing the routes electric circuits were to follow. There were boxes everywhere too, full of clothes and books and plates.

'Oh! Hello!' David said as he opened the door to me. 'I heard you were . . . you know, better.' His eyes were scanning my forehead just above my eyes; Greg must have told him about the plastic surgery on the scar.

'It's over the right one,' I said.

'Oh, right,' he answered. 'I hadn't . . . Here, let me get you a drink.'

He'd made some kind of punch. It was pink and sweet – perhaps sangria. There were bottles of beer too, and wine. I sipped at the pink punch and moved into the main room. My name was called out: it was Greg.

'Hey dude!' Greg said as he threw his arm around me. He was already pretty drunk. 'Where's Catherine?'

'In Oxford,' I told him. She'd gone there for the weekend. She bored me enormously now. Everybody bored me. Everything too. I'd spent the days since my meeting with Matthew Younger pondering what to do with the money. I'd run through all the options: world travel, setting up a business of my own, founding a charitable trust, splurging it all. None of them appealed to me in the least. What kind of charitable trust would I have founded? I didn't feel strongly about any issues. If I went out on a mad spending spree, what would I buy? I wasn't interested in art, or clothes, or drugs. The champagne I'd had the other day had tasted acrid, like cordite, and then I'd only bought it because Marc Daubenay had told me I should; I'd tried *foie gras* once, in Paris: it had made me sick. No: I'd picked up all the options, held each one like a child holding a cheap and crappy toy for a few seconds until, realizing that it's not going to spin, make music or in any way enchant him, he puts it down again. So I was bored – by people, ideas, the world: everything.

Greg lurched off to the kitchen to get more drink. I sat down on a sofa and looked around. It seemed a pretty boring party. I didn't know many of the people there and wasn't very interested in the ones I did know. David worked in PR or marketing or something like that; he bored me and his friends were boring too. I went and stood beside the window, two or so feet to its right. I stayed there for a while, then moved into the kitchen and topped up my glass. I'd hardly touched it, but it was something to do. I moved back to the main room and met Greg again.

'Hey dude!' he said, throwing the same arm round me. 'So where's Catherine?' He was slightly drunker than he'd been a quarter of an hour ago.

'She's in Oxford,' I said.

He lurched off again and I moved back to the sofa, then to the spot beside the window. This second spot was a better one. I'd become good at sensing which are good positions and which aren't when I'd been in hospital. It's because you can't move for yourself. In normal life, where you can move, you take being able to change your position for granted; you don't even think about it. But when you're injured and immobile, you have to go exactly where the doctors and nurses put you. Where they put you becomes terribly important – your position in relation to the windows, the doors, the TV set. The ward I spent most time in when I'd come out of intensive care was L-shaped. I was on the short side of the L, the foot, just inset from the corner where the long side hit it. It was a good spot: it had commanding views down both of the ward's avenues, clear sightlines to the nurses' enclave and the trolley station and the other little pockets of importance, crinkles in the flow of the ward's surfaces. In the ward after that I had a really bad spot, in a bed facing the wrong way, facing nowhere in particular, just wrong. Position has been important to me ever since. It's not just hospital: it's the accident as well. I was hit because I was standing where I was and not somewhere else – standing on grass, exposed, just like a counter on a roulette table's green velvet grid, on a single number, waiting . . .

I went back to the kitchen to top my glass up again, but realized that its level hadn't sunk at all since the last time I'd filled it, so I just stood in the doorway while two girls beside the punch bowl looked at me.

'You looking for something?' one of them asked me.

'Yes,' I said. 'I'm looking for a . . . for a thing.' I made a kind of twiddling motion with my fingers, a gesture somewhere between opening a bottle with a corkscrew and using a pair of scissors. Then I left the kitchen again.

I was heading down the hallway back towards the main room when I noticed a small room set off the circuit I'd been following up to now. I'd moved round the kitchen each time in a clockwise direction, and round the main room in an anticlockwise one, door-sofa-window-door. With the short, narrow corridor between the two rooms, my circuit had the pattern of an eight. This extra room seemed to have just popped up beside it like the half had in my settlement: off-set, an extra. I stuck my head inside. It was a bathroom. I stepped in and locked the door behind me. Then it happened: the event that, the accident aside, was the most significant of my whole life.

It happened like this. I was standing in the bathroom with the door locked behind me. I'd used the toilet and was washing my hands in the sink, looking away from the mirror above it – because I don't like mirrors generally – at this crack that ran down the wall. David Simpson, or perhaps the last owner, had stripped the walls, so there was only plaster on them, plus some daubs of different types of paint where David had been experimenting to see how the room would look in various colours. I was standing by the sink looking at this crack in the plaster when I had a sudden sense of déjà vu.

The sense of déjà vu was very strong. I'd been in a space like this before, a place just like this, looking at the crack, a crack that had jutted and meandered in the same way as the one beside the mirror. There'd been that same crack, and a bathtub also, and a window directly above the taps just like there was in this room – only the window had been slightly bigger and the taps older, different. Out of the window there'd been roofs with cats on them. Red roofs, black cats. It had been high up, much higher than I was now: the fifth or sixth or maybe even seventh floor of an old tenement-style building, a large block. People had been packed into the building: neighbours beneath me and around me and on the floor above. The smell of liver cooking in a pan had been wafting to me from the floor below – the sound too, the spit and sizzle.

I remembered all this very clearly. There'd been liver cooking on the floor below – the smell, the spit and sizzle – and then two floors below that there'd been piano music. Not recorded music playing on a CD or the radio, but real, live music, being played on a piano by the man who lived there, a musician. I remembered how it had sounded, its rhythms. Sometimes he'd paused, whenever he'd hit a wrong note or lost his place. He'd paused and started the passage again, running through it slowly, slowing right down as he approached the bit he'd got wrong. Then he'd played it several times correctly, running through it again, speeding it up again till he was able to play it back at speed without fluffing it up. I remembered all this clearly – crystal-clear, as clear as in a vision.

I remembered it all, but I couldn't remember *where* I'd been in this place, this flat, this bathroom. Or when. At first I thought I was remembering a flat in Paris. Not the one I'd stayed in when I did my course – that hadn't looked anything like the one unfolding in my memory, inside or outside: there'd been no cats on roofs, no liver and no piano music, no similar bathroom with an identical crack on the wall – but perhaps someone else's: Catherine's, or someone we'd both known, another student. But we hadn't visited any of the other students' places. No: it wasn't Paris. I searched back further in my past, right back to when I'd been a child. No use. I couldn't place this memory at all.

And yet it was growing, minute by minute as I stood there in the bathroom, this remembered building, spreading outwards from the crack. The neighbour who'd cooked liver on the floor below me had been an old woman. I'd passed her on the stairs most days. I had a memory of passing her outside her flat's door as she placed her rubbish on the landing. She'd say something to me; I'd say something back, then carry on past her. She'd been putting out her rubbish for the concierge to pick up. The building that I was remembering had had a concierge, just like Parisian apartment buildings have. The staircase had had iron banisters and worn marble or fake marble floors with patterns in them. I remembered what it had been like to walk across them: how my shoes had sounded on their surface, what the banisters had felt like to the touch. I remembered how it had felt inside my apartment, moving through it: from the bathroom with the crack in its wall to the kitchen and living room, the way plants hanging in baskets from the ceiling had rustled as I'd passed them, how I'd turned half sideways as I'd passed the kitchen unit's waist-high edge – turned sideways and then deftly back again in one continuous movement, letting my shirt brush the woodwork. I remembered how all this had felt.

Most of all I remembered this: that inside this remembered building, in the rooms and on the staircase, in the lobby and the large courtyard between it and the building facing with the red roofs with black cats on them – that in these spaces, all my movements had been fluent and unforced. Not awkward, acquired, second-hand, but natural. Opening my fridge's door, lighting a cigarette, even lifting a carrot to my mouth: these gestures had been seamless, perfect. I'd merged with them, run through them and let them run through me until there'd been no space between us. They'd been *real*; I'd been real – *been* without first understanding how to try to be: cut out the detour. I remembered this with all the force of an epiphany, a revelation.

Right then I knew exactly what I wanted to do with my money. I wanted to reconstruct that space and enter it so that I could feel real again. I wanted to; I had to; I would. Nothing else mattered. I stood there staring at the crack. It all came down to that: the way it ran down the wall, the texture of the plaster all around it, the patches of colour to its right. That's what had sparked the whole thing off. I had to get it down somehow – exactly, how it forked and jagged. Someone was knocking at the door.

'Hang on!' I called out.

'Hurry up!' a man's voice shouted back.

I looked around. Beside the bathtub were two paint cans; lying on one of their lids were a tape measure and a pencil. I picked up the pencil, tore off a strip of paper that was still clinging to the wall beneath the window and started copying the way the crack ran. I copied it really carefully. Meticulously. The knocking came again: two sets of knocks this time.

'We're bursting out here!' a girl's voice called through.

'Yeah: hurry up!' the same man's voice repeated.

I ignored them and carried on copying the crack. I had to start again two times – the first because I'd made the scale too big to fit the whole crack in, then once more when I realized that the flip side of the wallpaper was smoother than the bubbly side which I'd been drawing on, and so would make for a more accurate transcription. I copied it, meticulously, noting in brackets aspects such as texture and colour. After I'd finished copying the crack I stood there for a few more moments, letting the whole vision settle down inside me: bathroom, flat, staircase, building, courtyard, roofs and cats. I needed it to settle deep enough for it to stay. I closed my eyes for a few seconds, to see if I could see it in my mind, in darkness. I could. When I was satisfied of that I opened them again and left the bathroom.

'I'm bursting!' the girl told me again. It was one of the two girls who'd been in the kitchen earlier. She pushed past me into the bathroom.

'You been giving birth in there?' the man who'd told me to hurry up asked.

'I'm sorry?' I said.

'Giving birth. Is that what took you so long?'

'No,' I said. I took my coat and walked out of the party with my strip of wallpaper.

I walked down to the main Brixton intersection, where the giant box junction spreads across the tarmac from the town hall to the Ritzy cinema. It must have been midnight or so. Brixton was alive and kicking. There were red and yellow sports cars gridlocked on Coldharbour Lane, black guys in baseball caps touting for cab firms, younger black guys in big puffy jackets pushing cannabis and crack, black girls with curled and flattened hair and big round hips wrapped up in stretchy dresses screeching into mobiles, white girls queuing outside the Dogstar, chewing gum and smoking at the same time. They all came and went – people, lights, colours, noise – on the periphery of my attention. I walked slowly, with the strip of wallpaper, thinking of the room, the flat, the world I'd just remembered.

I was going to recreate it: build it up again and live inside it. I'd work outwards from the crack I'd just transcribed. The plaster round the crack was pinky-grey, all grooved and wrinkled from when it had been smeared on. There'd been a patch of blue paint just above it, to the left (its right), and, one or two feet to the left of that, a patch of yellow. I'd noted this down, but could remember it exactly anyway: left just above it blue then two more feet and yellow. I'd be able to recreate the crack back in my own flat – smear on the plaster and then add the colours; but my bathroom wasn't the right shape. It had to be the same shape and same size as the one David's had made me remember, with the same bathtub with its older, different taps, the same slightly bigger window. And it had to be on the fifth, sixth or seventh floor. I'd need to buy a new flat, one high up.

And then the neighbours. They'd been all packed in around me – below, beside and above. That was a vital part of it. The old woman who cooked liver on the floor below, the pianist two floors below her, running through his fugues and his sonatas, practising – I'd have to make sure they were there too. The concierge as well, and all the other, more anonymous neighbours: I'd have to buy a whole building, and fill it with people who'd behave just as I told them to.

And then the view across! The cats, the black cats on the red roofs of the building facing the back of mine across the courtyard. The roofs had been coated in slate tiles, and had risen and fallen in a particular way. If the building I bought didn't have roofs that looked like that facing the windows of the bathroom and kitchen of my fifth- or sixth- or seventh-floor flat then I'd have to buy the building behind it as well, and have its roofs changed until they looked that way. The building had to be tall enough too – the building behind mine, that is: not just one but two buildings of appropriate size and age would be needed. I thought all this through as I walked along Coldharbour Lane. I thought it through meticulously, still holding the strip of wallpaper.

I could do it all, of course. That was no problem. I had funds. I could not only buy my building and the building behind it, but also hire the staff. I'd need the old lady. She was growing more distinct in my mind: she had white, wiry hair and a blue cardigan. Every day she fried liver in a pan, which spat and sizzled and smelled rich and brown and oily. She'd be stooping down to lower her rubbish bag onto the worn marble or fake-marble landing floor, holding her back with one hand as she did this – and she'd turn to me and speak as I passed by. I couldn't quite remember what she'd say yet, but this didn't matter at this stage.

I'd need the pianist too. He was thirty-eight or so. He was tall and thin and very white, bald on top with fuzzy black hair sprouting at the sides. He was a fairly sad character: pretty lonely, didn't seem to get that many visitors – just children who he'd teach for money. At night he'd compose, slowly and tentatively. In the day he'd practise, pausing when he made mistakes, running over the same passages again and again, slowing right down into the bits that he'd got wrong. The music would waft up just like the smell of the old woman's liver. In the late afternoons you'd get the skill-less grind of his uninterested pupils, hammering out scales and trivial melodies. Sometimes, in the morning, he'd decide the lines that he'd composed the night before were worthless: you'd hear a discordant thump, then a chair scraping, a door slamming, footsteps dying away beneath the stairs.

The intersection by the telephone box from which I'd phoned Marc Daubenay came and went on the periphery of my attention as I thought these things through. There were people spilling out of a blue bar with blackened windows, old Jamaicans barbecuing chicken outside Movement Cars, more young guys pushing drugs. Then it was the tyre shop and café where the men had watched me as I'd jerked back and forth on the same spot in the street after setting out to meet Catherine; then, before the ex-siege zone, the street that ran parallel to the street perpendicular to mine. Then I was home. I sat on the sofa bed Catherine had half-folded away and carried on thinking these things through, holding the strip of wallpaper. Occasionally I'd look at the pattern I'd drawn across it. Mostly I just sat there holding it, letting the world that I'd remembered grow.

And grow it did. I started seeing the courtyard more clearly – the courtyard between my building and the one with undulating roofs with black cats on them. It had a garden in it, but the garden was pretty run-down. I scanned it in my mind, moving from left to right and back again.

'There's a motorbike in it!' I said aloud.

It was true: in a small patch of the courtyard, just outside my building's back door where no grass grew, sat a motorbike. The motorbike was propped up and had some of its lower bolts removed because – of course! It was another neighbour who was working on it. I remembered this man now: the motorbike enthusiast who lived on the first floor. He was in his twenties – quite good-looking, medium-length brown hair. He'd spend his weekends tending to his bike out in the courtyard: stripping bits away and cleaning them, then bolting them back on. Sometimes he'd run the engine for whole twenty-minute stretches, and the pianist would get pissed off: you'd hear his chair scrape back again, his feet pacing around his flat all agitated. This came back to me as I sat on the half-folded-away sofa bed.

I sat there on the sofa bed all night, remembering. Birds started singing outside; then came whirring milk floats, then blue and grey light seeping through the curtains. I remembered a nondescript middle-aged couple who lived on the floor above the motorbike enthusiast, the second floor. No kids. He left each day for work and she stayed in or went shopping or volunteered her time at Oxfam or somewhere like that. Then vaguer neighbours, people you don't really take much notice of. There was the concierge: I could clearly see the cupboard where she kept her brooms and buckets, but she herself didn't come to me – her face, her body. I saw the big staircase's wrought-iron banisters: they had a kind of oxidizing hue, all specked with green. The handrail running above them was made of black wood and had mini-spikes on, little prongs – perhaps for decoration or perhaps to prevent children sliding down them. Then the pattern in the floors: it was a black pattern on white – repetitive, faded. I couldn't quite make it out exactly, but I got the general sense of it, the way it flowed. I let my mind flow over it, floating above it – sinking into it too, being absorbed by it as though by a worn, patterned sponge. I fell asleep into the building, its surfaces, into the sound of liver sizzling and spitting, piano music wafting up the staircase, birds and milk floats, black cats on red roofs.

The next day was Sunday. This annoyed me. I wanted Monday and its open businesses. I'd need estate agents, employment agencies, who knew what else. And then what if my vision of the whole place faded before Monday came? How long would all the details stay lodged in my memory? I decided to safeguard them by sketching them out. I gathered all the unused paper I could find around my flat and started drawing diagrams, plans, layouts of room and floors and corridors. I blutacked each one to my living-room wall as I finished it; sometimes I'd run three or four or five into a big block, a continuous overview. When I'd run out of blank paper, I used the reverse side of letters, bills and legal documents – whatever came to hand.

I sketched my whole remembered flat outward from the crack running down the bathroom wall. The flat was modest but quite spacious. It had wooden floors with rugs covering parts of them. The kitchen was open plan, and ran into the main room. Its window faced the same way as my bathroom's window did: across the courtyard with the garden and the motorbike. The fridge was old, a 1960s model. Above it hung plants – spider plants, in baskets. I sketched the staircase, adding notes and arrows highlighting the banisters' spikes and oxidizing hue, the entrance to the flat of the old woman who cooked liver, the spot where she'd set her rubbish down for the concierge to pick up. I sketched the concierge's cupboard, drawing in the broom, the mop, the Hoover – how they stood together, which way each one leant. The concierge's face still didn't come to me, nor did the words the liver lady spoke to me as I passed her, but I let that lie for now. Whole sections of the building didn't come to me, in fact: stretches of staircase or lobby, the whole third floor landing. I left these vague, unfilled, with just a note in brackets next to inches of blank paper.

In the late afternoon I ordered pizza. While I was waiting for it to arrive, I remembered that Catherine would be arriving back that evening. It was her last evening here before she flew back to America. I transferred my giant, sprawling map from my living-room wall onto the wall of the bedroom, sheet by sheet. She turned up just after I'd eaten the last pizza slice. She looked tired but happy, flushed.

'How was Oxford?' I asked from the kitchen as I put the kettle on. Tea had become the main currency between us, a kind of milky, sickly sub-stitute for actual connection.

'Oxford rocks!' she said. 'It kicks ass! It's so . . . The way the kids, the students, ride their bikes around town. They're so cute. So enrowsed in being students . . .'

'So *what?*' I asked her as I brought the cups into the living room and set them down.

'Engrossed. In cycling around and talking to each other. I was thinking it'd be like great if you could shrink them down and keep them in a tank, like termites. You know those termite kits you get?'

'Yes,' I said. 'Yes I do.' I looked at her with interest and surprise. I thought that what she had just said was funny and intelligent – the first interesting thing she'd said since she'd arrived in London.

'You could go look at it twice a day and go: *Oh*

look! See, that one's studying! That one's riding his bike! And they don't even know you're watching them. It's just so . . .'

She paused there. She was really looking hard for the right word – and I wanted to hear it too, hear what she had to say.

'It's just so . . .' I repeated, slowly, prompting her to find it.

'Cute!' she said again. 'Just being students, doing what students do.'

I thought back to the time I'd been a student. I'd been conscious all the time that other people in the crappy provincial town, the people who weren't students, knew I was a student and expected me to be a certain way. I didn't know how exactly – but I felt this all through the three years I spent there, and this spoiled them. I once went on a demonstration, and the police and onlookers all watched us with a mixture of bemusement and contempt as we shouted out our slogans – and I shouted them out with conviction in time with the other demonstrators just because I knew that everyone was watching and expecting this. I can't even remember what the demonstration was about.

The kettle boiled. 'I'll go and pour it,' I said. I went back to the kitchen. I was pouring the water into the teapot when I realized that Catherine had followed me through. She was all wide-eyed, earnest. She looked at me and said:

'They were just really happy. Really innocent.'

84

I put the kettle down and said: 'Can I ask you a question?' I was looking straight at her.

'Yes,' she said, in a soft voice.

'What's the most intense, clear memory you have? The one you can see even if you close your eyes – really see, clear as in a vision?'

The question didn't seem to surprise her at all. She smiled peacefully, her eyes widened further and she answered:

'It's when I was a child. In Park Ridge, where I grew up, just outside Chicago. There were swings, these swings, on concrete, with a lawn around them. And there was a raised podium, a wooden deck, a few feet to the swings' right. I don't know what it was there for, this podium. Kids jumped on and off it. I did too. I was a kid, of course. But I can see the swings. Playing on them, swinging . . .'

Her voice trailed off. She didn't need to go on. I could see her seeing the swings. Her eyes were really, really wide and really sparkling. She looked beautiful. I felt a stirring in my trousers. Catherine knew. She shuffled over to me, opening herself up, waves opening outwards from her sparkling face. I would have kissed her right there if I hadn't heard a rustle from the bedroom. The evening breeze was tugging through the open window at the pages of my diagrams and sketches, trying to unpick them from the wall. I pushed off from the sideboard, brushed Catherine aside and hurried to my room to close the window.

I stayed in there all night, adding to the sketches, refining them, just staring at them. When morning came, I took Catherine and her big, dirty, purple rucksack down to Movement Cars, and put her in a taxi to the airport. Then I came home, took out the telephone directory and started making calls.

CHAPTER 5

Nazrul Ram Vyas came from a high-caste
family. In India they have a caste system,
with the Untouchables at the bottom and
the Brahmins at the top. Naz was a Brahmin. He
was born and grew up in Manchester, but his
parents came over from Calcutta in the Sixties. His
father was a bookkeeper. His uncle too, apparently.
His grandfather as well. And his father before him
too, I wouldn't be surprised. A long line of scribes,
recorders, clerks, logging transactions and events,
passing on orders and instructions that made new
transactions happen. Facilitators. That made sense:
Naz facilitated everything for me. Made it all
happen. He was like an extra set of limbs – eight
extra sets of limbs, tentacles spreading out in all
directions, coordinating projects, issuing instructions, executing commands. My executor.

Before he came into the picture I had endless
troubles. I don't mean with the practicalities:
without Naz I didn't even manage to get to a
stage where practicalities became an issue. No: I
mean with communicating. Making people
understand my vision, what it was I wanted to

do. As soon as Catherine had left, I started making phone calls, but these got me nowhere. I spoke to three different estate agents. The first two didn't understand what I was saying. They offered to show me flats – really nice flats, ones in converted warehouses beside the Thames, with open plans and mezzanines and spiral staircases and balconies and loading doors and old crane arms and other such unusual features.

'It's not *unusual* features that I'm after,' I tried to explain. 'It's *particular* ones. I want a certain pattern on the staircase – a black pattern on white marble or imitation marble. And I need there to be a courtyard.'

'We can certainly try to accommodate these preferences,' this one said.

'These are not preferences,' I replied. 'These are absolute requirements.'

'We have a lovely property in Wapping,' she went on. 'A split-level three-bedroom flat. It's just come on. I think you'll find . . .'

'And it's not one property I'm after,' I informed her. 'It's the whole lot. There must be certain neighbours, like this old woman who lives below me, and a pianist two floors below her, and . . .'

'This is the property you live in now?' she asked.

The third estate agent I spoke to vaguely got it – at least enough to understand the scale of what I was planning.

'We can't do that,' she said. 'No estate agent can. You need a property developer.'

So I called property developers. These are the people who go and find warehouses beside the Thames in the first place and gut them out, then turn them into open-plan units with mezzanines and spiral staircases and loading doors and old crane arms, and then get estate agents to flog them on to rich people who like that kind of thing. Developers don't usually deal with individual punters, with the purchaser. They deal in bulk, buying up whole complexes of buildings and hulks of disused schools and hospitals, knocking out units by the score.

'You want to buy a building off us?' the man in the head office of one developer said when I'd got through to him. 'Who are you with then?'

'I'm not with anyone,' I said. 'I want you to do a building up for me, in a particular way.'

'We don't do contract work for our competitors,' he said. He had a nasty voice – a cold, cruel voice. I pictured his office: the plywood shelves with files and ledgers full of fiddled numbers, then in the yard outside the workmen in their jeans stained white with sandstone and cement discussing politics or football or whatever it was they were discussing – anything, but not my project. They didn't care.

I phoned Marc Daubenay. He was out of his office when I called; the austere secretary told me he'd be back in half an hour. I used the time to go through what I'd say to him. With him I felt I could explain the whole thing: why I'd had the idea, why I wanted what I wanted. He'd been through the last five months with me. He'd understand.

He didn't, of course. When I eventually spoke to him, it came out garbled, just like it had when I'd imagined trying to explain it to my homeless person. I started going on about the crack in the wall of David Simpson's bathroom, my sense of déjà vu; then I backtracked to how ever since learning to move again I'd felt that all my acts were duplicates, unnatural, acquired. Then walking, eating carrots, the film with De Niro. I could tell from the deep silence at his end each time I paused that he wasn't getting it at all. I cut to the chase and started describing the red roofs with black cats on and the woman who cooked liver and the pianist and the motorbike enthusiast.

'This was a place you lived?' Marc Daubenay asked me.

'Yes,' I said. 'No. I mean, I remember it, but I can't place the memory.'

'Well, as we argued,' Daubenay said, 'your memory was knocked off-kilter by the accident.' He'd emphasized that in his pre-trial papers: how my memory had gone and only slowly returned – in instalments, like a soap opera, although he hadn't used that metaphor.

'Yes,' I said, 'but I don't think this was a straight memory. It was more complex. Maybe it was various things all rolled together: memories, imaginings, films, I don't know. But that bit's not important. What's important is that I remembered it, and it was crystal-clear. Like in . . .'

I hesitated there. I didn't want to use the word 'vision', in case Marc Daubenay got ideas.

'Hello? You still there?'

'Yes,' I said. 'I was saying it was crystal-clear.'

'And now you want to find this place?' he asked.

'Not find it,' I said. 'Make it.'

'Make it?'

'Build it. Have it built. I've been calling estate agents and property developers. None of them understands. I need someone to sort it all out for me. To handle the logistics.'

There was another long, deep silence at Daubenay's end. I pictured his office in my mind: the wide oak desk with the chair parked in front of it, the tomes of old case histories around the walls, the austere secretary in the antechamber, guarding his door. I gripped my phone's receiver harder and frowned in concentration as I thought about the wires connecting me to him, Brixton to Angel. It seemed to work. After a while he said:

'I think you need Time Control.'

'Time control?' I repeated. 'In what sense?'

'Time Control UK. They're a company that sort things out for people. Manage things. Facilitators, as it were. A couple of my clients have used them in the past and sent back glowing reports. They're the leaders in their field. In fact, they *are* their field. Give them a call.'

His voice had the same tone to it as when he'd

told me to drink champagne: kind but stern. Paternalistic. He gave me Time Control's number and wished me good luck.

Time Control UK were based up in Knightsbridge, near where Harrods is. What they did, essentially, was to look after people. Manage things for them, as Daubenay said. Their clients were for the most part busy executives: finance chiefs, CEOs, people like that. The odd film star too, apparently. Time Control ran their diaries for them, planned and logged their meetings and appointments, took and passed on messages, wrote press releases, managed PR. They also ran the more intimate side of their clients' lives: ordering meals and groceries, getting dry-cleaners to come and take their clothes away and bring them back again, calling in plumbers, phoning them up at eight twenty-five to get them showered and croissanted and shunted into the taxi Time Control had booked to take them to the nine-fifteen they'd set up. They'd organize parties, send birthday cards to aunts and nephews, buy tickets for the second day of the Fourth Test if they'd built a window in that afternoon in the knowledge that this particular client was partial to cricket. Their databases must have been incredible: the architecture of them, their fields.

I called Time Control in the late afternoon, almost immediately after I'd got off the phone to Daubenay. A man answered. He sounded relaxed but efficient. I couldn't quite picture their office, but I saw those blue and red Tupperware-type in- and out-trays in it somewhere, like the ones they have in nursery-school classrooms. I imagined it as open-plan, with glass or Pyrex inner walls. The background sound was fluffy rather than clipped, which suggested carpets and not floorboards. The man's voice assured me; I didn't feel the need to run through my explanation. I just said:

'I've been referred to you by my lawyer, Marc Daubenay of Olanger and Daubenay.'

'Oh yes,' the man said, very friendly. Olanger and Daubenay were a well-known firm.

'I need someone to facilitate a large project I have in mind,' I said.

'Wonderful,' the friendly man said. He seemed to understand exactly what I wanted without even asking. 'I'll put you through to Nazrul Vyas, one of our main partners, and you can tell him all about it. Okay?'

'Wonderful,' I said back. It was that word 'facilitate' that did it. Worked the magic. Marc Daubenay's word. As I waited to be put through to Vyas I felt grateful to Daubenay for the first time – not for getting me all that money, but for slotting that word, 'facilitate', onto my tongue.

Vyas sounded young. About my age: late twenties, early thirties. He had a fairly high voice. High and soft, with three layers to it: a Manchester base, an upper layer of southern semi-posh and then, on top of these, like icing on a cake, an Asian lilt. As he spoke his name then my name and then asked how he could help me, he sounded confident, efficient. I couldn't quite picture his office, but I saw his desktop clearly: it was white and very tidy.

'Hello,' I said.

'Hello,' said Nazrul Vyas.

A pause followed, then I went for it:

'I have a large project in mind,' I said, 'and wanted to enlist your help.' 'Enlist' was good. I felt pleased with myself.

'Okay,' said Naz. 'What type of project?'

'I want to buy a building, a particular type of building, and decorate and furnish it in a particular way. I have precise requirements, right down to the smallest detail. I want to hire people to live in it, and perform tasks that I will designate. They need to perform these exactly as I say, and when I ask them to. I shall most probably require the building opposite as well, and most probably need it to be modified. Certain actions must take place at that location too, exactly as and when I shall require them to take place. I need the project to be set up, staffed and coordinated, and I'd like to start as soon as possible.'

'Excellent,' Naz said, straight off. He didn't miss a single beat. I felt a surge inside my chest, a tingling. 'Let's meet,' Naz continued. 'When's convenient for you?'

'In an hour?' I said.

'One hour from now is fine,' Naz answered. 'Shall I come to you or would you like to come here?'

I thought about this for a moment. I had my diagrams at home, still stuck to the wall of the bedroom, but I didn't want to show these to him, or give him the back story with the party and the bathroom and the crack – let alone the carrots and the fridge doors. It was all working so well this way. I wanted it to carry on like this, neutral and clear. The image came to me of bubbly, transparent water, large clean surfaces and lots of light.

'In a restaurant,' I said. 'A modern restaurant with large windows and a lot of light. Can you arrange this?'

Within five minutes he'd phoned back to tell me that he'd booked a table for us in a place called the Blueprint Café.

'It's the restaurant of the Design Museum,' Naz explained. 'At Butler's Wharf, beside Tower Bridge. Shall I send you a car?'

'No,' I said. 'See you in an hour. What do you look like?'

'I'm Asian,' said Naz. 'I'll be wearing a blue shirt.'

I took a hurried bath, put on some clean, smart clothes and was just walking out of the flat when my phone rang. I'd already turned the answering machine on. It kicked in and I waited in the doorway to see who it would be.

It was Greg. 'You dude,' his voice said. 'Pity you left early Saturday. The party got, like, *todally awesome.*' He said this last word in a mock Californian accent, a Valley Girl voice. 'You boned

Catherine yet? Maybe you're boning her right now. You're pumping her and she's saying *Oh yes! Give me schools and hospitals! Give me wooden houses!*'

He went on like this for a while. I stood there listening to his voice coming through the answering machine's tinny speaker, simulating an orgasm. Before the accident I would have found this really funny. Now I didn't. It's not that I found it offensive or crass; I didn't find it anything at all. I stood there watching the answering machine while Greg's voice came from it. Eventually he hung up and I left.

It was just as well that Naz had told me what he would be wearing: there was another young Asian guy in the Blueprint Café. I'd have known which one was Naz, though, after all. He looked just like I'd imagined him to look but slightly different, which I'd thought he would in any case. He was sitting at a table by the window, keying something into a palmtop organizer. He had an interesting face. For the most part it was frank and open – but his eyes were dark: dark, sunk and intense. He rose to greet me, we shook hands and then we sat down.

'No problems getting here?' he asked.

'No, none at all,' I said. The Blueprint Café's walls were hung with photographs of eminent British designers. This was good, very good. A waiter appeared and Naz asked for a large bottle of mineral water.

'Shall we eat?' he asked me.

I wasn't particularly hungry. 'What do you think?' I asked him back.

'Something light,' he replied.

We ordered kedgeree and two small bowls of fish soup. No wine. The waiter walked away towards the kitchen, which was visible behind a large round window. It was designed that way – not totally open, so diners could see every last thing the chefs were doing, but open enough to give them glimpses of the kitchen: blue flames jumping out of frying pans, fingers raining herbs down over dishes, things like that.

'Before we begin realizing your project,' Naz said, 'we need to get a sense of scale. What size of building do you have in mind?'

'A big one,' I said. 'Six or seven floors. Have you ever been to Paris?'

'I was there two weeks ago,' said Naz.

'Well, the way buildings are there,' I told him. 'Large tenement buildings, with lots of flats stacked on top of one another. That's the type of building I need. My flat must be on the top floor but one.'

'And the building opposite? If I remember rightly, you indicated that you'd probably need that building too.'

'That's right,' I said. 'It should be almost the same height. Perhaps one floor lower. When I say 'opposite' I mean facing at the back. Across a courtyard. I need that building for two things only: red tiles on its roofs and black cats walking over this.'

'Roofs plural?' he asked.

'They go up and down,' I told him. 'Rise and fall. In a particular way. We might have to modify them. We'll certainly need to modify lots of things throughout the building and the courtyard.'

'Yes, so you told me,' Naz said. 'But tell me about the people you propose to fill the building with. The primary building, I mean. Will they be actually living there?'

'Well, yes,' I answered. 'They can actually live there too. They'll have to get used to being in two modes, though: *on* and *off*.'

'How do you mean?' asked Naz.

'Well, *on* when they're performing the tasks I'll ask them to perform. The rest of the time they can do what they want. Like soldiers: they're on parade at one moment, then afterwards they go and smoke their cigarettes in the guardroom, and have baths and maybe change into civilian clothes. But then a few hours later they have to be back on parade again.'

The waiter came. Naz's palmtop organizer was lying in front of him. It was a Psion – one of the companies Matthew Younger and I had bought stocks in. It was lying face up on the table, but Naz wasn't using it. Instead, he was logging my requirements in his mind, translating them into manoeuvres to be executed. I could tell: something was whirring back behind his eyes. For some reason I thought of scarab beetles, then of the word 'scion'. The thing behind Naz's eyes whirred for a while, then he asked:

'What tasks would you like them to perform?'

'There'll be an old woman downstairs, immediately below me,' I said. 'Her main duty will be to cook liver. Constantly. Her kitchen must face outwards to the courtyard, the back courtyard onto which my own kitchen and bathroom will face too. The smell of liver must waft upwards. She'll also be required to deposit a bin bag outside her door as I descend the staircase, and to exchange certain words with me which I'll work out and assign to her.'

'Understood,' said Naz. 'Who next?'

'There'll also be – what does the word 'scion' mean?'

'I don't know,' Naz said. 'Let's find out. I'll contact a colleague and tell him to look it up.'

He took a tiny mobile from his pocket, switched it on and composed a text message. The phone beeped as he typed each letter in. He laid the phone down on the table top and let it send its message. I pictured his office again: the blue and red Tupperware in- and out-trays, the glass inner walls, the carpets. I traced a triangle in my mind up from our restaurant table to the satellite in space that would receive the signal, then back down to Time Control's office where the satellite would bounce it. I remembered being buffeted by wind, the last full memory I have before the accident.

'There'll also be,' I went on, 'on the floor below this old lady, a pianist.'

'So who else lives on her floor?' Naz asked.

'No one,' I said. 'No one specific, I mean. Just anonymous, vague neighbours.'

'These vague neighbours: they don't have to be on parade? On, I mean? They can be off the whole time?'

'No,' I said. 'All the . . . performers – no, not performers: that's not the right word . . . the partic-ipants, the . . . staff . . . must be . . . I mean, we'll need complete . . . jurisdiction over all the space.'

'But go on,' Naz said. 'Sorry I interrupted you.'

'You did?' I asked him. I was slightly flustered now; I felt my tone was slipping. I thought of the last formal word I'd used and then repeated it, to bring my tone back up. 'Well, yes: jurisdiction. On the floor below the liver lady, or perhaps two floors below, there has to be a pianist. He must be in his late thirties or early forties, bald on top with tufts at the side. Tall and pale. In the day he practises. The music has to waft up in the same way as the liver lady's cooking smell does. As he's practising he must occasionally make mistakes. When he makes a mistake he repeats the passage slowly, over and over again, slowing right down into the bit that he got wrong. Like a Land Rover slowing down for bumpy terrain – a set of potholes, say. Then in the afternoons he teaches children. At night he composes. Sometimes he gets angry with . . .'

Naz's mobile gave out a loud double beep. I stopped. Naz picked it up and pressed the 'enter' button.

'Heir or descendant,' he read. 'From the Middle English *sioun* and the Old French *sion*: shoot or twig. First citation 1848. Oxford English Dictionary.'

'Interesting,' I said. I took a sip of my mineral water and thought of the scarab beetle again. 'Anyway,' I continued after a moment, setting the glass down, 'this guy sometimes gets angry with another person who I'll need, this motorbike enthusiast who tinkers with his bike out in the courtyard. Fixes it and cleans it, takes it apart, puts it back together again. When he has the motor on, the pianist gets angry.'

Naz processed this one for a while. His eyes went vacant while the thing behind them whirred, processing. I waited till the eyes told me to carry on.

'Then there's a concierge,' I said. 'I haven't got her face yet – but I've got her cupboard. And some other people. But you get the idea.'

'Yes, I get it,' Naz said. 'But where will you be while they're performing their tasks – when they're in *on* mode.'

'I shall move throughout the space,' I said, 'as I see fit. We'll concentrate on different bits at different times. Different locations, different moments. Sometimes I'll want to be passing the liver lady as she puts her rubbish out. Sometimes I'll want to be out by the motorbike. Sometimes the two at once: we can pause one scene and I'll run up or down the stairs to be inside the other. Or a third. The combinations are endless.'

101

'Yes, so they are,' said Naz.

The fish soup came. We sipped it. Then the kedgeree. We ate it. I explained more things to Naz and he processed them. When his eyes told me to wait I waited; then the whirring behind them stopped and I'd go on again. He never once asked why I wanted to do all this: he just listened, processing, working out how to execute it all. My executor.

Before we left the Blueprint Café Naz outlined the rate he'd charge. I told him fine. I gave him my banking details and he told me how to contact him at any time: he'd supervise my project person-ally, on a full-time basis. At ten the next morning he called me and told me how he thought we should proceed: we should first find a building that approximated to the one I had in mind – at least enough for it to be converted. That was the first step. While this was going on, he'd contact architects, designers and, of course, potential performers.

''Performers isn't the right word,' I said. 'Staff. Participants. Re-enactors.'

'*Re*-enactors?' he asked.

'Yes,' I told him. 'Re-enactors.'

'Would you like me to take charge of seeking out the property?' he asked.

'Well, yes,' I said.

As we hung up I got a clearly defined picture of my building again: first from the outside, then the lobby, my faceless concierge's cupboard, the main staircase with its black-and-white recurring pattern floor, its blackened wooden handrail with spikes on it. Then Naz's office superimposed itself over that: the plastic blue and red, the windows, his people walking across the carpets as they set out to look for my place. These people were carrying the image of Time Control's office out into the city, not the image of my building. This second image started fading in my mind. A sudden surge of fear ran through the right side of my body, from my shin all the way up to my right ear. I sat down, closed my eyes and concentrated on my building really hard. I kept them closed and concentrated on it till it came back and eclipsed the image of the office. I felt better. I stood up again.

I understood then that there was only one person who could take charge of seeking out the property, and that was me.

CHAPTER 6

In school, when I was maybe twelve, I had to do art. I wasn't any good at it, but it was part of the syllabus: one hour and twenty minutes each week – a double period. For a few weeks we were taught sculpture. We were given these big blocks of stone, a chisel and a mallet, and we had to turn the blocks into something recognizable – a human figure or a building. The teacher had an effective way of making us understand what we were doing. The finished statue, he explained, was already there in front of us – right in the block that we were chiselling away at.

'Your task isn't to create the sculpture,' he said; 'it's to strip all the other stuff away, get rid of it. The surplus matter.'

Surplus matter. I'd forgotten all about that phrase, those classes – even before the accident, I mean. After the accident I forgot everything. It was as though my memories were pigeons and the accident a big noise that had scared them off. They fluttered back eventually – but when they did, their hierarchy had changed, and some that had had crappy places before ended up with better ones: I remembered them more clearly; they seemed more important. Sports, for example: they got a good spot. Before the accident I'd never been particularly interested in sports. But when my memory came back I found I could remember every school basketball and football game I'd played in really clearly. I could see the layout of the court or pitch, the way I and the other players had moved around it. Cricket especially. I remembered exactly what it had been like to play it in the park on summer evenings. I remembered the games I'd seen on TV: overviews of the field's layout with diagrams drawn over them showing which vectors were covered and which weren't, slowmotion replays. Other things became less important than they had been before. My time at university, for example, was reduced to a faded picture: a few drunken binges, burnt out friendships and a heap of half-read books all blurred into a big pile of irrelevance.

The art teacher fluttered back into a good, clear spot of memory. I even remembered his name: Mr Aldin. I thought a lot about what he'd said about stripping away surplus matter when I was learning to eat carrots and to walk. The movement that I wanted to do was already in place, I told myself: I just had to eliminate all the extraneous stuff – the surplus limbs and nerves and muscles that I didn't want to move, the bits of space I didn't want my hand or foot to move through. I didn't discuss this with my physio; I just told it to myself. It helped. Now, as I wondered how to find my building, I thought of Mr Aldin again. The building, I told myself, or he told me, or to be precise my image of the school art room told me, in a voice hovering around paint-splashed wooden tables – the building was already there, somewhere in London. What I needed to do was ease it out, chisel it loose from the streets and the buildings all around it.

How to do this? I'd need to see the block, of course, the slab, London. I had a grotty, dog-eared *A-Z* but couldn't get any sense of the whole town from that. I'd need a proper map, a large one. I was about to go and buy one in the nearest newsagent when it struck me that I wasn't thinking big enough. To do this properly I'd need coordination, back-up. I phoned Naz back.

'I'd like to hire a room,' I told him.

'What kind of room?' he asked.

'A space. An office.'

'Right,' said Naz.

'I'd like to organize the search from there,' I continued. 'With maps on the walls, things like that. A kind of military operations room.'

'You'd like to organize the search yourself?' he asked. 'I thought I was to . . .'

'I'd like to take charge, but I'd like you to work with me.'

There was a pause, then Naz said:

'Fine. An office, then.'

'Yes,' I said.

'Any other specifications?'

'No,' I answered. 'Just a normal office with a couple of desks in it. Light, windows. Just usual.'

An hour later he'd got me an office in Covent Garden. It had a fax machine, two phone lines, a laptop, marker pens, white sheets of A1, two giant maps of London, some pins to stick one of the maps to the wall and some more pins to stick into it to mark locations. Naz had bought pins of several different colours and some thread to wrap round these, like cheese wire, slicing the town into blocks and wedges.

Naz and I devised a method: we'd cordon off an area of the wall-mounted map with pins and thread, then scan the same area from the second map into the laptop, then, cutting away adjacent streets using the software, send the resulting image to mobiles Naz's people were carrying. We isolated six main areas we thought most likely to contain my building: Belgravia, Notting Hill, South Kensington, Baron's Court, Paddington and King's Cross. Each of these had plenty of tall, tenement-style buildings – not to mention flowing, unbroken streets which, with the slight exception of some buildings round the stations, had escaped the bombing raids of World War Two pretty unscathed.

We set our plan to work. Naz put five of his people on the case: it was their job to walk around each block and wedge of streets we sent to them. We worked methodically, marking off, scanning in and zapping out each section; Naz's people would then go and walk around it, calling the office each time they saw a building they thought might approximate to mine. Each of them moved up each street in his or her block, then down the next, up the next and so on. One of our phones would ring from time to time:

'I've found a large apartment building with a blue façade near Olympia,' the searcher would say.

'What street?' we'd ask.

'Corner of Longridge Road and Templeton Place.'

'How many floors?'

'. . . *three, four, five* – Six!'

'Longridge Road, Templeton Place,' I or Naz would repeat to the other; the other would find the intersection on the wall-mounted map, stick a purple pin in it, then enter the particulars – six floors, blue façade and so on – into a spreadsheet Naz had created on the laptop. Sometimes both phones rang at once. Sometimes neither of them rang for several hours.

By five or so on the first day the map had nine purple pins stuck in it.

'Let's go and look at them,' said Naz. 'I'll call us a car.'

'Tomorrow,' I said.

By five o'clock the next day we had fifteen buildings. I'd knocked the car's arrival back to six, but when it came I told Naz:

'I prefer to wait until tomorrow morning.'

'As you wish,' he said. 'I'll send another car round to your flat at nine.'

I phoned him the next morning at eight-thirty.

'I prefer to make my own way there,' I said.

'I'll meet you there, then.'

'No. I prefer to go alone.'

'How will you know which places to look in?' he asked.

'I remember them all,' I said.

'Really?' Naz sounded incredulous. 'All the exact locations?'

'Yes,' I told him.

'That's impressive,' he said. 'Phone me as and when you need me.'

I didn't remember each location, of course. But I'd become increasingly aware of something over the last two days: these people wouldn't find my building. No matter how well I described it to them or how thoroughly they looked, they wouldn't find my building for a simple reason: it wouldn't be my building unless I found it myself. By noon on the second day of their search I'd been certain of this.

Why hadn't I called the search off, then? you might ask. Because I liked the process, liked the sense of pattern. There were people running through the same, repetitive acts – consulting their mobiles, walking up one street, down the next one and up a third, stopping in front of build-ings to make phone calls – in six different parts of town. Their burrowing would get inside the city's block and loosen it, start chiselling away at surplus matter: it would scare my building out, like beaters scaring pheasants out of bushes for a Lord to shoot – six beaters advancing in formation, beating to the same rhythms, their movements duplicating one another. As I started out that day I imagined looking on from overhead, from way above the city, picking out Naz's people, each one with a kind of tag on them, a dot like police cars have to help police helicopters pick them out. I imagined looking down and seeing them all – plus me, the seventh moving dot, my turning and redoubling etching out the master pattern that the other six were emulating. I imagined looking down from even higher up, the edges of the stratosphere. I stopped for a moment in the street and felt a light breeze moving round my face. I turned the palms of my hands outwards and felt a tingling creeping up the right side of my body. It was good.

I started with Belgravia. I'd walk up one street, down the next and up a third just like Naz's people had been instructed to do, so as not to miss any out. After two hours of this, though, I realized that my building wasn't in Belgravia. The area's clean, white houses with raised proches and white columns didn't strike any chords with me, even if technically they met the criteria I'd given to the searchers. King's Cross was the same. So was South Kensington. Paddington came closest: several buildings round there looked like mine. They *looked* like mine but weren't mine. Don't ask me how I could tell that: I just could.

In the late afternoon I phoned Naz.

'How were they?' he asked.

'Oh, I didn't go to the ones our people short-listed,' I told him. 'I decided I should look for it myself.'

'I see,' said Naz. 'I'll tell them to discontinue their searches, then.'

'No,' I said. 'Tell them to carry on. When we've exhausted our original six areas, we'll broaden out.'

There was a pause at Naz's end. I pictured the behind of his eyes, the whirring. After a while he said:

'I'll do that if that's what you want.'

'Good,' I said. Process: it was necessary.

I didn't find my building that day. Or the next. When I got home that evening there were two messages for me: one from Greg and one from Matthew Younger. Greg wanted me to call him. Matthew Younger wanted me to call him too: the sectors we'd bought into had climbed ten per cent in value over the last week, presenting us with a great opportunity to top-slice and diversify. I listened to their messages as I lay on the sofa. All the walking I'd done had exhausted me. I took a bath, put a plaster on a blister that had appeared on my right foot and went to bed.

111

I had a vivid dream. I dreamt that streets and buildings were moving past me, like the commuters had the day I'd stood still outside Victoria Station asking for spare change. The streets and buildings were moving past me on conveyor belts like those long ones that carry you along the corridors of airports. There were several of these moving belts connected to each other – converging and branching off, criss-crossing, ducking behind or under one another like a giant Spaghetti Junction, conveying houses, pavements, lampposts, traffic lights and bridges past me and around me.

My building was in there, being carried along somewhere in the complex interlacings. I caught glimpses of it as it slipped behind another building and was whisked away again to reappear somewhere else. It would show itself to me then slip away again. The belts were like magicians' fingers shuffling cards: they were shuffling the city, flashing my card, my building, at me and then burying it in the deck again. They were challenging me to shout 'Stop!' at the exact moment it was showing: if I could do that, I'd win. That was the deal.

'Stop!' I shouted. Then again: 'Stop . . . Stop!' But I timed each shout just wrong – only a tenth or even hundredth of a second off, but wrong nonetheless. I'd shout 'stop' each time I saw my building, and the system of conveyors would grind to a halt – but this took a few seconds, and by the time it was completely still my building had become submerged again.

After a while I closed my eyes, my dream-eyes, and tried to *sense* when it was coming up. I sensed the rhythm things were moving at, the patterns they were following, and let my imagination slip inside them. I could sense when my building was about to come by. I waited for it to go by twice, and just before it reappeared a third time shouted:

'Stop!'

I knew even as I shouted it that it would work this time. As the conveyors ground to a halt again, my building came to rest directly in front of me. I stepped forward and entered it. I got to see it all even more clearly than I had on the night of David Simpson's party – got to move around it, relishing its details: the concierge's cupboard and the staircase with its worn floor, the black-and-white recurring pattern in it, the oxidizing wrought-iron banisters, the black handrail with its spikes. I saw the pianist's door and the door of the lady who cooked liver, the spot beside it where she placed her rubbish as I passed her, my own flat above her with its open kitchen and its plants, its bathroom with a cracked wall and a window that looked out across a courtyard to a building with red roof tiles and black cats. I got to fully occupy it – not for long, but for a while, until the scene changed and I found myself inside a library negotiating travel prices with a grumpy waitress who was Yugoslavian.

In the morning, after I'd woken up, I started understanding why I hadn't found my building in the four days I'd been working on it: I'd been rational about it. Logical. I needed to go irrational on the whole thing. Illogical. Of course! I'd probably passed it at some point over the last few years already – which meant that it would be recorded somewhere in my memory. Everything must leave some kind of mark. And then even if I hadn't passed it already, I'd only manage to stalk it down if I moved surreptitiously: not in straight lines and in blocks and wedges but askew – diagonally, slyly, creeping up on it from sideways.

I cooked myself some breakfast and pondered how best to make my search irrational. The first idea that came to me was to I-Ching the map: to close my eyes, turn round a few times, stick a pin in blindly and then go and look in whatever area it happened to have landed on. The more I thought about that method, though, the less sly it seemed. Random's not the same as sly, is it? I tried it with my A-Z, just to see what would happen: Mitcham. I tried it a second time: Walthamstow Marshes. So much for the Wisdom of the Orient.

Colours was the next idea I had: following colours. I could decide to go where, say, yellow things went: a van, an advertising hoarding, someone's clothes. I could start somewhere, anywhere, and walk down the street the yellow van went down, then wait beside a yellow shop front till a woman wearing yellow trousers went by and I'd follow her. It was completely arbitrary – but it might prompt something, get me looking at things in a way I wouldn't normally, open chinks up in the camouflage behind which my place was hiding.

Then, following on from that idea, I thought of walking jerkily, erratically. I don't mean in my walk itself, my gait: I mean that I would start off down one street, then double back suddenly, like I had when I'd set out to Heathrow to meet Catherine but realized that I'd left her flight details behind. Or I'd pretend to be heading one way, waiting to cross a certain road by a pedestrian crossing – then, when the green man appeared, I'd veer off in some other direction, like a striker when he takes a penalty in football and sends the goalkeeper the wrong way.

I also considered following a numerical system: starting from point zero I'd turn down the first street on the right, then take the second left, the third right, fourth left and so on. The system could be much more complicated than that, of course: I could bring in fractions and algebra and differentials and who knows what else. Or I could devise a corresponding process using the alphabet: go down the first street I came to whose name starts with *a*, then carry on until I find a *b*, a *c* etc. Or I could apply numeric principles to an alphabetic process: start on a street that began with an *a*, then advance along the alphabet by the same number of letters contained in the street's name and find the nearest street whose name began with that new letter. Or I could . . .

The phone rang while I was in the middle of these deliberations. It was Matthew Younger.

'How are you?' he asked.

'Fine,' I told him. 'I'm looking for a building. What's *top-slice*?'

'Ah!' he answered, his voice booming down the line to me. 'Top-slicing is what you do when your shares in a certain company have appreciated – risen – and you slice the profit off by selling some until the value of your holding represents what it did when you bought it.'

'Why would you want to do that?' I asked.

'In order,' he explained, 'to invest the top-sliced money in another company, thus diversifying your holdings. Now your shares in the technology and telecommunication companies we selected recently have risen overall by a staggering ten per cent in little over one week. While I know how much you favour those two sectors, I just felt that if we top-sliced that ten per cent profit we could invest it in another sector while in no way diminishing your commitment to technology and tele . . .'

'No,' I told him. 'Keep them where they are.'

There was a pause at his end. I pictured his office: the polished mahogany table, panelled walls and corniced ceiling, the portraits of frail and wealthy men. After a while he came back:

'Fine,' he said. 'Jolly good. Just touching base,

really, with a suggestion – but it's your call entirely.'

'Yes,' I answered.

I hung up and went back to pondering methods of looking for my building in an irrational manner. I'd thought up so many by midday that I'd lost track of half of them. By early afternoon I'd realized that none of them would work in any case, for the good reason that implementing any one of them methodically would cancel its irrational value. I started to feel both dizzy and frustrated, and decided that the only thing to do was walk out of my flat with no plan at all in mind – just walk around and see what happened.

I left my flat, walked down the perpendicular street past my dented Fiesta, then turned into the ex-siege zone, passed the tyre place and café, then the phone box I'd called Marc Daubenay from. I walked to the centre of Brixton, the box junction between the town hall and Ritzy. Normally I'd have turned right to the tube at this point, but today I carried on up towards David Simpson's road. I don't know why: I felt like carrying on that way, is all. And then to stay south of the river: that felt sly. All Naz's people were on the north side; anywhere south was well out of the search's official radius, and therefore more fruitful hunting ground. If someone knows people are looking for him in a certain place, he finds another place to hide in.

I went up towards Plato Road, but ducked down a street parallel to it before reaching it. To go right back there might have short-circuited things, I reasoned. I turned right, then turned left to balance things up. Then I overshot a turning to the right but doubled back and took it after all. I came across some men laying wires beneath the street and stopped to watch them for a while. They were connecting wires to one another: blue, red and green ones, making the connections. I watched them, fascinated. They knew I was watching, but I didn't mind. I had eight and a half million pounds, and could do what I wanted. They didn't seem to mind either – perhaps because they could tell from how I watched them that I respected them. For me, they were Brahmins: top of the pile. More than Brahmins: gods, laying down the wiring of the world, then covering it up – its routes, its joins. I watched them for an age, then walked away with difficulty, really concentrating on each muscle, every joint.

A little after this I found a sports track. It was tucked into a maze of back streets and fenced in by knitted green wire. Inside the first fence another one caged in a beautiful green asphalt pitch. The pitch was multipurpose. All sorts of markings cut and sliced across it: semicircles, circles, boxes, arcs – in yellow, red and white. It was beautiful for me, but to anyone else it would just have looked shoddy and run-down. Two smaller, decrepit cages stood at either end of this pitch: two football goals. Between the caged-in pitch and the green outer fence a red track ran. The tracks I'd seen in my coma had been like this one: red, with white lines marking out the lanes. A couple of loudspeakers were dangling from poles beside the track; they looked like they weren't used any more, and probably didn't work. I stood against the green fence, looking in and thinking about the commentaries I'd had to give during my coma. I stood there thinking for a while, then turned around – and saw my building.

It was my building alright. I knew that instantly. It was a large tenement building, seven floors tall. It was quite old – maybe eighteen nineties, nineteen hundred. It was a dirty cream colour. Off-white. I'd come to it from a strange angle, from the side, but I could see that it had large white windows and black drains and balconies with plants on them. These windows, drains and balconies repeated themselves as the side façade ran on, high and imperious, behind a wall, then turned away and out of sight. Oh, it was definitely mine.

The building had a compound round it, a kind of garden space, but I was separated from this by the wall. In front of me was an iron side door. I tried it: it was shut. It was one of those doors with an electronic keypad and a CCTV camera mounted above it. I moved out of the camera's field of vision and waited to see if anyone would come through. Nobody did. After a while I walked around the sports track, passed beneath a railway bridge and came to the building from the front.

Oh yes: it was my building. My own, the one that I'd remembered. It was big and old and rose up seven floors. It was off-white at the front too, with windows but no balconies. Its main entrance had a kind of faded grandeur: wide, chequered steps ran from the street to a double doorway above which was carved in stone relief the building's name: Madlyn Mansions.

I stood in the street looking at my building. People were coming and going through the double doors pretty regularly: normal-looking people, old and young, half white and half West Indian. Residents. After a while I walked up the chequered steps to the door and peered inside.

The building had a lobby. Of course. Almost straight away I saw my concierge's cleaning cupboard – the one I'd sketched out in my diagram, with broom and mop and Hoover leaning across one another inside. It was six or so feet to the right of where it should have been, but it was the right kind of cupboard. On the lobby's other side was a little concierge's booth: a cabin with a sliding window in it. I could see a concierge, a small black man, talking to someone inside the cabin. Both these men's backs were turned on the main doors – which opened now as a middle-aged West Indian man came out and, seeing me standing there, held one of them for me.

'You going in?' he asked.

I glanced towards the concierge again: his back was still turned.

'Yes,' I said. 'Thank you.'

I took the door from the West Indian man and stepped into the lobby.

The street's sounds disappeared, replaced by the hollow echo of this tall, enclosed space. The sudden change felt like it does inside an aeroplane that suddenly descends, or when a train enters a tunnel and your ears go funny. There were footsteps echoing from somewhere up above and then the murmur of the voices of the concierge and the man he was talking to. The lobby's floor was grainy – maybe granite. It wasn't quite right, but I'd be able to change it. I strode quickly and lightly over it, still glancing at the concierge. He was more of a porter than a concierge, but I'd change that too. I'd replace him: it had to be a woman. I could picture her body now: it was middle-aged and pudgy. Her face was still blank.

At the far end of the lobby from the street doors the floor turned into a large, wide staircase. This was perfect. The patterning on its floor wasn't right either – but the dimensions were perfect. The banister was too new, but I'd get it ripped out and replaced in no time. Looking up, I saw it dwindling and repeating as it turned into each floor. I stood at its base for a moment, watching it dwindling and repeating. It was exciting: the motorbike enthusiast's flat was just a floor away, the pianist's only two; two floors above that was the liver lady. I could even see the edges of my own landing as I craned my head back and looked up. I felt a tingling start up in my right side.

Eventually I looked down again and saw a door at the foot of the staircase. Above the door, carved in relief just like the building's name above the front door, only slightly smaller, was the word *Garden*. I tried this door: it was open, and I stepped into a courtyard. Perfect too: it was large, with trees and bushes, enclosed on all four sides by buildings, by their backs. To my left were several sheds; I'd have those pulled down to make way for the patch of ground the motorbike enthusiast would use. When I stepped further out into the courtyard and turned round to look up at the building, I could see the pianist's window; three floors above that, the windows to my bathroom and my kitchen. The building facing mine on the courtyard's far side was similar to mine – equally tall but not identical.

'Good,' I said quietly to myself. 'Very good. What colour are its roofs, though?'

This question couldn't be answered straight away: from here the angle up to the facing building's roof was too sharp to see the slates, or whether their level rose and fell. I could see hut-like bits protruding from it, though, their tops.

That was good too, I thought: they'd have doors in them, most probably, for access to the roof. Just what I needed for the cats: to get them out there so that they could lounge around.

I took one last look at the courtyard, breathed in deeply, went back through the garden door and started up the staircase. The black-on-white recurring pattern wasn't there, as I mentioned earlier; nor were the wrought-iron banisters with their oxidizing hue and blackened wooden rail above them, but their size and movement – the way they ran and turned – was perfect. The flats started on the first floor. Their front doors were the wrong size: too small. Another thing to change. I recognized my pianist's one, though. I stood and listened at it for a while. A kind of grating was coming from inside – very subdued, probably pipes and water.

I moved up the staircase, past the boring couple's flat, on up to where the liver lady lived. Her door was the wrong size, like all the doors, but the spot beside it where she'd place her rubbish bag for the concierge to pick up as I went by: that was just right – minus the pattern, of course. I listened at her door as well and heard a television playing. I walked around the spot she'd place her bag on, looking at it from different angles. I saw where I'd come down the staircase just as her door was opening. Standing there now, I could picture her in greater detail: her wiry hair wrapped in a shawl, the posture of her back as she bent down, the way the fingers of her left hand sat across her lower back and hip. The tingling started up again.

It just remained for me to walk up to my floor. I did this and stood outside my own flat. I listened at the door: no sound. The occupants were probably out at work. I tried to X-ray through the door – not to see what was actually inside but to project what would be: the open-plan kitchen with its Sixties fridge and hanging plants, the wooden floors; off to the right the bathroom with its crack, the pink-grey plaster round it, grooved and wrinkled, the blue and yellow daubs of paint. Then the bit of wall without a mirror where David Simpson's mirror had been, the bathtub with its larger, older taps, the window that the scent of frying liver wafted in through.

I stood there, projecting all this in. The tingling became very intense. I stood completely still: I didn't want to move, and I'm not sure I could have even if I had wanted to. The tingling crept from the top of my legs to my shoulders and right up into my neck. I stood there for a very long time, feeling intense and serene, tingling. It felt very good.

What snapped me out of it eventually was a door closing with a bang on a lower floor. I could hear someone coming out and walking down the staircase. I moved on to the end of my landing; there was a floor above it, with two normal doors and then a smaller, padlocked one. Cat access huts as well, perhaps, I reasoned. Seven or so feet to my door's right there was a window: I leant against it and, forehead on pane, looked out across the courtyard. From here I could see that the facing roof was flat, not staggered. It wasn't red either. There were three cat access sheds on it in all, ten or so feet apart. I pictured the cats lounging: two or three of them at any given time, spread out across the roofs I'd have made staggered – lounging, languorous and black against their red.

I'd seen all I needed to see. I spun off from the window and walked straight down to the lobby without pausing. I walked straight across this, too, and out into the street. I found a phone and called Naz.

'Any luck?' he asked.

'I've found it, yes,' I told him.

'Excellent,' he answered. 'Where?'

'In Brixton.'

'In Brixton?'

'Yes: Madlyn Mansions, Brixton. It's behind a kind of sports track. Near a railway bridge.'

'I'll find it on the map and call you back. Where are you now?'

'I'm on my way home,' I told him. 'I'll be there in twenty minutes.'

I walked back to my flat. There was a message on my answering machine already, but when I played it, thinking it would be from Naz, it turned out to be from Greg. I lay down on the folded-away sofa bed and waited. Eventually Naz phoned.

'The building is privately owned,' he said, 'and leased out to tenants. The owner is one Aydin

Huseyin. He manages this and two other proper-
ties in London.'

'Right,' I said.

'Shall I enquire whether or not he's interested
in taking offers on this property?' Naz asked.

'Yes,' I said. 'Buy it.'

We got it for three and a half million. A snip,
apparently.

CHAPTER 7

We hired an architect. We hired an interior designer. We hired a landscape gardener for the courtyard. We hired contractors, who hired builders, electricians and plumbers. There were site managers and sub-site managers, delivery coordinators and coordination supervisors. We took on performers, props and wardrobe people, hair and make-up artists. We hired security guards. We fired the interior designer and hired another one. We hired people to liaise between Naz and the builders and managers and supervisors, and people to run errands for the liaisers so that they could liaise better.

Looking at it now, with the advantage – as they say – of hindsight, it strikes me that Naz could probably have devised a more efficient way of doing it. He could have chosen one place, one specific point to start from, and worked out from there in logical procession: chronologically, in a straight line, piece by piece by piece. The approach he took instead was piecemeal – everything springing up at once but leaving huge gaps in between and creating new problems of alignment and compatibility that in their turn required more supervising, more co-ordination.

'There's a problem with the windows on the third floor,' Naz told me one day, several weeks into the works.

'I thought all the windows had been finished,' I said.

'Yes,' said Naz, 'but now the windows in the main third-floor flat have to come out again so we can lift the piano in.'

Another time we realized we'd got the courtyard ready too soon: trucks would have to drive across it as they removed detritus from the building, ruining the landscaper's creation.

'Why didn't we think of that?' I asked Naz.

Naz smiled back. I started suspecting then that his decision to opt for the piecemeal approach was deliberate. As we were driven from one meeting to another – from the site itself, say, to our office in Covent Garden, or to our architect's office in Vauxhall, or to the workshop of the metallurgist who was making our banisters, or from a Sotheby's auction of Sixties' Americana at which we'd been looking at fridges back to the site via Lambeth Town Hall (palms were greased – I'll say no more) – each time we left the building or came near again we'd see trucks piled high with rubble, earth or ripped-out central-heating units pulling out from its compound and other trucks arriving with scaffolding or new earth or long strips of pine. There'd be small vans full of wiring, caterers' vans,

vans belonging to experts in fields I didn't know existed: stone-relief consultants, acoustic technicians, non-ferrous-metal welders – London's premier in the art since 1932, this third outfit's van announced proudly on its side.

'So what's your position in the ferrous-metal league?' I asked them.

'We don't do ferrous-metal welding,' they replied.

'And where did you rank before '32?'

'I don't know that. You'll have to ask the boss.'

Then there'd be behemoths: giant cranes on wheels, crane lifts with crane-grab limbs, all skeletal and menacing and huge. We'd carry plaster on our clothes into a Mayfair piano salesroom, then carry the contrasting chimes and tinkles of four types of baby grand still humming in our ears on to a used furniture warehouse. We'd receive faxes on the machine we had in our car and stuff them into the back-seat glove compartment as the driver raced us to another meeting, then forget that we'd received them and have them re-faxed or go back to the same office or the same warehouse again – so the humming in our ears was constant, a cacophony of modems and drilling and arpeggios and perpetually ringing phones. The hum, the meetings, the arrivals and departures turned into a state of mind – one that enveloped us within the project, drove us forwards, onwards, back again. I've never felt so motivated in my life. Naz understood this, I think now, and cultivated a degree of chaos to keep everybody involved on their toes, fired up, motivated. A genius, if ever there was one.

Not that motivation was otherwise lacking: the people we'd hired were being paid vast amounts of money. What was lacking, if anything, was comprehension: making them understand exactly what it was that was required of them. And making them understand at the same time how little they needed to understand. I didn't need to make them share my vision, and I didn't want them to. Why should they? It was my vision, and I was the one with the money. They just had to know what to do. This wasn't easy, though – making them understand what to do. They were all London's premiers: the best plumbers, plasterers, pine outfitters and so on. They wanted to do a really good job and found it hard to get their heads round the proposition that the normal criteria for that didn't apply in this case.

The thickest groups by far were actors and interior designers. Morons, both. To audition the actors we hired the Soho Studio Theatre for a couple of days after placing an ad in the trade press. It read:

Performers required to be constantly on call in London building over indefinite period. Duties will include repeated re-enactment of certain daily events. Excellent remuneration. Contact Nazrul Ram Vyas on etc. etc.

Naz and I arrived on the first day to find a big crowd in the lobby. We'd got our driver to drop us off round the corner from the theatre rather than right outside, so as not to make an ostentatious entrance: that way, we figured, we'd be able to walk round the lobby incognito for a while, sizing people up.

'That one looks worth auditioning for the motorbike enthusiast,' I mumbled to Naz.

'The one in the jacket?' he mumbled back.

'No, but he looks worth auditioning too, now you mention it. And that frumpy woman over there: a possible concierge, I think.'

'What about the others?' Naz asked, still mumbling.

'We'll need extras too: all the anonymous, vague neighbours. Those two black guys look vaguely familiar.'

'Which ones?'

'Those two,' I told him, pointing – and right then they all started clicking, wising up. A heavy silence fell across the lobby; everybody glanced at us, then turned away and started pretending to talk again, but in reality they were still glancing at us. One guy came right up to us, held his hand out and said:

'Hello there! My name's James. I'm really looking forward to this enterprise. You see, I need to fund my studies at RADA, where I've been given a place. Now I've prepared . . .'

'What's RADA?' I said.

'It's the Royal Academy of Dramatic Arts. I auditioned, and the tutor told my local authority that I was gifted – his words, not mine.' At this point in his spiel James held his hand up to his chin in an exaggerated manner, and I could tell he'd practised the gesture in the same way as the gay clubbers I'd watched several weeks ago had practised theirs. 'But,' he went on, 'they wouldn't give me a grant. So I welcome this whole enterprise. I think it will help me expand. Learn things. My name's James.'

He still had his hand out. I turned to Naz.

'Can you get rid of half these people?' I asked him. 'And give audition slots to the ones I pointed out – and to any others you think might be right. I'm going to get a coffee.'

I went to the very place I'd sat in when I'd watched the clubbers, media types, tourists and homeless people, the Seattle-theme coffee shop just like the one at Heathrow: it was just round the corner from the theatre. I asked for a cappuccino.

'Heyy!' the girl said. It was still a girl, but it was a different girl this time. 'Short cap coming up! You have a . . .'

'Ah yes!' I said, sliding it out. 'Absolutely I do! And it's edging home.'

'I'm sorry?' she asked.

'Eight cups stamped,' I told her. 'Look.'

She looked. 'You're right,' she said, impressed. She stamped the ninth cup as she handed me my coffee. 'One more and you get a free drink of your choice.'

'Plus a new card!' I said.

'Of course. We'll give you a new card as well.'

I took my cappuccino over to the same window seat I'd had the last time and sat there looking out onto the intersection of Fifth Street and Old Compton Street. There was a homeless person there, but it wasn't my one. The new one didn't have a dog – but he did have friends who sallied over to him from their base up the street just like my homeless person's friends had; but then these didn't seem like the same people either. The sleeping bag that the new guy had wrapped around him seemed identical to my one's sleeping bag, though. So did his sweat top.

I'd forgotten about the loyalty-card business. Now I'd been reminded I was really excited by it. I was so close! I gulped my cappuccino down, then strode back to the counter with the card.

'Another cappuccino,' I told the girl.

'Heyy!' she answered. 'Short cap coming up. You have a . . .'

'Of course!' I said. 'I was just here!'

'Oh yes!' she said. 'Sorry! I'm a zombie! Here, let me . . .'

She stamped the tenth cup on my card, then said:

'So: you can choose a free drink.'

'Cool,' I said. 'I'll have another cappuccino.'

'On top of your cap, I mean.'

'I know,' I said. 'I'll have another one as well.'

She shrugged, turned round and made me a new one. She pulled out a new card, stamped the first cup on it and handed it to me with my two coffees.

'Back to the beginning,' I said. 'Through the zero.'

'Sorry?' she asked.

'New card: good,' I told her.

'Yes,' she said. She looked kind of depressed.

I took my two new coffees back to my seat by the window. I set them side by side and took alternate sips from each, like Catherine had with her drinks in the Dogstar, oscillating between pre-clock and post-clock cups. This was a good day, I decided. I finished my coffees and went back up to the Soho Studio Theatre.

The first person Naz and I saw was the second man I'd picked out as a possible for the motorbike enthusiast. He looked about right: early to mid twenties, brown hair, fairly handsome. He'd prepared a passage to perform for us: some piece of modern theatre by Samuel Beckett.

'We don't want to hear that,' I said. 'We just want to chat for a while, fill you in on what you'll need to do.'

'Okay,' he said. 'Shall I sit here, or stand, or? . . .'

'Whatever,' I said. 'What we're looking for is this: you'd need to be a motorbike enthusiast. You'd have to be available on a full-time basis – a live-in full-time basis – to occupy a flat on the first floor of an apartment building. You'd need to

spend a lot of time out in the building's courtyard tinkering with a motorbike.'

'Tinkering?' he asked me.

'Fixing it,' I said.

'What do I do once it's fixed?'

'You take it apart again. Then fix it back.'

He was quiet for a while, thinking about this.

'So you don't need me to act at all?' he asked
eventually.

'No,' I told him. 'Not act: just do. Enact. Re-enact.'

He didn't get the part, as it turned out. The
next-but-one motorbike enthusiast possible did.
He wasn't one of the ones who'd been in the
lobby. He had less acting experience than the
other two – almost none. His movements and his
speech seemed less false, less acquired. On top
of that he had a bike and knew a bit about them.
By the end of the first day I'd found him, plus
the husband in the boring couple, plus two or three
vague, anonymous neighbours. That was it, though:
no one else had been right. Back in the car I said
to Naz:

'I'm not so sure the theatre world is the right
place to look for re-enactors.'

'You think so?' said Naz.

We discussed it as we were driven to Aldgate –
we were meeting a wholesaler of rare and
outmoded light fittings. By the time we'd got there
I'd become convinced it wasn't.

'Where else, though?' I wondered aloud as we
left Aldgate for Brixton.

'Community centres?' Naz ventured as he stuffed the receipts for the order we'd just made into the glove compartment. 'Swimming pools? Supermarket notice boards?'

'Yes,' I said. 'Those sound like the right kind of places.'

We cancelled the next day's audition, and Naz had notices distributed in the new venues. These ones brought us a much broader sweep of people. The old woman who became the liver lady saw it at her bridge evening, the boring couple's wife at a yoga class. The pianist we hooked in a musicians' journal – he was doing a Ph.D. in musicology. He was just right for the part: quiet, gloomy, even bald on top. He nodded glumly as I explained to him how he'd have to make mistakes:

'You make mistakes,' I told him, 'then you go over the passage you got wrong again, slowing right down into the bit where you messed up. You play it again and again and again – and then, when you've got down how to do it without messing up, play it some more times, coming back to normal speed. And then you carry on – at least until you hit your next mistake. You with me?'

'I make the mistakes deliberately?' he asked, looking at the floor. His voice was vacant and monotonous, completely without intonation.

'Exactly,' I said. 'In the afternoons you teach young students. School children. Pretty basic stuff. In the evenings you compose. There's more, but that's the gist of it.'

'I'll do it,' he said, still looking away. 'Can I huf an obvos?'

'What did you say?' I asked him. He'd mumbled his last phrase into his collar.

He looked up for an instant. He really looked miserable. Then his eyes dropped again and he said, only slightly more clearly:

'Can I have an advance? Against the first two weeks.'

I thought about that for a moment, then I answered:

'Yes, you can. Naz will see to that. Oh – but you'll have to grow your hair out at the sides. Is that acceptable?'

His eyes moved slowly from one corner of their sockets to another, trying half-heartedly to catch a glimpse of the hair on either side of his pale head. They gave up pretty quickly; he looked down at the floor and nodded glumly again. He was perfect. He signed his contract, Naz gave him some money and he left.

Interior designers were the other nightmare group. We interviewed several. I'd explain to them exactly what I wanted, down to the last detail – and they'd take this as a cue to start creating décor themselves!

'What I'm getting from you is a downbeat, retro look,' one of them told me. 'And that's exciting. Full of possibilities. I think we should have faux-flock wallpaper throughout – Chantal de Witt does a fantastic line in this – and lino carpeting along the hallways. That's what I'm seeing.'

'I don't care what you're seeing,' I told him. 'I don't want you to create a look. I want you to execute the *exact* look I'll dictate to you.'

This one stormed out in a huff. Two others agreed in principle to execute the look I wanted but balked when it came to the blank stretches. I'd left blank stretches in my diagrams, as I mentioned earlier – stretches of floor or corridor that hadn't crystallized inside my memory. Some of these had since come back, but others hadn't, any more than the concierge's face, and I'd decided that these parts should be blank in reality, with doorways papered and cemented over, strips of wall left bare and so on. Neutral space. Our architect loved this, but the designers found it quite repulsive. One of them agreed to do it, so we hired him; but when it came to actually realizing it he snapped.

'I don't care what you're paying me,' he shouted. 'It will destroy me professionally if this gets out. It's just so *ugly*!'

We had to fire him. He sued us. Marc Daubenay came in and dealt with him. I don't know how it turned out. Perhaps the case is still running today, who knows.

So in the end we found a set designer. It was Naz's idea: a brilliant one. Frank, his name was. He'd designed sets for movies, so he understood the concept of partial décor. Film sets have loads of neutral space – after all, you only have to make the bit the camera sees look real; the rest you leave unpainted, without detail, blank. Frank brought a props woman called Annie with him. She turned out to be vital in the later stages.

Matthew Younger came once to the building during the setting-up period. I'd had him sell four million pounds worth of stocks when I'd first bought the building. It had cost just over four in all: the three and a half price tag, plus conveyancing fees, stamp duty and all that stuff, plus the bribes of two grand each we'd given some of the long-standing tenants to get them to waive their rights and move straight out. Only two had refused, and they'd both changed their minds within a week. I didn't enquire how they'd been persuaded.

The amazing thing, though, is that by the time Matthew Younger visited me on the site a few weeks later, my portfolio's value had risen back almost to the level it had been at before he'd sold the shares.

'It's like yoghurt,' I said, 'or a lizard's tail, that grows back if you yank it off.'

'Speculation!' he said, smiling from ear to ear. His voice boomed up the stairwell, zinging off the loose iron banisters that were being ripped out one by one. They'd looked right in the catalogue, but didn't any more once we'd installed them, so they were being ripped out and replaced. 'The technology and telecommunications sectors are experiencing a boom just now,' he went on. 'They're going stratospheric. This is great, but

139

you must understand that your level of exposure is enormous.'

'Exposure,' I repeated. 'I like exposure.' I turned the palms of my hands outwards and raised them both – almost imperceptibly, but still enough to feel a muffled tingling in my right side.

'I've prepared you a chart,' said Matthew Younger, taking a large piece of paper from his dossier, 'that takes the mean performance of these aggregated sectors over eight years. If you look . . .'

I felt another type of tingling on my upturned palms – not one coming from inside me but an exterior one, a sensation of lots of little particles falling on it. I looked up: granite crumbs were tumbling from the stairs above us.

'Let's go outside,' I said.

I led Matthew Younger out into the courtyard. Swings were being installed that day. I hadn't seen swings in my original vision of the court-yard – but they'd grown there later, as I thought about it further: a concrete patch with swings on and a wooden podium a few feet to its right. Workmen had laid down the cement and were now planting the swings' bases in it while it was still wet. Matthew Younger held his map up against the sky.

'Look,' he said. 'In this first four-year period this chart covers . . . just here, see? – they rose pretty sharply. But then here, over the next two years, they drop again – and just as sharply, even dipping lower than they were back here. From here they rise again, and from the time when we bought into them their upward thrust has been phenomenal. But if they choose to plummet again . . .'

'Is there any reason they should?' I asked.

'No,' he said. 'All the signs suggest they'll rise still more. But one can never completely second-guess the market.'

'Isn't that your job?' I said.

'Well, of course,' he said. 'To a large extent. But there is a small degree of randomness – a capricious element that likes occasionally to buck expectations, throw a spanner in the works.'

'A shard,' I said.

'I'm sorry?' he said.

'Go on,' I told him.

'Oh. Right. Well: caution – and above all diversification – can largely neutralize this element. Which brings us back to the question of exposure. Now if . . .'

'Shh!' I said, holding my hand up. I was looking at the jagged line that ran across his chart: how it jutted and meandered. As his lecture had moved off the figures and onto the randomness stuff he'd let the left side of his chart drop, so the value line was running vertically, like my bathroom's crack. I let my eyes run up and down it, following its edges and directions.

Matthew Younger saw that I was looking at it and straightened it up.

'No!' I said.

'I'm sorry?' said Matthew Younger.

'It was better when you . . . Can I keep this chart?'

'Of course!' he boomed back. 'Yes, have a proper look at it in your own time. I'll leave you some stock profiles I've prepared here should you wish to diversif . . .'

His booming was drowned out by drilling coming through an open window on the second floor. Matthew Younger handed me the chart and then a wad of papers, then I showed him out.

'Could you have the word 'speculation' looked up?' I asked Naz as we were driven to a glazier's that afternoon.

'Of course.' He took his mobile out and tapped in a text message.

The reply came ten minutes later:

'The faculty of seeing,' Naz read; 'observation of the heavens, stars, etc.; contemplation or profound study of a subject; a conjectural consideration; the practice of buying and selling goods. From the Latin *speculari*: spy out, watch, and *specula*: watch tower. First citation . . .'

'Watch tower,' I said; 'heavens: I like that. You could see the heavens better from a watch tower. But you'd be exposed.'

'Yes, I suppose you would,' Naz answered.

On the way back to my building from the glazier's we detoured via my flat. I was still sleeping there while waiting for my building to be ready, but I was hardly ever there: I'd leave early each morning and return late at night, sleep for a few hours and then take off again. That morning I'd left a tiling catalogue behind; I told the driver to pass by there so that I could pick it up.

When we arrived there, Greg was ringing at my front door. I'd already got out of the car when I saw him – otherwise I might have made the driver drive me round the block and loop back a few minutes later. Greg turned round and saw me: I was trapped.

'My God!' Greg shouted. 'Nice car dude!'

I didn't say anything. It was a nice car, I suppose. It was quite long and had these doors that opened in the middle of the back. It wasn't ostentatious, though – and anyway I only had it because my Fiesta wouldn't have taken a desk and fax machine. As soon as everything was up and running I'd get rid of this car and go back to the Fiesta.

Greg stood on my steps, a few feet from me.

'So,' he said. 'What's new? You haven't called me in six weeks.'

'I've been . . .' I told him, 'you know . . . busy.'

'Doing what?' asked Greg.

'Getting ready to move into a new place.'

'Where?' he asked.

'The other side of Brixton,' I said.

'Other . . . side . . . of Brixton,' he repeated.

'Yes,' I said.

We stood there facing one another. After a while I said:

'I've got to pick up this tile catalogue, and then go off to a meeting.'

Greg looked past me into the car where Naz was sitting.

'Sure,' he said. 'Well . . .'

'I'll give you a call,' I told him as I walked past him into my flat. 'Later this week. Or early next.'

I didn't call him – not that week, nor the next, nor the next one either. My project was a programme, not a hobby or a sideline: a programme to which I'd given myself over body and soul. The relationships within this programme would be between me and my staff. Exclusively. Staff: not friends.

Soon after that day we moved our central office from Covent Garden to Brixton. Our activities were pretty localized there by this point. We rented the top floor of a modern blue-and-white office building a few streets away, just off the main drag. It looked modern and official in a dated kind of way – like some Eastern European secret-police headquarters. There were metal blinds drawn crookedly across most of its windows when we took it over, and metal tubes emerging from its sides – air ducts, laundry chutes, who knows what. On the roof were aerials, antennae. Naz set up his headquarters and coordinated things from there while I spent more and more time in my building itself, working on the smaller details with the staff members to whom specific areas of the project had been delegated.

Annie came to play more and more of an

important role the further the project progressed, as I mentioned earlier. She and I would run around together finding the right brooms and mops, say, for the concierge's cupboard. Or we'd get in ashtrays for the hall and work out where to place them, then find that their position clashed with the way doors opened, so have them moved again. Working out compatibility became our main activity. With the piano, for example: this had been delivered and installed, but we still had to find the right degree of absorbency for its flat's walls. Too much and I wouldn't hear it at all; too little and it wouldn't be muffled enough – it had been slightly muffled when I'd first remembered it. To fine-tune things like this we needed everyone to be in sync: the drillers to stop drilling, hammers hammering, sanders sanding and so on, while the pianist started playing.

'How's that?' Annie asked me as we stood in my flat listening to the music.

'It's fine,' I said. 'But is his window open or closed right now?'

'Is his window opened or closed?' Annie repeated into a two-way radio.

'Closed,' the reply came.

'Closed,' she repeated to me.

'Tell them to open it now,' I said.

'Open it up now,' she repeated.

And so on. We went through several episodes like that. Two-way radios came into play a lot.

Mobiles had been good for one-on-one communication, but by now we often needed one-to-several – several-to-several too. So I'd telephone Naz over in his headquarters, and Naz would radio three of our people while he talked to me; then one of them would radio Annie and she'd radio Naz on another channel, and he'd call me back; or I'd call Annie and she'd radio her back-up, or – well, you get the picture. By the final stages, Annie had four support staff directly under her: their radios were tuned to her frequency exclusively.

You could see Naz's office from the top floors of my building – and, of course, vice versa. We had a telescope installed beside Naz's main window – a powerful one. Naz had wanted to use CCTV, but I'd told him no: I didn't want cameras anywhere. I'd made them take away the one mounted at the side gate by the sports track that I'd stood by on the day I'd first discovered the building. The only camera I allowed on site was Annie's Polaroid. She used it to capture positions and arrangements: what was where in relation to what else. It was quicker than sketches or diagrams. More accurate too. If we'd got something just right but then had to move it while we carried something else through its space, Annie would take a Polaroid snap; then, when we wanted to reinstate whatever it was, we'd just stand in the position she'd taken the snap from holding up the photo while directing people to place such and such an object right, left, a bit further back and so on till it matched the photo. Smart, precise. She was a nice girl.

One afternoon I stood in Naz's office gazing through the telescope. I gazed for a long time, watching people move around behind my building's windows. Then I lowered it and gazed at trucks and vans coming and going. They were mostly going, taking stuff away. It amazed me how much had needed to be got rid of throughout the whole project: earth, rubble, banisters, radiators, cookers – you name it. For every cargo that arrived, large or small, another cargo had to be taken away. At least one. If it were possible to gather together and weigh everything brought in over the weeks of set-up and then do the same to everything that had been carried out, I'm pretty sure the second lot would weigh more. This would be true from the beginning, when we were dealing with skipfuls of clutter, right through to the end, when we went round picking up bits of paper with our fingers, making absolutely sure that everything apart from what was meant to be there was removed.

'Surplus matter,' I said, still gazing through the telescope.

'What's that?' asked Naz.

'All this extra stuff that needs to be carted away,' I said. 'It's like an artichoke – the way there's always more of it on your plate after you've finished than there was before you started.'

'I like artichokes,' said Naz.

'Me too,' I said. 'Right now I do, at least. Let's eat some for supper this evening.'

'Yes, let's,' Naz concurred. He got onto his phone and told someone to go and buy us artichokes.

It really took shape in the final two weeks. The hallways had been laid, the courtyard landscaped and re-landscaped, the flats fitted or blanked out as my diagrams had stipulated. Now we had to concentrate on the minutiae. We had to get the crack right, for example: the crack in my bathroom wall. I still had the original piece of paper that I'd copied it onto back at that party – plus the diagrams that I'd transcribed it onto over the next twenty-four hours, of course. Frank and I and a plasterer called Kevin spent a long time getting the colour of the plaster all around it right.

'That's not quite it,' I'd tell Kevin as he mixed it. 'It should be more fleshy.'

'Fleshy?' he asked.

'Fleshy: grey-brown pinky. Sort of like flesh.'

He got there in the end, after a day-or-so's experimenting.

'Not like any flesh I've seen,' he grunted as he smeared it on.

That wasn't the end of it, though: when it dried it darkened, ending up a kind of silver brown. We had to backtrack and remix it so that it would turn out dry the colour that the last mix had when wet. Nor was that the end of it: we hadn't realized how difficult it would be to get plaster to crack the way we wanted it to.

'I mix plaster so it won't crack,' Kevin sniffed.

'Well, do wrong what you usually do right, then,' I said.

He mixed it much drier – but then cracks are sort of random: you can't second-guess which way they'll go. It took another day of experimenting: trying salt and razor blades and heat and all sorts of devices to get it to crack the right way. Kevin whistled the same tune for hours while he did this: a pop tune, one I thought I recognized. He didn't whistle the whole tune – just one bit of it, over and over.

'What is it?' I asked him after several hours of whistling and crack-forming, rubbing over and reforming.

'What's what?'

'That song.'

'*History Repeating*,' he said. 'By the Propeller-heads.' He raised his eyebrows and his voice climbed as he half-sang and half-spoke the line that he'd been whistling: '"All, just-a, little, bit-of, history re-peat-ing." See?' Then, stepping back, he asked: 'How's that?'

'It's quite nice,' I said. 'I've heard it on the radio.'

'No,' Kevin said. 'The crack.'

'Oh! Quite good. Not quite sharp enough, though.'

Kevin sighed and went at it again. Several hours later a scalpel dipped in a mix of TCP and varnish managed to cut and set it in the formation we wanted.

'Satisfied?' asked Kevin.

'Yes,' I answered. 'But there's still the blue and yellow patches to daub on.'

'Not my job,' Kevin said. 'I'm out of here.'

We didn't have much problem finding the right type of large taps for the bathtub – the problem was with making them look old. We had this problem often, as you might imagine: making things look old. The hallway had to be scuffed down with sandpaper and smeared with small amounts of grease-diluted tar. The banisters had to be blasted with vaporized ice to make them oxidize. And then the windows were too crisply transparent: the courtyard and the roofs didn't look right through them. I couldn't work out why at first, nor express what was wrong with them: I just kept telling my staff that the courtyard didn't look right.

'So what's not right about it?' asked the landscape gardener.

'Nothing's not right about it: it's the way it looks through these windows. Too crisp. That's not how I remembered it.'

'Remembered it?' he asked.

'Whatever,' I said, waving him away. Annie came over and looked. She solved it instantly:

'It's the type of glass,' she said. 'Not old enough.'

Bingo. New glass is totally consistent, doesn't gloop and run and crimp the things you see through it like old glass does. We had all the panes removed and older ones brought in.

My living room and kitchen came together nicely. We'd knocked interior walls down to get the right open-plan shape. Now we got cracking on the furnishings. I brought the right type of plants in – eventually. That Portuguese woman! Formidable: her voice, her stark physique. She stomped out of her van lugging these beautiful, lush, healthy ferns and spider plants that seemed to cascade out of white ceramic pots.

'These are no good,' I said to Annie. 'They're too lush, too green.'

'Waz wrong wiz zem?' the Portuguese plant woman thundered. 'My planz healzy! My planz good!'

'I know they're good,' I said. 'That's just the problem. I need old and shabby ones in tinny baskets.'

'Baskez no good for zem!' she said, slapping the back of her hand against my arm. 'They needz zpaze, zupport. I know waz good for zem!'

Behind her, through the window and across the courtyard, men on the facing roofs were busily replacing the tiles we'd had laid down. They'd been too blood-red, not orangey enough. The Portuguese plant woman took a frond between her fingers, held it up to me and slapped my arm with the back of her free hand again.

'Look! Zmell! My planz iz very healzy!'

I escaped and went to Naz's while Annie got rid

of her. Later that day we picked up some half-dead plants in some old junk shop.

The fridge arrived the next day. We netted it not from the Sotheby's Americana auction that I mentioned earlier but from an auction site Naz had found on the internet. It looked just right – but its door slightly caught each time you opened it, just like Greg had said all fridge doors do outside of films.

'That sucks!' I said. 'That really fucking sucks! You'd have thought that with all of their alleged craftsmanship' (they'd played this aspect of the fridge up on the website) 'they could have made one whose door didn't catch like this. I mean, what's the whole point of doing all this if it's still going to catch?'

'What do you mean?' asked Annie.

'It . . . Just, well . . .' I said. 'It bloody shouldn't!'

I sat down. I was really upset.

'Don't worry,' said Annie. 'It just needs new rubber.'

Someone was dispatched to get new rubber. While we waited for that to arrive, we tested for the smell of liver frying. An extractor fan had been installed above the liver lady's stove, its out-funnel on the building's exterior turned towards the windows of my kitchen and my bathroom. Liver had been bought that day – pig's liver; but we found that frying just one panful didn't produce enough smell. Someone else was dispatched to buy more frying pans and a lot more liver. They cooked it in four frying pans at once. Annie and I waited in my flat.

'How's that?' she asked.

'It's great,' I told her. 'The spit and sizzle is exactly the right volume. There's just one thing not quite . . .'

'What?' she asked.

'The smell is kind of strange.'

'Strange?' she repeated – then, into her cackling radio: 'Wait a minute. Strange?'

'Yeah,' I said. 'Sort of strange. A bit like cordite.'

'Cordite? I've never smelt cordite. You know what I think it is, though? It's that the pans are new.'

'Bingo again,' I told her. 'That must be it.'

The last two days were 'sweep' days. I, Naz, Annie and Frank moved through the building sweeping it for errors: inconsistencies, omissions. We found so many that we thought we'd have to delay the whole thing. The recurring black-on-white floor pattern had continued through a bit of neutral space on the second floor; the door to the concierge's cupboard had been painted – things like that. Smaller details too: the tar-and-grease coat in the hallway, under the outmoded lights, had too much sheen; it was obvious that the putty holding the new old windows in place had been set only days ago; and so on. And then often fixing one thing just offset another. All the neighbours had been trained up by now and were practising their re-enacted gestures *in situ* – but then they'd disturb our carefully contrived arrangements as they moved around rehearsing. Crossed wires. One of Annie's people even mis-understood the word 'sweep'.

'What are you doing?' I asked when I found her literally sweeping down the staircase after we'd spent ages lightly peppering it with bus tickets and cigarette butts.

'I'm . . .' she said; 'I thought you . . .'

'Annie!' I called up the stairwell.

Even after we'd got it all just right we did four more sweeps. We'd jump from one detail to another to see if we'd catch a mistake unawares. We'd move from the bottom to the top and down again, across the courtyard, up the façade of the facing building, back and up the staircase again, over and over and over.

'Feeling nervous?' Naz asked on the final day before the date we'd set to put the whole thing into action.

'Yes,' I told him. I was feeling very nervous. I hadn't been sleeping well all week. I'd lie awake for half the night, running in my imagination through the events and actions that we were to go through in reality when the time came. I could run through them in a way that made them all work really well, or in a way that made them all mess up and be an abject failure. Sometimes I'd run the failure scenario and then the good one, to cancel the bad one out. At other times I'd be running the good one and the bad one would cut in and make me break out in a panicky sweat. This went on every night for a whole week: me, lying awake in my bed, sweating, nervously rehearsing in my mind re-enactments of events that hadn't happened but which, nonetheless, like the little bits of history in Kevin's pop song, were on the verge of being repeated.

CHAPTER 8

The day of the first re-enactment finally arrived. July the eleventh.

We'd decided to begin at 2 p.m. I spent the morning in Naz's office, then ate a final light lunch with him. The air there was solemn, its heavy silence punctured only by the occasional ringing phone or crackling radio which one of Naz's staff would answer in hushed tones.

'What is it?' I'd ask Naz each time.

'Nothing,' he'd answer quietly. 'Everything's under control.'

At half-past one I left. Naz's people stood by the door as I made my way out – three or four of them on each side, forming a kind of tunnel – and wished me luck, their faces grave and sober. Naz took the lift down to the street with me, then, when the car pulled up, turned to face me and shook my hand. He was staying behind to direct all activities from his office. His dark eyes locked on mine while our hands held each other, the thing behind the eyes whirring deep back inside his skull.

Our driver drove me from the office to the building. It was just two minutes' walk away, but he took me there in the car we'd gone around in while setting all this up. I sat in the back seat and watched the streets slide by: the railway bridge, the sports track with its knitted green wire fence, its battered football goals, its yellow, red and white lane markings, boxes, arcs and circles. I turned my head to look out of the rear window just in time to see the top of Naz's office disappear from view. Then I turned back – and, as I did, my building slid up to the car and loomed above me like a sculpted monolith, the words *Madlyn Mansions* still carved in the stone above its front door.

The driver brought the car to a halt in front of it. Annie was waiting on the pavement. She opened the car door and I stepped out.

'All ready?' she asked.

I didn't know what to answer. Was it ready? Everything had seemed to be in place the evening before. Annie had been there all morning: she'd know better than me if it was ready. Or had she meant was I ready? I didn't know. How could you gauge these things? What standard would we have gauged them by? A slight ripple of dizziness ran through me, so I let these thoughts go. I smiled back at Annie weakly and we walked up the stone steps into the building.

The same quiet, uneasy atmosphere was reigning here as had reigned in Naz's office. The bustle and hum of scores of people going about tasks that I'd grown so accustomed to over the last weeks and months had disappeared and been replaced by earnest, hushed, last-minute concentration. The concierge re-enactor was standing in the lobby, while one of the costume people fiddled with the strappings of her face mask. Her face had never come to me – or, to be precise, it had come to me, but only as a blank – so I'd decided she should wear a mask to blank it out. We'd got one of those masks that ice-hockey goaltenders wear: white and pocked with little breathing holes. I stopped in front of her.

'You understand exactly what it is you have to do?' I asked her.

There was a pause behind the mask, then she said:

'Yes. Just stand here.'

Her voice, behind the plastic, was unnatural: it rattled and distorted like those tinny children's toys that emit cow sounds or little phrases when you shake them. I liked that.

'Exactly. Stand here in the lobby,' I repeated. I nodded at her and the costume person, then moved on towards the stairs.

The glum pianist was already practising up in his third floor flat. We'd chosen something by Rachmaninov for him to play – at first, at least. He'd played me sample pieces by several composers, and I'd liked this one by Rachmaninov best. It was called *Second* or *Third Concerto* or *Sonata in A Major* or *B Flat, Minor, Major* – something along those lines. What I liked about it was the way it undulated: how it bent and looped. Plus it was very difficult to play, apparently, which was good: he'd really make mistakes. I heard him hit his first snag as I moved onto the staircase. I stood still and grabbed Annie by the arm:

'Listen!' I whispered.

We listened. The pianist paused, then went at it again, slowing right down as he entered the passage that had tripped him up. He repeated it several times, then picked his pace up and returned to the beginning of the sequence, clocking it – then again, a little faster, then again and again and again, speeding it up each time until he was back almost at full speed. Eventually he accelerated out of the passage and on into the rest of the sonata.

'That's just right,' I said to Annie. 'Just right.'

We moved on, up past the motorbike enthusiast's flat. He wasn't there, of course: he was out in the courtyard tinkering with his motorbike. I hoped he was, at least: that's where he was supposed to be. Then past the boring couple's flat. On the floor above this, the fourth floor, we found Frank. He was standing on the landing with a diagram in his hands, checking the walls and floor – the distribution of filled-in and blank space – against this. Seeing me, he nodded his head in a way that implied he was satisfied with his check, let the hand holding the clipboard drop to his side and told me:

'Everything in order. Good luck.'

159

We continued upwards. Members of Frank and Annie's crews were moving off the stairs, retreating behind doors with radios in their hands. We passed the liver lady's door: I could hear several people shuffling around behind it, and the sound of soft, uncooked liver being laid out on cutting boards. Then we were on my floor. Annie entered my flat with me to check everything was right here, too. It was: the plants were scraggly but alive; the floorboards were scuffed but warm, neither shiny nor dull but somewhere in between; the rug was lying in the right place, slightly ruffled. Annie and I stood facing one another.

'All yours,' she said, smiling warmly. 'Call Naz when you're ready to go.'

I nodded. She left, closing the door behind her.

Before phoning Naz I stood alone in my living room for a while. The layout of the sofas and the coffee table, of the kitchen area – the plants, the counter and the fridge: all this was correct. Below me I could hear radios and TV sets being switched on throughout the building. At least one Hoover was in use. I stepped into the bathroom and looked at the crack on the wall. Just right too: not just the crack but the whole room – taps, wall, colours, crack, everything: perfect. I stepped back into my living room, picked up the phone and called Naz.

'Ready?' he asked.

'Yes,' I said.

'Good,' he replied. 'I'll start the liver and the cats. We'll take it from there.'

160

'Fine,' I said, and hung up.

I walked over to the kitchen window and looked out. Above the staggered, red-tiled rooftops of the facing building, the doors of two of the little cabins opened and two cats were shunted out of each. Three of them started meandering slowly around the roofs, each in his own direction; the fourth just sat down and stayed still – although if I slightly moved my head a centimetre or so to the left the kinked glass made him elongate and slither. A crackle came from downstairs: the snap of wet liver landing on hot oil; then came another one, a third, a fourth. For a few seconds it sounded as though fireworks were being let off a few streets away; then the crackles quietened down into a constant sizzle punctuated by the occasional pop. I wandered back into the bathroom and looked at the cats from there while I waited for the liver's smell to reach me.

When it did, I stepped back into the living room and called Naz.

'It's not right,' I said.

'What's not?' he asked.

'That smell,' I said. 'I thought Annie had made sure they'd broken the pans in. So they weren't new, I mean.'

'I'll check that with her now,' he said. 'Hold on.'

I heard him radio Annie and repeat to her what I'd told him. I heard her radio crackle to his radio and back down the phone line to me. I heard her tell him:

'They are broken in. We went through all this.'

'She says they are broken in,' Naz told me. Then there was a crackle and I heard Annie's voice ask Naz:

'What's not right about the smell?'

'What's wrong with it?' repeated Naz.

'It's got that sharp edge,' I told him. 'Kind of like cordite.'

'A bit like cordite,' I heard him tell her.

'That's what he said before,' I heard her voice say. 'Tell him to give it a few minutes. It should settle down once it gets cooking.'

'Give it a few minutes,' Naz said. 'It should . . .'

'Yes, I heard,' I told him.

I hung up again and walked over to my kitchen area. The plants rustled in their baskets as I passed them, just like I'd first remembered them rustling. I went over to the window. The cats were widely dispersed now, black against the red. I could see three of them: the fourth must have slunk off behind a chimney pot. I brushed past the kitchen unit's waist-high edge, the same way I'd remembered brushing past it when I'd first remembered the whole building – turning half sideways and then back again. My movement wasn't deft enough, though, and my shirt caught slightly on the corner as I passed – not violently, snagging, but still staying against the wood for half a second too long, hugging it too thickly. This wasn't right – wasn't how I remembered it: my memory was of passing it deftly, letting the shirt brush the woodwork lightly, almost

162

imperceptibly, like a matador's cape tickling a bull's horns. I tried it again: this time my shirt didn't touch the woodwork at all. I tried it a third time: walking past the unit, turning sideways and then back again, trying to make my shirt brush fleetingly against the woodwork as I turned. This time I got the shirt bit right, but not the turning. It was difficult, this whole manoeuvre: I would need to practise.

I moved over to the fridge and pulled the door towards me. The door gave without resistance, opening in a smooth and seamless flow. I closed it, then pulled it towards me again. Again it opened smoothly. I did it a third time: again, faultless. Downstairs the pianist was coming out of a corrective loop, speeding up as he took off for new territory. I opened the fridge faultlessly once more, then closed it for the last time: I was ready to go.

I called Naz again.

'I'd like to leave my flat now,' I told him. 'I'll walk down past the liver lady's.'

'Okay,' Naz said. 'Count thirty seconds from now and then leave your door. Exactly thirty seconds.'

He hung up. I hung up too. I stood in the middle of my living-room floor, counting thirty seconds with my hands slightly raised, palms turned slightly outwards. Then I left my flat.

Moving across the landing and down the staircase, I felt like an astronaut taking his first steps – humanity's first steps – across the surface of a previously untouched planet. I'd walked over this stretch a hundred times before, of course – but it had been different then, just a floor: now it was fired up, silently zinging with significance. Held beneath a light coat of sandy dust within a solid gel of tar, the flecks of gold and silver in the granite seemed to emit a kind of charge, as invisible as natural radiation – and just as potent. The non-ferrous-metal banisters and the silk-black wooden rail above them glowed with a dark, unearthly energy that took up the floor's diminished sheen and multiplied its dark intensity. I turned the first corner, glancing through its window as I moved: light from the courtyard bent as it approached me; a long, thin kink travelled across the surface of the facing building, then shot off away to wrinkle more remote, outlying spaces. The red rooftiles were disappearing as I came down, eclipsed by their own underhang as the angle between us widened. Then I turned again and the whole façade revolved away from me.

I continued down the stairs. Sounds travelled to me – but these, too, were subject to anomalies of physics, to interference and distortion. The pianist's music ran, snagged and looped back on itself, first slowing down then speeding up. The static crackle of the liver broke across the orphaned signals cast adrift from radios and television sets. The Hoover moaned on, sucking matter up into its vacuum. I could hear the motorbike enthusiast clanging down in the courtyard, banging at a nut to loosen it. The clanging echoed off the facing building, the clangs reaching me as echoes almost coinciding with the clangs coming straight up from his banging – almost but not quite. I remembered seeing a boy once kicking a football against a wall, the distance between him and the wall setting up the same delay, the same near-overlap. I couldn't remember where, though.

I moved on down the staircase. As I came within four steps of the fifth-floor landing I heard the liver lady's locks jiggle and click. Then her door opened and she moved out slowly, holding a small rubbish bag. She was wearing a light-blue cardigan; her hair was wrapped up in a headscarf; a few white, wiry strands were sprouting from its edges, standing out above her forehead like thin, sculpted snakes. She shuffled forward in her doorway; then she stooped to set her bag down, holding her left hand to her back as she did this. She set the bag down carefully – then paused and, still stooped, turned her head to look up at me.

We'd spent ages practising this moment. I'd showed her exactly how to stoop: the inclination of the shoulders, the path slowly carved through the air by her right hand as it led the bag round her legs and down to the ground (I'd told her to picture the route supporting arms on old gramophone players take, first across and then down), the way her left hand rested on her lower back above the hip, the middle finger pointing straight at the ground. We'd got all this down to a *t* – but we hadn't succeeded in working out the words she'd say to me. I'd racked my brains, but the exact line had never come, any more than the concierge's face had. Rather than forcing it – or, worse, just making any old phrase up – I'd decided to let her come up with a phrase. I'd told her not to concoct a sentence in advance, but rather to wait till the moment when I passed her on the staircase in the actual re-enactment – the moment we were in right now – and to voice the words that sprung to mind just then. She did this now. Still stooped, her face turned towards mine, she released her grip on the bag and said:

'Harder and harder to lift up.'

I froze. *Harder and harder to lift up*, she'd said. I thought about this as I stood there facing her. *Harder and harder to lift up*. I liked it. It was very good. As she got older, her bag of rubbish was becoming harder and harder to lift up. She smiled at me, still slightly stooped. It felt just right: all just as I'd imagined it. I stood still, looking back at her, and said:

'Yes. Every time.'

The words just came to me. I spoke them, then I moved on, turning into the next flight of stairs. For a few seconds I felt weightless – or at least differently weighted: light but dense at the same time. My body seemed to glide fluently and effort-lessly through the atmosphere around it – grace-fully, slowly, like a dancer through water. It felt very good. As I reached the third or fourth step of this new flight, though, this feeling dwindled.

By the fifth or sixth one it was gone. I stopped and turned around. The liver lady's head was disap̶ back into her flat and her hand was ̶ ̶oor to behind it.

̶ ̶d.

̶ ̶opped closing and the liver lady ̶ad back out. She looked quite ̶ came from behind her, inside the

̶cellent,' I said. 'I'd like to do it

̶e said.

̶ top of the first flight,' I told her.

̶ain, shuffled back out towards
hei̶ ̶ picked it up, then shuffled back
into̶ ̶n and closed the door. I started
up t̶ ̶ but before I'd reached the bend
I he̶ ̶r open again behind me and a
faster̶ ̶erson step out onto the landing.

'Wa̶ ̶e,' said a man's voice.

I tur̶ ̶d. It was one of Annie's people.

'Wha̶ ̶ asked.

'If yo̶ ̶ng to start from the top of your
own flig̶ ̶er than back in your flat,' he said,
'how wil ² ̶ know when to open the door?'

I thought about this. It was a fair question. Annie
appeared behind this man.

'What's the problem?' she asked.

I told her. She pondered it for a while, then said:
'We need someone to watch you and signal to

Sam

Comhlacht neamh̶
faoi Acht an Reifrin
agus neodrach a chu
chun an Bunreacht

Is iad comhaltaí an

An Breitheamh On

An tUasal Seamus

An tUasal Peter T.

An tUasal Peter Fi

An tUasal Martin

An Coimisiún F

18 Sráid Líosai
Teileafón:
Íosghlao:
Ríomhpho
Suíomh

@
f
i

us when the time comes to send her out. But no one can really do that without getting in the way themselves.'

'The cat people!' I said.

'Of course!' said Annie.

The people who'd pushed the cats onto the facing building's roof would be able to see me from the top-floor windows of that building as I turned the staircase bend: there was a window there.

'They need to watch for me, and radio you when I'm on the – let's see: when did the door open?' I walked back to the step I'd been on when the liver lady's locks had clicked and jiggled. 'The third one down,' I said.

'I'm not directly linked to them,' said Annie, holding up her radio. 'We'll have to go through Naz.'

She radioed him and the chain of communication was set up. The cat people would watch me from their building as I passed the window on the banister bend and, when I hit the third step of the next flight, give the order to open the door – this via Naz, who'd act as the join between the two parties from his office a few streets away. It took ten or so minutes to set this up. When all the links were in place, everyone apart from me went back into the liver lady's flat, her door was closed again and I walked back up the stairs to the top of the first flight.

I stood there for a while, rocking very slightly

forwards and backwards on my planted feet. I felt the point of pressure shifting from my heels to my toes via the arched tendon in between, the plantar fascia, then back again, a three-part chain. I rocked slightly back then slightly forward several times, then headed down the stairs again.

This time I paused in front of the window by the first bend. I even leant against it, resting my forehead on the glass like I had one floor up on the day I'd found the building. I couldn't see the spotters in the facing building, the two cat men – but I knew they were there. If they'd been marksmen, snipers, they'd have had a clear shot at me right now. I slid both arms slightly up against the window pane. The tingling started in my right hip and seeped upwards, up my spine. I looked at the top branches of a tree below me in the courtyard: a light breeze was buffeting its leaves, making them dance.

I pulled my head away and made to move on down – but hesitated when I noticed a small patch of black moving quite fast against the facing building. It was gone so quickly that I thought it must have been another optical effect, a quirk of the kinked glass. I tried to reproduce it by pressing my forehead back onto the window pane and pulling it away again, but couldn't make the black patch reappear. I tried it several times without success. I hadn't imagined it, though: there'd been a streak of black moving fast against the facing building.

Eventually I gave up and moved on down. As I hit the third step I heard a buzz or scrape that came from behind the liver lady's door. It could have been a radio or it could have been her rubbish bag scraping the floor. An instant later came the jiggle of her latch; then the door opened and she shuffled out again, her rubbish bag in her hand. Once more she stooped to set her bag down, holding her left hand to her lower back as she did this; once more she looked up at me and pronounced her phrase:

'Harder and harder to lift up.'

I answered her as before. Again I felt the sense of gliding, of light density. The moment I was in seemed to expand and become a pool – a still, clear pool that swallowed everything up in its calm contentedness. Again the feeling dwindled as I left the zone around her door. As soon as I'd reached the third step of the next flight I turned round, as before, and said:

'Again.'

We did it again – but this time it didn't work. She'd steered the rubbish bag through its horizontal arc around her legs and, stooping, started to lower it to the ground when suddenly it slipped out of her hand and fell with a loud clunk. She bent over to pick it up but I stopped her.

'Don't bother,' I said. 'It's broken the . . . you know: it won't be right. Let's take it from the top again. Someone should clean that patch up, too.'

Her bag had leaked from its bottom right corner,

leaving a wet, sticky-looking patch on the floor. Someone came out and mopped this up.

'It looks too clean now,' I said when they'd done this.

Annie came out again and looked.

'We'll have to dust and sand it again,' she said.

'How long will that take?' I asked.

'A good hour till it looks just like it did before.'

'An hour?' I repeated. 'That's too . . . I need it to . . .'

My voice petered out. I was quite upset. I wanted to slip back into it now, right now: the pool, the lightness and the gliding. There was nothing I could do, though: it wouldn't be right if the floor wasn't the right texture. I gathered myself together and announced:

'Okay: do it. I'll move on.'

I'd come back to the liver lady later. And besides, she was just part of the re-enactment: I had a lot still to do, a lot more space to cover.

I walked past the pianist's flat. The sound of his music grew crisper and sharper as I passed his door, then once again soft and floaty as I moved down from his floor. On the landing below his I passed the boring couple's flat. This is where the Hoover noise was coming from. The Hoover was being shunted back and forth across a carpet, by the sound of it. The wife re-enactor would be doing it. I moved on, through a patch of neutral space, down past the motorbike enthusiast's flat. His clangings were still coming from the courtyard, but with less of an echo now: maybe the trees and the swings were getting in the way down here. I carried on down to the lobby.

Here the sensation started returning: the same sense of zinging and intensity. My concierge was standing as instructed – standing quite still in the middle of the lobby with her white ice-hockey mask on. Behind her, to her left – my right – there was a cupboard; beside that, another strip of white, neutral space. As I walked around her in a circle, looking at her from all sides, her stumpy arms and featureless face seemed to emanate an almost toxic level of significance. I cocked my head to one side, then the other; I crouched to the ground and looked at her from there. She looked like a statue in a harbour, towering above the granite – or a spire, a reactor, a communications mast. Being this close to her I felt overexposed after a while – so I opened up her cupboard door and stepped inside.

Here were the broom, the mop and bucket and the industrial Hoover, all in the positions that I'd first remembered and then sketched them in. There was another object, too: a strangely shaped machine for cleaning granite floors. It hadn't come to me initially – but then when I'd found it stored in there one morning it hadn't seemed wrong, either, so I'd kept it. I stayed in the cupboard for a long time. In here it felt intimate, warm. I felt I'd burrowed to one of the innermost chambers of the vision I'd had realized all around me. It was a good position: well placed, with good sightlines. The cupboard door was slightly ajar: I looked out through its slit at the concierge standing in the lobby. She was standing with her back turned to me, the mask straps fastened at the back of her head. Her shoulders rose and fell as she breathed. The view I had of her was like a murderer's view – hidden, looking through a thin slit at her back.

After a while I stepped back out of the cupboard, crossed the strip of neutral space and came back to the bottom of the staircase. I was about to step into the garden when I heard the main door open behind me, the one that led onto the street. I turned round. A small boy had just walked in: he was one of the pianist's pupils, arriving for a lesson. He walked across the lobby, towards where the concierge was standing – then caught sight of me and hesitated. He must have been ten or eleven years old. On his back he wore a little satchel – one of Annie's props, that. He had straight, brown hair and freckles. We stood facing one another, me and him, completely still – three people completely still there in the lobby: myself, this small boy and the concierge. He looked frightened. I smiled at him and said:

'Just carry on. It will all be fine.'

At this the small boy started moving again. He walked past me and started up the staircase. I looked at his satchel as he passed me, his scuffed leather shoes. I watched him walk up and away from me, turning and dwindling. He disappeared from view on the second floor and his footsteps stopped. I heard a muffled bell ring; then the piano music stopped too. I heard the pianist's chair being scraped back, then his footsteps heading for his door. I waited till the boy was safely in before I went out to the courtyard.

This was full of outdoor noises: distant cars and buses, trains and planes, the general subdued roar that air in cities has. Upstairs on the third floor the child started playing scales. These spilled out of the pianist's window but, not walled in like his own playing had been in the stairwell, dissipated in the summer air. I could see smoke piping from the vent outside the liver lady's kitchen almost directly above me. I could see my bathroom window sill but not the glass itself: the angle was too sharp. I looked down again. The motorbike enthusiast was three yards to my left. He had stopped banging at his bolt and was now turning it, unscrewing something. On the earth beneath the engine of his bike a patch of oil had formed: it looked kind of like a shadow, but more solid. I stood by his bike for a while, looking at the patch, then said:

'Leave that there when you've finished.'

'Leave what?' he asked, looking up at me and slightly squinting.

'Leave that patch,' I said.

'How leave it?' he asked.

'Don't let it be smudged or covered over. I might want to capture it later.'

'Capture it?' he asked.

'Whatever,' I said. 'Just don't let it get wiped out. Understand?'

'Yes,' he said. 'Okay.'

I left him and walked over to the swings. It wasn't his business to make me explain what I meant by 'capture'. It meant whatever I wanted it to mean: I was paying him to do what I said. Prick. I did want to capture it, though: its shape, its shade. These were important, and I didn't want to lose them. I thought of going back up to my flat to get a piece of paper onto which to transcribe the patch, but decided to do it later, when he wasn't there. If it rained, though . . . I sat down on one of the swings and looked up at the sky. It didn't look like rain: it was blue with the odd billowing cloud. I slid off the swing after a while, pushed it so it continued swinging to and fro and lay on my back beneath it, watching it swing above my head against the sky. The billowing clouds were moving slowly and the swing was moving fast. The blue was still – but two high-up aeroplanes were slicing it into segments with their vapour trails, like Naz and I had done to the city with our pins and threads. Lying on my back, I let my arms slide slightly over the grass away from my sides, turned my palms upwards till the tingling sensation crept through my body again. I lay there for a very long time, tingling, looking at the sky . . .

Later that evening I was lying in my bath, soaking, gazing at the crack. The pianist's last pupil had

175

gone, and he'd started composing, playing a phrase then stopping for a long time before playing it again with a new half-phrase tagged onto the end. Liver was crackling and sizzling downstairs. I could smell it. It still wasn't quite right – still had that slightly acrid edge, like cordite. I brought that up again with Naz when we spoke after my bath.

'We'll try to get that right,' he told me. 'Apart from that, though, how did you think it went?'

'It went . . . well, it went . . .' I started. I didn't know what to tell him.

'Was it a success, in your opinion?' he asked.

Had it been a success? Difficult question. Some things had worked, and some things hadn't. My shirt had slightly caught against the cutting board, but then the fridge had opened perfectly. The liver lady had come up with that fantastic line but then dropped her rubbish bag when she'd tried to re-enact her movements for a third time. Then there was the question of the smell, of course. But had it been a success? A success at what? Had I expected all my movements to be seamless and perfect instantly? Of course not. Had I expected the detour through understanding that I'd had to take in order to do anything for the last year – for my whole life – to be bypassed straight away: just cut off, a redundant nerve, an isolated oxbow lake that would evaporate? No: that would take work – a lot of work. But today my movements had been different. Felt different. My mind too, my whole consciousness. Different, better. It was . . .

'It was a beginning,' I told Naz.

'A beginning?' he repeated.

'Yes,' I said. 'A very good beginning.'

That night, I dreamt that I and all my staff – Naz, Annie, Frank, the liver lady and the pianist and the motorbike enthusiast and concierge and piano pupil, plus all Naz's, Frank's and Annie's people, the coordinators lurking behind doors, the spotters in the facing building and their back-up people too – I dreamt that all of us had linked ourselves together: physically, arm in arm and standing on each other's shoulders like a troupe of circus acrobats. We'd linked ourselves together in this way in the formation of an aeroplane. It was an early, primitive plane: a biplane, of the type an early aviator might have used for a record-setting transatlantic flight.

We'd taken off in this formation and were flying above my building and the streets around it. We could look down as we flew and see the courtyard with its trees and swings, its patch of oil beneath the engine of the motorbike. We could see ourselves, our re-enacted doubles, in the courtyard too: the motorbike enthusiast, banging and unscrewing; myself, lying beneath the swings. We could see the cats slinking around the red roofs. If we banked north and glided for a while we could see Naz's building with its blue-and-white exterior, the aerials on its roof. Through its top windows we could see doubles of Naz's office team coordinating events in my building. We could see these events too, through walls which had become transparent: the liver lady laying her bag down, talking to me as I passed her, the pianist practising his Rachmaninov, the concierge, the pupil – the whole lot.

We banked again and saw the sports track with its white and red and yellow markings. There were athletes running around this, just like there had been in my coma. I was commentating again. Everything was running smoothly, happily, until I noticed, lying beside the goalposts, these old, greasy escalator parts – the same ones that I'd seen laid out at Green Park Station. As soon as I saw them the whole thing went out of kilter: events in my building, Naz's people, the athletes and the commentary – the lot. Athletes tripped over, crashing into one another; my flow of words faltered and dried up; the liver lady's rubbish bag broke, scattering putrid, mouldy lumps of uneaten liver all over the courtyard; the swings' chains snapped; black cats shrieked and chased their tails. And then our plane – the plane that we'd formed from the interlinking of our bodies: it was stalling, nose-diving towards the ground, whose surface area was crumpling like old tin . . .

Just before the crash I woke up cold with sweat to the unpleasant smell of congealed fat.

CHAPTER 9

Fat became quite a problem, as it goes. Over the next days and weeks the liver lady fried her way through a small mountain of pig liver. She had three or four frying pans on the go at any given time. She might not have been doing it herself: it might have been the back-up, Annie's people, tossing it all on, slab after slab, letting them slide around and sizzle, turning them over and taking them off again. Whoever was doing the actual cooking, the sheer amount of vaporized fat rising from the frying pans hung around the building. It clogged up the extraction fan, whose out-vent pointed towards my bathroom window. To have this outer part cleaned turned out to be difficult: you couldn't get at it from inside. We had to hire those window cleaners you see dangling from the tops of skyscrapers to come and scrape the fat out while they hung beside it. It was pretty nerve-wracking to watch. I had the courtyard below them cleared, just in case. I know all about things falling from the sky.

These men didn't fall – but the cats did. That's what I'd seen on the day of the first re-enactment, when I'd pressed my cheek against the window by the turning between my floor and the liver lady's and then pulled it away: the black streak I'd thought was an optical effect. It wasn't: it was one of the black cats falling off the roof. By the end of the second day of re-enactments three had fallen. They all died. We'd only bought four in the first place; one wasn't enough to produce the effect I wanted.

'What do you want to do?' asked Naz.

'Get more,' I said.

'How many more?'

'At a loss rate of three every two days, I'd say quite an amount. A rolling supply. Just keep putting them up there.'

'Doesn't it upset you?' Naz asked two days later as we stood together in my kitchen looking down into the courtyard at one of his men sliding a squashed cat into a bin bag.

'No,' I said. 'We can't expect everything to work perfectly straight away. It's a learning process.'

A more serious problem was the pianist. This one did upset me, plenty: I caught him out red-handed one day, blatantly defrauding me. I'd spent an afternoon concentrating on the lower sections of the staircase, studying the way light fell from the large windows onto the patterned floor. The floor had a repetitive pattern, as I mentioned earlier: when sunlight shone on it directly, which it did on the second floor for three hours and fourteen minutes each day, it filled the corridors of white between the pattern's straight black lines like water flooding a maze in slow motion. I'd already observed this happening on the top floors, but was working on the lower floors now. I'd noticed that the light seemed deeper down here – more dense and less flighty. Higher up it had more dust specks in it: these were borne upwards by the warm air in the stairwell; when they reached the top floors they hung around like small stars in massive galaxies, hardly moving at all, and this made the air seem lighter.

So anyway, I was lying on the floor observing this phenomenon – speculating, you might say – while the piano music looped and repeated in the background when I saw the pianist walk up the stairs towards me.

This, of course, was physically impossible: I was listening to him practising his Rachmaninov two floors above me at this very moment. But impossible or not, there he was, walking up the stairs towards me. As soon as he caught sight of me he jolted to a standstill, then started to turn – but it was too late: he knew the game was up. He became static again. His eyes scampered half-heartedly around the floor's maze as though looking for a way out of the quandary he found himself in while at the same time knowing that they wouldn't find one; the bald crown of his head went even whiter than it usually was. He mumbled:

'Hello.'

'What are you . . .' I started, but I couldn't finish

the sentence. A wave of dizziness was sweeping over me. The piano music was still spilling from his flat into the sunlit stairwell.

'I had an audition,' he murmured.

'Then who . . .' I asked.

'Recording,' he said, his eyes still moping at the floor.

'But there are mistakes in it!' I said. 'And loop-backs, and . . .'

'A recording of me. I made it myself, especially. It's the same thing, more or less. Isn't it?'

It was my turn to go white now. There were no mirrors in the building, but I'm sure that if there had been and I'd looked in one I would have seen myself completely white: white with both rage and dizziness.

'No!' I shouted. 'No, it is not! It is just absolutely not the same thing!'

'Why not?' he asked. His voice was still monotonous and flat but was shaking a little.

'Because . . . It absolutely isn't! It's just not the same because . . . It's not the same at all.' I was shouting as loud as I could, and yet my voice was coming out broken and faint. I could hardly breathe. I'd been lying on my side when he came up the stairs towards me, and had only half-risen – a reclining posture, like those dying Roman emperors in paintings. I tried to stand up now but couldn't. Panic welled up inside me. I tried to be formal. I forced a deep breath into my lungs and said:

'I shall pursue this matter via Naz. You may go now. I should prefer to be alone.'

He turned around and left. I made straight for my flat. No sooner had I got there than I threw up. I lurched into the bathroom and stood holding the sink for a long, long time after I'd finished puking. When I could, I raised my eyes up to the crack; this oriented me again, stopped me feeling dizzy. The building was on my side, even if this bad man wasn't. When I felt well enough to move, I went into the living room, sat down on my sofa and phoned Naz.

'It's totally unacceptable!' I told him after I'd explained what had just happened. 'Completely totally!'

'Shall I fire him?' asked Naz.

'Yes!' I said. 'No! No, don't fire him. He's perfect – in the way he looks, I mean. And in the way he plays. Even the way he speaks: that vacant mono-tone. But give him hell! Really bad! Hurt him! Metaphorically, I mean, I suppose. He has to understand that what he's done just won't fly any more. Make him understand that!'

'I'll talk to him immediately,' Naz said.

'Where are you now?' I asked him.

'I'm in my office,' he said. 'I'll come over. Can I bring you anything?'

'Some water,' I said. 'Sparkling.'

I hung up – then phoned him back straight away.

'Find out how often he's pulled this one, when you talk to him,' I said.

Naz turned up with the water after half an hour. Apparently the pianist was sorry: he hadn't realized how vital it was that he should actually be playing the whole time. He'd only used the cassette two times before, when he'd needed to do something else, and . . .

'Something else?' I interrupted. 'I don't pay him to do other stuff! Three times, no less!'

'He's agreed not to do it again,' Naz said.

'He's agreed, has he? That's nice of him. Shall we give him a raise?'

Naz smiled. 'Shall I stick a surveillance camera on him?' he asked.

'No,' I said. 'No cameras. Find some other way of making sure he's doing it properly, though.'

The thing behind Naz's eyes whirred for a while and then he nodded.

It wasn't unreasonable to expect this guy to play when he'd been paid to play – been paid enormous amounts of money, at that. And the hours weren't that bad: I generally put the building into *on* mode for between six and eight hours each day – mostly in stretches of two hours. Sometimes there'd be a five-hour stretch. Once I went right through a night and half the next day. That was my prerogative, though: it had been written in the contracts that all re-enactors and all back-up staff had signed – written right there in big print for them to read.

I moved through the spaces of my building and its courtyard as I saw fit, just like I'd told Naz I would when we'd first met. I roamed around it as my inclination led me. On some days I felt like gathering data: sketching, measuring, transcribing. So I'd copy the patch of oil beneath the motorbike, say – how it elongated, how its edges rippled – then take the drawing over to Naz's office, have it photocopied several times, then stick the copies in a line across my living room wall, rotating the patch's formation through three-sixty. I captured lots of places this way: corners, angles against walls, bits of banister. Sometimes instead of sketching them I'd press a piece of paper up against them and rub it around so that their surface left a mark, a smear. Or I measured the amount of time it took the sunlight to first flood and then drain from each floor in the afternoon, or how long it would take for the swings, if pushed with such and such a strength, to come to a complete standstill.

At other times I lost all sense of measure, distance, time, and just lay watching dust float or swings swing or cats lounge. Some days I didn't even leave my flat: instead, I sat in my living room or lay in my bath gazing at the crack. I'd keep the building in *on* mode while I did this: the pianist had to play – really play – and the motorbike enthusiast hammer and bang; the concierge had to stand down in the lobby in her ice-hockey mask, the liver lady fry her liver – but I wouldn't move around and visit them. Knowing they were there, in *on* mode, was enough. I'd lie there in my bath for hours and hours on end, half-floating while the crack on the wall jutted and meandered, hazy behind moving wisps of steam.

I worked hard on certain actions, certain gestures. Brushing past my kitchen unit, for example. I hadn't been satisfied with the way that had gone on the first day. I hadn't moved past it properly, and my shirt had dragged across its edge for too long. The shirt was supposed to brush the woodwork – kiss it, no more. It was all in the way I half-turned so that I was sideways as I passed it. A pretty difficult manoeuvre: I ran through it again and again – at half-speed, quarter-speed, almost no speed at all, working out how each muscle had to act, each ball and socket turn. I thought of bull-fighting again, then cricket: how the batsman, when he chooses not to play the ball, steps right into its path and lets it whistle past his arched flank millimetres from his chest, even letting it flick the loose folds of his shirt as it shoots by. I put the building into *off* mode for a whole day while I practised the manoeuvre: striding, half-turning as I rose to my toes, letting my shirt brush against it – grazing it like a hover-craft does water – then turning square again as I came down. Then I tried it for real the next day, with the building in *on* mode. After the two days I had three separate bruises on my side – but it was worth it for the fluent, gliding feeling I got the few times it worked: the immersion, the contentedness.

I worked hard on my exchange with the liver lady too. Not that anything – dropped bag apart – had been wrong with it on the first day we'd done it: I just felt like doing it again and again and again. Hundreds of times. More. No one counted – I didn't, at any rate. I'd break the sequence down to its constituent parts – the changing angle of her headscarf and her stooped back's inclination as I moved between two steps, the swivel of her neck as her head turned to face me – and lose myself in them. One day we spent a whole morning going back and back and back over the moment at which her face switched from addressing me with the last word of her phrase, the *up*, to cutting off eye contact, turning away and leading first her shoulders then eventually her whole body back into her flat. Another afternoon we concentrated on the instant at which her rubbish bag slouched into the granite of the floor, its shape changing as its contents, no longer suspended in space by her arm, rearranged themselves into a state of rest. I laid out the constituent parts of the whole sequence and relished each of them, then put them back together and relished the whole – then took them apart again.

One day, as I stood by my kitchen window looking down into the courtyard, I had an idea. I phoned Naz to tell him:

'I should like,' I said, 'a model of the building.'

'A model?'

'Yes, a model: a scale model. Get Roger to make

it.' Roger was our architect. 'You know when you go into public buildings' lobbies when they're being developed and you see those little models showing how it'll all look when it's finished . . .'

'Ah yes, I see,' Naz said. 'I'll get on to him.'

Roger delivered the model to me a day and a half later. It was brilliant. It was about three feet high and four wide. It showed the courtyard and the facing building and even the sports track. There were little figures in it: the motorbike enthusiast next to his bike, the pianist with his bald pate, the liver lady with her headscarf and her snaky strands of hair, the concierge with her stubby arms and white mask. He'd even made a miniscule mop and Hoover for her cupboard. You could see all these because he'd made several of the walls and floors from see-through plastic. On the ones that weren't see-through he'd filled in the details: light switches and door-knobs, the repeating pattern on the floor. The stretches of neutral space he'd made white. Sections of wall and roof came off too, so you could reach inside. As soon as Roger had left my flat I called Naz.

'Give him a big bonus,' I said.

'How much?' Naz asked.

'Oh, you know: big,' I told him. 'And Naz?'

'Yes?'

'I'd like you to . . . Let's see . . .'

The figures of the characters were moveable. I'd picked up the liver lady one while talking and was making it bobble down the stairs and out into the courtyard.

'I'd like you to get the liver lady to go down the stairs and visit the motorbike enthusiast.'

'Now?' he asked.

'Now,' I said, 'yes.'

Two minutes later I was standing at my window watching her – the real liver lady – shuffling out into the courtyard. I dragged Roger's model over to the window so I could see both it and the courtyard at the same time. I picked up the motorbike enthusiast figure and placed him on one of the swings.

'Now,' I told Naz, 'I'd like the motorbike enthusiast to go sit on the swing closest to him.'

Not half a minute later I saw the real motorbike enthusiast look up towards my building's doorway. He was talking to someone; I couldn't hear what was being said because the pianist was playing his Rachmaninov – but then I didn't need to. The motorbike enthusiast looked up towards my window, then rose to his feet, walked over to the swing and sat on it.

'I'd prefer him to kneel on it,' I told Naz.

'Kneel?'

'Yes: kneel rather than sit. He should kneel in exactly the same position as he kneels beside his bike in.'

The figure had been cast in that position. Its limbs didn't move. A few more seconds, and the real motorbike enthusiast changed his position on the swing so he had one knee on the seat.

'And now . . .' I said. 'The pianist! He can go and watch.'

I made the pianist figure do just that: cross over to his window and peer out. Seconds later the piano music stopped below me; then the sound of a chair being pushed back, then footsteps – then his real bald pate popped out of his real window. I lifted the model up and rested it against the window sill so I could look down on the model's head poking out at the same time as I looked at the real one. The distance made them both look the same size.

Before I sent them all back to their posts, I had the motorbike enthusiast give the swing a hard push. As he did this I did the same thing to the model swing. I watched them both swing. The model swing swung about two and a half times for each time the real swing swung. It also stopped before the real one did. I stayed at my window for a long time, watching the diminishing movements of the real swing. I remembered wind-up musical toys, Fisher Price ones, how they slow down as their mechanism unwinds right out to its end, until it seems that no more music will come from them – but then if you nudge them just a little, they always give one last half-chime, and another half-half-chime, and still more, less and less each time, for up to hours – or weeks – after they first ground to a halt.

The next day I placed my model on my living-room floor. I moved the figures around once more and issued instructions down the phone to Naz as I did this – only today I didn't go and look. Just knowing it was happening was enough. I had the concierge pick up the liver lady's rubbish bag, the motorbike enthusiast kneel in the lobby for two hours, the pianist sit on the closed lid of his piano facing his window for another two – and all the while, as they did this for real, I sat in the same spot on my living-room floor. The day after that I lay beside the model looking at it from the same angle as the sun did. My gaze burst in through the upper staircase window and flooded the floor's patterned maze, then slowly – very slowly, almost imperceptibly – glazed, lost its focus, darkened and retreated, disappearing from the furthest edge of floor four hours and seven minutes after it had first entered. I did this for each floor I'd previously measured: four hours and seven minutes for the top down to three hours and fourteen minutes for the second.

I only left the building – the whole re-enactment area, I mean: the building and the courtyard and the stretch of streets between there and Naz's office, with its bridge and sports track – twice during the next month. The first time was to go shopping. I'd been having all that done for me, but one day I got an urge to go and check up on the outside world myself. Nothing much to report. The second time was when I noticed that my old, dented Fiesta which was parked beside the sports track had a flat tyre. I hadn't driven it in months, and didn't plan to any time soon – but when I saw the flat tyre I remembered the tyre place beside my old flat: the one I'd paused beside the day the Settlement came through, uncertain whether to go home or press on to the airport.

As soon as I'd remembered it, I started seeing the tyre shop clearly in my mind: its front windows, the pavement where its sign stood, the café next to it. I remembered that a garish model baked-beans tin was mounted on the cafés roof beside a pile of tyres. More tyres had been lined up on the street outside, parked upright in a rack. As these details came back to me, the whole place – which when I'd lived beside it had seemed to me so mundane that I'd barely even noticed it – took on the air of something interesting. Intrigued, I decided to visit it. I borrowed some tools from the motorbike enthusiast, replaced the flat tyre with the spare one and then drove back to where I used to live to have the flat one fixed.

The place didn't seem to have changed since I'd last seen it. It still had tyres lined up in a rack on the street outside and more tyres piled up on its roof beside the large-scale garish model baked-beans tin that advertised the next door café. The tyres were normal tyres, real ones, and looked miniature next to the giant tin, like toys. More tyres were leaning in stacks against the shop front, like you see at go-kart tracks. Behind these, painted announcements advertised special deals on tyres both new and part-worn or free fitting. On the pavement outside, a small rectangular contraption stood upright: a waist-high board skewered by a pole set into a heavy base. In the breeze the board span quickly round the pole, flashing two messages at passers-by in quick succession. Both messages said 'TYRES'.

There was a more elaborate advertisement swaying around on the pavement a few feet away: a child dressed in a Michelin Man suit. The suit gave him an obese white tyre-girth that swayed as he moved. He was maybe ten, eleven. I could tell it was a boy because he wasn't wearing the suit's head. Two older boys had this: these two were standing by the tyre shop's entrance, kicking the head to one another like a football. As I pulled up they stopped kicking it and sauntered over to my car. They looked at my tyres very earnestly, craning their necks in an exaggerated way – imitating their parents, doubtless, or whoever it was that owned this shop.

I stepped out of the car. 'You've got a dent,' the oldest boy said. He must have been fifteen.

'I know that,' I told him. 'That's not why I'm here. I'm here because I've got a flat tyre.'

The slightly younger boy who'd been kicking the head with him had moved round the car to check the tyres on the passenger side.

'It's in the boot,' I told them.

I walked round to the back of the car and opened

193

it up. The two boys peered inside, like gangsters in movies – in those scenes where the gangsters open up a car boot in which they've stashed a body or a cache of guns. These boys were thinking of those scenes too as I opened up the boot for them: I could tell. They peered in; then the oldest one reached in and lifted the tyre out. The younger tried to help him, but he brushed his hand aside. The youngest one, the one in the Michelin Man suit, had waddled over and tried to join in, but the middling one shoved him away again.

'You're meant to stand out in the street!' he told him, raising his voice.

'You're not in charge of me!' the youngest one shouted back.

'Shut up, both of you!' the oldest told them.

The middling one looked down. His face flushed red with hurt. The youngest one swaggered triumphantly beside him in his suit. The oldest boy carried the tyre into the shop. I followed him. The middling boy slouched in behind me but stayed in the doorway, keeping the youngest out. There was no one else in the shop.

'Where are the real people?' I asked.

'I'm real,' the oldest boy said. He looked offended.

'You know . . . the . . . the owners,' I said.

'Off to lunch,' he answered.

'Café next door,' added the middling one.

'Well, I could come back when . . .' I began – but

stopped because the oldest boy had dunked my tyre into a tub of water and was slowly turning it round. He seemed to know what he was doing. He stared into the murky water, his eyes taut with concentration. I stared too: it was absorbing, watching the tyre's bottom edge entering the water and slowly revolving. After a few seconds the boy stopped turning it and pointed:

'There's your puncture,' he said.

I followed his finger with my eye. Bubbles of air were rising from a silvery slit on the rubber's surface. It was like mineral water, only dirty.

'Will they be able to fix it?' I asked. 'When they come back, I mean.'

'I can fix it,' said the boy.

He hoisted the tyre out of the water and carried it over to a kind of lathe. The tyre was pretty big in proportion to him: he had to half-support it with his knee. Black grime was rubbing off it onto his clothes, which were already smeared with grime all over. He sat down at the lathe and pressed a pedal with his foot, which made a series of clamps tighten round the tyre. Then his foot pressed another pedal and the tyre deflated with a bang. He started daubing glue on from a tin. His hand moved quickly as he did this, dipping and daubing, flashing the brush one way then another. The exaggerated manner he'd had when he sauntered over to the car was gone, eclipsed now by his earnest concentration, his artisanal skill. The middling boy watched him from a few feet away. The youngest boy watched too. The eyes of both of them were full of admiration – longing, almost – as they watched him flick the brush.

He pressed a pedal with his foot; the lathe revolved a quarter-turn between his hands, and he brushed an adjoining spot with glue. He pressed another pedal, and the wheel turned back for him to brush the spot on the other side of the puncture. When he'd brushed all he wanted, he dipped his hand into to the tub again, scooped up some water and patted this on the tyre while the three of us stood still, reverent as a congregation at a christening, watching him at his font.

Effortlessly the boy's hand rose and flipped a lever at the lathe's side. The lathe hissed as its clamps released my wheel and glided back. The same hand reached up to beside his shoulder to take hold of a blue tube. The tube was hanging just beyond his field of vision, but the hand didn't need help: it knew just where it was. Its fingers jabbed the tube into my tyre and its thumb depressed a catch; air started flowing into it. A minute later the tyre was mended, inflated and rolling across the tarmac back towards my car. He took it to the boot again and lifted it back in.

'Shouldn't we put it back on?' I asked. 'Drive on it, I mean?'

'No. Keep it as a spare,' he said. 'You should rotate them.'

'Rotate, yes,' I said. 'Okay.'

He could have told me anything and I'd have said 'Okay'. I stood there looking at him for a while longer. We all did. A truce seemed to exist now between the other two boys. After a while I asked him:

'Shall I pay you, then, or . . .'

'Yes. Pay me,' he said. 'Ten pounds.'

I paid him ten pounds. I remembered that my wind-screen washer reservoir was empty and I asked him for some fill-up. He glanced at the middling boy and slightly raised his chin; the middling boy ran into the shop and came out with a litre of blue liquid which he and the youngest boy poured into the windscreen washer reservoir for me, operating in sync together now, the youngest one holding the lid off while the middling one poured, then passing the lid over for the middling one to screw on while he, the youngest one, carried the empty bottle over to a bin. They closed the bonnet for me and I got back into my car.

Before I drove off I pushed the windscreen spurter button to make sure it worked. Liquid should have squirted out onto the glass, but nothing happened. I pushed it some more. Still nothing. I got out, opened the bonnet again and checked the reservoir. It was empty.

'It's all gone!' I said.

The boys peered in. The oldest one got down on his knees and looked under the car.

'There's no patch,' he said. 'It hasn't leaked. It should be there.' He turned to the middling boy and said: 'Go get another bottle.'

Another bottle was brought out and poured into the reservoir. Once more I climbed inside the car and pressed the spurter button. Once more nothing happened – and once more, when we looked inside the reservoir, we found it empty.

'Two litres!' I said. 'Where has it all gone?'

They'd vaporized, evaporated. And do you know what? It felt wonderful. Don't ask me why: it just did. It was as though I'd just witnessed a miracle: matter – these two litres of liquid – becoming un-matter – not surplus matter, mess or clutter, but pure, bodiless blueness. Transubstantiated. I looked up at the sky: it was blue and endless. I looked back at the boy. His overalls and face were covered in smears. He'd taken on these smears so that the miracle could happen, like a Christian martyr being flagellated, crucified, scrawled over with stigmata. I felt elated – elated and inspired.

'If only . . .' I started, but paused.

'What?' he asked.

'If only everything could . . .'

I trailed off again. I knew what I meant. I stood there looking at his grubby face and told him:

'Thank you.'

Then I got into the car and turned the ignition key in its slot. The engine caught – and as it did, a torrent of blue liquid burst out of the dashboard and cascaded down. It gushed from the radio, the heating panel, the hazard-lights switch and the speedometer and mileage counter. It gushed all over me: my shirt, my legs, my groin.

CHAPTER 10

I should have jumped out of the car as fast as I could, but I sat there instead, letting the blue liquid gush all over me. When it had finished gushing it trickled, then dribbled, then dripped. I sat impassive while it ran itself out. It took a long time: even when it seemed to have dripped itself dry it still managed to grind out another half-drip a few seconds later, and another half-half-drip a few seconds after that.

Slowly, tentatively, the three boys edged over to the car and peered in. The youngest one gasped when he saw my trousers soaked in the sticky blue liquid. The other two said nothing: they just stared. I stared too: we all stared at the dashboard and my legs. We stayed there, static like that, for a long while. Then I drove back to my building.

When I got there, I took off my wet clothes and had a bath. I lay in my bath looking at the crack and thinking about what had happened. It was something very sad – not in the normal sense but on a grander scale, the scale that really big events are measured in, like centuries of history or the death of stars: very, very sad. A miracle seemed to have taken place, a miracle of transubstantiation – in contravention of the very laws of physics, laws that make swings stop swinging and fridge doors catch and large, unsuspended objects fall out of the sky. This miracle, this triumph over matter, seemed to have occurred, then turned out not to have done at all – to have failed utterly, spectacularly, its watery debris crashing down to earth, turning the scene of a triumphant launch into the scene of a disaster, a catastrophe. Yes, it was very sad.

I lay there in my bath replaying the event in my mind, scouring its surfaces. There'd been the garish model tin and piled-up tyres, the spinning sign, the swaying tyre-suit of the youngest boy, the lathe with its clamps and pedals and the blue tube full of air. I remembered how the boy had carried the tyre from my car boot to the shop, how grime had rubbed onto his shirt; then how his hands had whipped around it daubing glue on, re-inflating it. I lay for so long remembering that the bath turned cold and my skin wrinkled. After an age I got out and phoned Naz.

'I'd like you to facilitate another project I'm considering,' I said.

'Certainly,' Naz replied. 'Tell me about it.'

'I should like a certain area,' I said, 'to be reproduced exactly.'

'A small section of the building?' he asked.

'No,' I said. 'Another place. A tyre repair shop.'

'That shouldn't be a problem,' Naz said. 'If you

tell me where it is, I'll give Roger a call right now and get him to knock you up another model.'

'It's not a model I require,' I told Naz. 'It's a full-scale reproduction. I should like Roger to reproduce this tyre shop exactly, down to the last detail. Furthermore, I shall require re-enactors to run through a certain event which I'll outline later. These re-enactors must be children: three of them, aged fifteen, thirteen and eleven. Plus one man of my age. Four people in all, plus back-up. I shall require them to run through this event constantly, round the clock.'

There was a pause at Naz's end. I pictured his office in the blue-and-white building, how the desks were laid out, the telescope by the window. After a while he said:

'How can they do that?'

This was a good question, but I had the answer:

'We'll have several teams,' I told him, 'relieving one another, in relay.'

'In relay?' he said.

'Yes,' I answered. 'We rotate them.'

There was another pause at Naz's end. I concentrated on his office again, clasping the phone. Eventually he answered:

'Fine.'

His people found a warehouse out at Heathrow. It was on the outskirts of the land owned by the airport – one of a row of old hangars for small private aircraft that the corporation running the whole place hired out. It was large enough to contain a full-scale reproduction of the tyre shop itself – including roof with tyres and garish model baked-beans tin – and of the road outside it where the boy in the Michelin Man suit had swayed beside the spinning sign that said 'TYRES TYRES' – and where, of course, the sticky liquid had exploded from my dashboard and cascaded over me.

They also paid the real tyre people, the men who'd been inside the café when the episode had happened, half a grand – nothing – to let Roger, Frank and Annie come and detail everything about the shop: the layout of the shelves, the products on them, their positions, age and state of wear, the dimensions of the garish model baked-beans tin, the lathe inside with its pedals and its clamps, the blue tube full of air and so on. The instruments all had to work, of course. The owner of the real tyre place, a round man of forty-odd, came out and taught us how to use all the equipment. He trained up a team of ten fifteen-year-old boys until they knew how to dip tyres in water and look out for silky bubbles, how to clamp and turn the wheel with their feet while daubing glue on, how to reach their hand behind them to collect the tube of air and guide it to the valve without needing to turn their heads. It took a while.

As far as positions and movements were concerned: I took care of these myself, as before. I showed the Michelin Man boy re-enactor where to stand and sway, and the other two how to kick his head between them. I made them kick it with a minimum of movement, hammering it with their legs mechanically, like zombies or robots. The driver, the person re-enacting my role, had to get out slowly. Like the concierge, he wore a white ice-hockey goaltender's mask, so as not to overrun my personality with his – or, more precisely, so as not to impose any personality at all. I just wanted the motions and the words, all deadpan, neutral – wanted the re-enactors to act out the motions without acting and to speak the words without feeling, in disinterested voices, as monotonous as my pianist. The oldest boy had to take the tyre from the boot, carry it over to the lathe and fix it; the middling one had to attempt to help him lift it and the oldest had to push his hand away; the youngest one had to come over and then lurk outside the door. I showed them where to step, to lift, to kick, to stand. Most of the time they only had to stand, completely static.

We were ready to go after ten days. I'd had a raised viewing platform built, a little like an opera box, because I'd enjoyed watching the action in my building from above and wanted to have a similar option here. I'd established that I might roam around the re-enactment area itself, and that the re-enactors shouldn't be put off by this. I chose to begin watching the re-enactment from the platform, though. At some point in the afternoon of the tenth day after the original event, Naz signalled up to me that everything was ready; I nodded back down to him and it began.

A strong fan was switched on in front of the TYRE-TYRE sign, to make it spin. Seconds later the blue Fiesta drove slowly across the warehouse floor past the Michelin Man boy and pulled up next to where the two older boys were kicking his head to one another. The driver, wearing a white ice-hockey mask, stepped out. Slowly, in a mono-tone, the oldest boy intoned the words:

'*You've – got – a – dent.*'

There was a pause before the driver answered:

'*I – know – that – that's – not – why – I'm – here.*'

There was another pause. This was good, very good. They were avoiding all eye contact with one another, just as I'd instructed them. I experienced a sensation that was halfway between the gliding one I'd felt when my liver lady had spoken to me on the staircase during the first re-enactment in my building and the tingling that had crept up my right side on several other occasions. This mixed sensation grew as we reached the part where the boy intoned the words:

'*I – am – real.*'

When the sticky blue liquid exploded, I'd meant to leave my box and go down to the car to watch, but found myself fixated where I stood. I could see the re-enactor playing me splattered in the driving seat: his legs spread, his arms raised beside the wheel, his body powerless as the two litres descended on it. The mixed sensation grew still stronger, and I was riveted to my spot on the plat-form. I made it down the second time round, when the sensation had subsided. This time I stood beside the car and watched the liquid gush out. Frank and Annie had created a whole mini plumbing system in the car, that siphoned the blue liquid off into a sack which was triggered to rupture when the engine was turned on a second time. It wasn't gushing out quite right, but it was complicated. It took two more run-throughs to tweak that bit. There were other minor hitches: the air in the blue tube hadn't been set at the right pressure; the spare tyre wasn't dirty enough to stain the boy's overalls adequately – pretty minor things. On the whole it went well – very well.

The first team ran through it six times. Each run-through took twenty minutes, give or take a minute either side, plus a change-over of six or so minutes. I didn't mind the change-over: I kind of liked the pause, the hovering as the sequence clocked itself, ran through the zero, started again. The first team did it for three hours, then the second team took over. I watched them do it six times too, then watched the third team do it twice. In the small hours of the morning I decided to leave.

'Shall I tell them to stop?' Naz asked me as I put my jacket on.

'No,' I said. 'Absolutely not. They should continue. When they've done three hours replace them with the third team. Keep rotating them.'

'For how long?' he asked.

'Indefinitely,' I said. 'Round the clock. And Naz?'
'Yes?'

'When you leave here yourself, have someone you trust stay and supervise, so no one does a pianist on us.'

'But he won't be able to supervise it indefinitely,' Naz said.

A good point. I thought about it for a moment, then told him:

'So select several people, and have them work in shifts just like the re-enactors. Rotate them as well.'

I went back five times over the next two weeks to watch the liquid blue explosion and the events leading up to it being re-enacted. In some of the sessions I was pretty analytical, concentrating on several things simultaneously. They were short enough to do that. So three minutes in I'd pay particular attention to what happened just after the oldest boy pushed aside the middling boy's hand – how the middling boy turned aside to confront the youngest one. Or I'd watch for the car's route. Its tyres left markings on the warehouse floor; as the sequence was repeated it drove back over its own tracks – sometimes slightly to the left or right, sometimes more or less exactly covering a previous set. On my third visit I had an idea:

'I'd like the car's route to be changed,' I told the driver re-enactor.

'How do you mean?' he asked. He looked very tired.

'Instead of reversing out this way when you go to take up your position at the end of every sequence,' I said, 'I want you to drive the car on forwards, and turn round, and leave along there, and then turn round the other way to come back in.'

'So I'd be doing a figure of eight?' he asked.

'Exactly,' I said.

The change was implemented. Over the following hours and days the car deposited across the floor an eight – a thick black line of run-together turrets and plateaux out of whose edges individuated lines and corners slightly rose, records of the wildest routes. Just to the right of this a large, sticky patch made by the repeated gushing of hundreds of litres of blue liquid stained the floor. I sketched small parts of line and patch in detail, and pressed sheets of paper straight onto them to make prints, which I then stuck to the walls of my flat. If I stared at them for long enough they took on shapes: birds, buildings or the interlocked sections of space stations – and my whole mood would slide from analytical to dreamy. The same slide happened at the re-enactment scene itself. One minute I'd be really concentrating on an aspect of the sequence and the next I'd let the movements mesmerize me, like a bird charmed by a snake: the Fiesta slowly rolling through its well-worn eight, the tyre floating on the boy's knee to the workshop, his hand pushing the hand of the other boy away, the gliding clamps, the gushing blue – monotonous, hypnotic, endlessly repeating.

In these moments the episode's sounds took on the aspect of a lullaby. The re-enactors' voices echoed off the corrugated ceiling; above this, low-flying aeroplanes passed by, whistling and groaning as they left for or arrived from who knows where. The exploding liquid made a rushing, then a trickling sound. The fan hummed from before the beginning of each run-through to after the end. Other sounds emerged from the scene's edges, from beneath its surfaces – sounds hidden in the enclave where the scraping of the middling boy's foot met the rustle of the youngest one's Michelin Man suit, or where the gush of liquid met the roof's vibrations. Occasionally these sounds seemed to become voices, speaking words and phrases I never quite managed to make out.

I spent a lot of time there, watching, I also spent a lot of time sitting in my living room staring at the sketches and prints, or lying in my bath thinking about the re-enactment, knowing that it was continuing, constantly, on a loop. Sometimes I really concentrated on each moment, each manoeuvere; but sometimes I thought of other matters altogether. For a couple of days I returned to the study of my building, keeping the whole place in *on* mode for two ten-hour stretches with only two hours' break between them. Then I drove back out to Heathrow and watched the tyre sequence through fifteen times.

On this particular day I requested another

change to be implemented. I called Frank and Annie out to the warehouse and asked them:

'Is there any way that you could make the blue liquid not gush out?'

'Well, of course,' said Frank. 'We just don't make it gush. We de-activate the trigger.'

'Yes, but then the liquid would stay in the reservoir, right?' I said.

He nodded yes. I told him:

'That's no good. I want it so that it disappears from the reservoir, then doesn't reappear again. Just disappears.'

Annie and Frank looked at one another. Then Annie said, sheepishly:

'But that's impossible.'

'I know,' I said, 'but that's the . . . I mean, isn't there some way you could make it happen?'

There was another pause, then Frank replied:

'Not really, no.'

'I want it to go up,' I said, 'even if it's harder – hard, I mean. Disappear upwards. Become sky.'

They both thought about this for a while. Then Frank said:

'We could make the liquid travel upwards. In a tube, for example. We could lead a tube up from the holding tank towards the ceiling. We could even feed it through the roof and have it all sprayed upwards in a fine mist. But that's . . .'

'I like that,' I said. 'Try it. Try some other things along those lines too. See what you can come up with.'

Driving back to Brixton that day, I decided to detour past the original tyre shop. I was alone, driving my Fiesta. As I approached the railway bridge just before the shop, I noticed that the traffic in front of me was being held up. Some cars were turning round and heading back in the direction I'd just come from. I understood why when I was twenty or so feet from the traffic lights beside the bridge: there was a police cordon beyond them, demarcated by a line of yellow-and-black tape. It was the same type of tape they'd used to demarcate the siege zone two months before the accident – only that had been a hundred or so yards away, beyond the tyre shop. This new zone started near the phone box I'd called Marc Daubenay from, and ran down Coldharbour Lane, which was empty save for policemen standing and walking around.

I drove up to the tape and, ignoring a traffic officer's signal to turn round, pulled my Fiesta to one side, stepped out and walked up to him.

'What's happened?' I asked.

'Incident,' he answered. 'If you'd like to turn round and go back to the next intersection . . .'

'What type of incident?' I asked.

'Shooting,' he said. 'Please go back to your car and . . .'

'Who was shot?' I asked.

'A man,' he said. 'We don't hand information out to onlookers. If you'd please return to your car and proceed back up to the next intersection . . .'

The small radio on his shoulder crackled, and a voice said something I couldn't pick up. I peered beyond him. There were two police motorbikes standing in the middle of the street, plus several cars: three normal white police cars, a white police van, one of those special red cars and an unmarked metallic blue car with a magnetized light mounted on its roof. Two men in white boiler suits were walking down the middle of the road.

'You have to go back,' the traffic policeman told me. 'You can't leave your car there. You'll have to detour via Camberwell or the centre of Brixton.'

'Detour,' I said. 'Yes, of course.'

I snatched one more look across his shoulder, then got back into my car and drove off. When I walked into my flat, I heard Naz's voice on my answering machine, leaving a message. I picked my phone up.

'It's me,' I said. 'The real me. I've just walked in.'

'I was just leaving you a message about Frank and Annie's idea. They've devised this idea for the liquid. You requested . . .'

'Listen,' I said. 'I'd like to find out about something.'

'Oh yes?' Naz said.

'There's been some kind of incident on Coldharbour Lane,' I told him. 'A shooting. I should like to know what happened.'

'I'll see what I can learn,' Naz said.

He called back an hour later. Someone had indeed been shot. Details were vague, but it seemed to be drugs-related. It had happened outside Movement Cars. A black man in his thirties. He'd been on a bicycle, and two more black men had pulled up in a car and shot him. He'd died on the spot. Did I want to know more?

'Do you know more?' I asked Naz.

'Not yet,' he said. 'But I can keep up to date on information as it comes out. Would you like that?'

I pictured the black man dying beside his bicycle outside the phone box I'd called Daubenay from the day the Settlement came through. I pictured the two other black men shooting him from their car. Had they stayed inside their car? I didn't know. I remembered a man wheeling a coke machine into the cab office as the box's display counted down the seconds. *Movement Cars. Airports, Stations, Light, Removals.*

'Hello?' Naz's voice broke in.

'Yes,' I told him. 'Keep me up to date. And Naz?'

'Yes?'

'I'd like you to procure the area once the police are done with it.'

'Procure it?' he repeated.

'Hire it. Obtain permission to use it.'

'What for?' Naz asked.

'A re-enactment,' I said.

CHAPTER 11

Forensic procedure is an art form, nothing less. No, I'll go further: It's higher, more refined, than any art form. Why? Because it's real. Take just one aspect of it – say the diagrams: with all their outlines, arrows and shaded blocks they look like abstract paintings, avant-garde ones from the last century – dances of shapes and flows as delicate and skilful as the markings on butterflies' wings. But they're not abstract at all. They're records of atrocities. Each line, each figure, every angle – the ink itself vibrates with an almost intolerable violence, darkly screaming from the silence of white paper: something has happened here, someone has died.

'It's just like cricket,' I told Naz one day.

'In what sense?' he asked.

'Each time the ball's been past,' I said, 'and the white lines are still zinging where it hit, and the seam's left a mark, and . . .'

'I don't follow,' he said.

'It . . . well, it just is,' I told him. 'Each ball is like a crime, a murder. And then they do it again, and again and again, and the commentator has to commentate, or he'll die too.'

'He'll die?' Naz asked. 'Why?'

'He . . . whatever,' I said. 'I've got to get out here.'

We were in a taxi going past King's Cross. Naz was on his way to meet someone who knew a policeman working in forensics. I was going to the British Library to read about forensic procedure. I'd done this for days now, while I waited for Naz to lay the ground for the re-enactment of this black man's death. I think I'd have gone mad otherwise, so strong was my compulsion to re-enact it. We couldn't re-enact it properly until we'd got our hands on the report about it – the report written by the police forensic team who were dealing with the case. Naz trawled through all the contacts in his database to try to find a way of getting access to this and, while he did, I staved off my hunger for it by devouring every book about forensics I could find.

I read textbooks for students, general introductions meant for members of the public, papers delivered by experts at top-level conferences. I read the handbook every professional forensic investigator in the country has to learn by rote, and learnt it by rote too. It was laid out in paragraphs headed by numbers, then by capital letters, then by roman numerals, then by lower-case letters as they indented further and further from the left-hand margin. Each indentation corresponded to a step or half-step in the chain of actions you must follow when you conduct a forensic search. The whole process is extremely formal: you don't just go ahead and do it – you do it slowly, breaking down your movements into phases that have sections and sub-sections, each one governed by rigorous rules. You even wear special suits when you do it, like Japanese people wearing kimonos as they perform the tea ceremony.

Patterns are important. You move through the crime area in a particular pattern that the head investigator chooses in advance. It could be that he tells you to move forward in straight lanes, like competition swimmers. Or he might cut up the area by laying a grid across it and assigning each investigator one of the grid's zones. Or he might order a spiral search. Me, if I were a head investigator, I'd plump for a figure of eight, and have each of my people crawl round the same area in an endlessly repeating circuit, unearthing the same evidence, the same prints, marks and tracings again and again and again, recording them as though afresh each time.

Patterns are everywhere in forensic investigations. Investigators have to find and recognize the imprints made by, for example, trainers, fingers and tyres. So with tyres you get ribbed patterns, with two pairs of jagged lines; you get aggressive ribbed ones – the same as ribbed but with prongs sticking from the corners of the lines; then you get cross bar – hexagonal blocks with inverted *v*s in them (my Fiesta's tyres were cross bar); directional – a brick pattern, like two adjoining walls seen from a corner; block – same as directional but all cubistic – and curvilineal, which show a gridded net bending and twisting out of shape. Trainers leave hundreds of types of pattern. Fingerprints are the most complicated: the variations in the whorls and deltas found in them are infinite – no two are ever the same.

Well, all these patterns have to be recorded. Captured, like I'd captured the mark beneath the motorbike that day. You capture fingerprints by sprinkling powder over them, blowing lightly across this to remove the powder not stuck to the miniature wet ridges that the finger's touch has left, then pressing tape onto the remaining powder and removing it again: the pattern sticks to it. Shoe and tyre prints are captured by pouring plaster into the mould the rubber promontories have cut in the earth or mud, letting it set and then lifting it away again, turning space hollowed out by action into solid matter. If the prints are made by wet shoes or by tyres on concrete, then you have to sketch. You're supposed to make constant sketches as a matter of course, in order to record the dimensions of furniture, doors, windows and so on, and the distances between objects and bodies to entrances and exits, just like I had both when I'd first remembered my building and after the re-enactments had begun.

You're supposed to constantly photograph too, like Annie had when we'd been setting my building up. You have to take four types of photographs: close-ups of individual items of evidence, medium-distance ones to record the relative positions of closely related items, long-distance ones that include a landmark to establish the crime scene's location and, finally, ones from other observation points – although it strikes me that the third and fourth types are more or less the same. If I were interested in photos, which I'm not, I'd want to take aerial ones too: first from a crane, then from a circling blimp – one high enough to enable the viewer to make out among the crime scene's larger patterns images and shapes that maverick archaeologists will claim in years to come were put there to guide the spaceships of a master race of aliens down to earth.

Each day, as soon as I got turfed out of the library, I phoned Naz, to see how his efforts were progressing. He'd hooked up with this person on the police force and bribed him a lot of money to make us a copy of the forensic report on this particular shooting.

'So where is it, then?' I asked him after a week.

'Expected end of next week,' Naz said.

'End of next week! That's an eternity away. Can't our man get us a sneak preview?'

'That is a sneak preview,' Naz told me. 'It hasn't been written yet.'

'What the fuck do I pay taxes for?' I asked.

'Oh,' said Naz, 'Matthew Younger's been looking for you.'

'Fuck him,' I said, and hung up.

The next day I went back to the library. I'd read all there was to read about crime-scene searches, so I started reading about guns. I pored over a report by one Dr M. Jauhari, M.Sc. Ph.D., F.A.F.Sc. and Director of the Central Forensic Science Laboratory, Calcutta. At least he was in 1971, when the report was published. Dr Jauhari explained that a firearm functions like a heat engine, converting the chemical energy stored in the propellant into the kinetic energy of the bullet. By way of illustration he compared and contrasted the workings of a firearm with the workings of the internal combustion engine. In the latter, vaporized gasoline is compressed in the cylinder by the piston; then the spark plug fires the gasoline charge, converting it into expanded gas; the pressure resulting from this gas's expansion in turn results in the pressure which drives the piston. That's how a combustion engine works, or how it worked in 1971. A firearm, Dr Jauhari explained, is similar: the primer, the propellant, the chamber and the bullet correspond to the spark plug, the gasoline, the cylinder and the piston – only instead of returning to its starting point and firing off again, the bullet continues right on out into the air. An engine is like a single shot that endlessly repeats itself.

Dr Jauhari was thorough. Before describing types of guns he sketched their function:

A firearm,

he wrote,

> *provides a means by which a missile can be hurled from considerable distances with considerable velocity. Its capability to deliver a death blow to a human being even at long ranges of firing makes it a weapon of choice for homicidal purposes. It is occasionally found to get involved in suicidal and accidental shootings also.*

People never stop to think about these basic facts when they watch wars and cop shows on the television. People take too much for granted. Each time a gun is fired the whole history of engineering comes into play. Of politics, too: war, assassination, revolution, terror. Guns aren't just history's props and agents: they're history itself, spinning alternate futures in their chamber, hurling the present from their barrel, casting aside the empty shells of past.

One other thing about guns: their beauty. As I flicked past the photos, diagrams and illustrations Dr Jauhari used to show the evolution of guns over the ages and the differences between pistols, rifles, machine guns and sub-machine guns, it grew on me how beautiful an object a gun – any gun – is. Some are more beautiful than others, of course, depending on the sleekness of their finish, the curvature of the handle, the thickness of the hammer and a dozen other factors. But just being guns makes them all beautiful. That things so small, so pleasing to the eye, so friendly to the touch – so passive – can contain such force is breathtaking. Then the way they hang just off the body, cradled tenderly like babies, sleeping – till the moment they erupt and carry beauty to another level. No beauty without violence, without death.

Our mole came through eventually. Naz brought the report over to my flat one evening.

'When we ask the Council for permission to use the space,' he said as he handed it to me, 'we'll have to decide what type of licence to apply for. We could . . .'

'Later,' I said. I took the report and closed the door on him.

It had come in a sealed, unmarked envelope. As I opened this I felt that tingling spreading outwards from the base of my spine. The pages were flaky and the text badly aligned; it had been Xeroxed in a hurry. The language it was written in was clear, which surprised me. I'd expected it to be full of police terminology – people 'proceeding' instead of moving, 'perpetrators' instead of people and with every noun and action prefaced by 'alleged'. In fact, it was stark and straightforward:

The killers,

it said,

> *parked their car beside the Green Man public*
> *bar, stepped out and opened fire with Uzi sub-*
> *machine guns. The victim got onto his bicycle*
> *and tried to ride away, but turned too sharply*
> *into Belinda Road and fell onto the tarmac as*
> *the front wheel twisted under him.*

I pictured the front wheel twisting and him going down. He must have known then that it was all up. He'd got up again, the report said, and taken two or three more steps down Belinda Road while the killers fired on him some more. Then he'd gone down a final time. He'd been dead by the time the ambulance arrived.

There were pages of detailed diagrams. They showed the layout of the area in which the shooting had happened: the phone box, the street, kerb, bollard, even a puddle into which some of the victim's blood had flowed. They showed his position first as he stood in the phone box, then as he tried to escape, then as he fell, got up and fell again. They showed the killers' positions as they parked their car and walked towards him, firing. The three men were drawn in outline with numbers inside the outlines, like you get in children's colouring books. There were arrows indicating movement and direction.

The longer I stared at these pictures, the more intense the tingling in my upper body grew. It had moved into my brain, like when you eat too much monosodium glutamate in a Chinese restaurant. My whole head was tingling. The diagrams seemed to be taking on more and more significance. They became maps for finding buried treasure, then instructions for assembling pieces of furniture, then military plans, the outline of a whole winter's arduous and multi-pronged advance across mountains and plains. I drifted off into these plains, these mountains, floating alongside the generals and foot soldiers and cooks and elephants. When I looked up from the diagrams again, Naz was there, standing in front of my sofa with another man.

'When did you come in?' I asked him. 'Who's this?'

'This man's a doctor,' said Naz. 'I've been here for the last hour and a half.'

I tried to ask him what he meant by that, but the words were taking a long time to form. The other man opened a bag and took a pen or torch out.

'You were just sitting here,' said Naz. 'You'd gone completely vacant. You didn't notice me, or hear me. I waved my hand in front of your face and you didn't even move your eyes.'

'How long ago was this?' the doctor asked.

'I'm fine,' I said.

'The whole last hour and a half,' Naz told him. 'Until just now, when you came in.'

'Has he experienced any kind of trauma recently?' the doctor asked. He switched his torch-pen on. 'What's his name?'

'I'm fine,' I said. 'Send this man away.'

'Keep your head still,' the doctor said.

'No,' I said. 'Send this man away, Naz, now. Get off my property or I'll have you arrested.'

'I can't help you if you won't let me help you,' he said.

I looked past his ear and thought I saw another cat fall off the roof. I told this man:

'I'm ordering you to leave my property this instant.'

He stood still for a while. Naz did too. The three of us were static for several moments – and while we were I didn't mind this doctor being here. I'd even have let him stay if he'd only behaved himself and not moved. Eventually, though, he turned to Naz and motioned with his eyes towards the door, then slipped his torch-pen back into his bag and left. Naz saw him out. I heard the two men murmuring together as I went into the bathroom and washed my face. I washed it in cold water and didn't dry it straight away, but let it drip while I stared at the crack on the wall. I watched the crack as I listened to the doctor walking down the stairs.

When I went back into the living room, Naz was there and the flat's door was closed. Naz said:

'I think it would be a good idea for you to . . .'

'Where have you managed to get us to?' I asked him.

He'd got the re-enactors, the car and bicycle and the replica sub-machine guns. He'd rung up to tell me all this, but I hadn't answered.

'When did you ring?' I asked him.

'Several hours ago. Didn't you hear the phone?'

'No,' I said. 'Not that one.'

I did have a vague memory of ringing – but it was of the phone the black man with the bicycle had used in the phone box outside Movement Cars. His last words would still have been buzzing in his head as he left the phone box, and in the head of the person he'd talked to, their conversation only half-decayed at most. Then he'd have caught sight of his killers. Did he know them? If he did, he still might not have known they'd come to kill him – until they took their guns out. At what point had he realized they were guns? Maybe at first he thought they were umbrellas, or steering-wheel locks, or poles. Then when he realized, as his brain pieced it together and came up with a plan of escape, then changed it, he found out that physics wouldn't let him carry out the plan: it tripped him up. Matter again: the world became a fridge door, a broken lighter, two litres of blue goop. That's when he was first hit: as he went over. The first round of bullets struck him in his body, not his head, the report said. They didn't even make him lose consciousness. He would have known he'd been hit but not really felt it, nor the scrapes he'd received from hitting the ground as he went over the handlebars – would have just vaguely understood that something had occurred, something had changed, that things were different now.

'. . . and a further licence from the local police,' Naz was saying, 'which won't be a great problem now the Council have given the nod, although the status of the event needs to be determined pretty quickly.'

'What?' I asked him. 'What are you saying?'

Naz looked at me strangely, then started again:

'Lambeth Council are happy to give permission for the re-enactment to proceed, but there's confusion about what type of licence they need to give us,' he said. 'It's not a demonstration and it's not a street party. The activity that it most closely resembles is filming.'

'No,' I said. 'No cameras. No filming. You know that.'

'Yes,' said Naz, 'but we should *apply* for it under filming. We need to designate it as a recognized type of event so they can grant us permission to do it. Filming's the easiest route. We apply to use the area for a film shoot and then just don't have any cameras.'

'I suppose so,' I said. 'As long as we don't actually film. How soon can we do it, then?'

'Next week,' said Naz.

'No, that's not soon enough!' I said.

'There's not much we can . . .'

'It needs to be done sooner!' I said. 'Why can't we do it tomorrow?'

226

'Licence certificates can take days to process,' he explained, 'even with the type of bribes we're paying.'

'Pay bigger bribes, then!' I said. 'It won't last if we wait a whole week!'

'What won't last?' he asked.

I looked past his head. I could see three cats on the red roof on the far side of the courtyard, which meant that the people over there had replaced the one I'd seen falling. I looked back at Naz.

'Day after tomorrow at the latest!' I said. 'The very outside latest!'

He got it all together for the day after that. He got the licence from the Council and the license from the police, organized all the staff and back-up staff, the caterers and runners and who knows what else. It struck me as I waited that all great enterprises are about logistics. Not genius or inspiration or flights of imagination, skill or cunning, but logistics. Building pyramids or landing space-craft on Jupiter or invading whole continents or painting divine scenes over the roofs of chapels: logistics. I decided that in the caste scale of things, people who dealt with logistics were higher even than the ones who made connections. I decided to get Matthew Younger to invest in the logistics industry, if there was one.

While I waited I also got Roger to build me a model of the area in which the shooting had taken place: the phone box, pavement, bollards, street, shops and pubs. The model had little cars that you could move around, and a little red bicycle. It also had little human figures: the two killers with their sub-machine guns, the victim. Roger delivered it to me the evening before we did the re-enactment. I removed his model of my building from the coffee table in the living room and placed this new model there instead. I stayed up all night looking at it. I placed the human figures in the positions indicated by the forensic report's diagrams. I made the two killers park their car, step into the street and advance forward. I made the dead man leave the phone box, climb onto his bicycle, fall off, stumble a few steps forwards and collapse. I watched each phase of the sequence from all angles.

Why was I so obsessed with the death of this man I'd never met? I didn't stop to ask myself. I knew we had things in common, of course. He'd been hit by something, hurt, laid prostrate and lost consciousness; so had I. We'd both slipped into a place of total blackness, silence, nothing, without memory and without anticipation, a place unreached by stimuli of any kind. He'd stayed on there, gone the whole hog, while I'd been sucked back, via vague sports stadiums, to L-shaped wards and talks of Settlement – but for a short while we'd both stood at the same spot: stood there, lay there, floated there, whatever. Persisted. We'd both stood at the same spot in a more plain sense, too: in the phone box I'd called Marc Daubenay from the day the Settlement came

through, this cabin out of whose miniature duplicate I was making the little model of him step
again and again and again. Our paths had diverged
as soon as we'd left it: I'd stepped out – two times,
then passed by it a third and gone up to the
airport, whereas he'd stepped out and died; but
for a while we'd both stood there, held the receiver,
looked at the words *Airports, Stations, Light.*

To put my fascination with him all down to our
shared experience, though, would only be telling
half the story. Less than half. The truth is that,
for me, this man had become a symbol of perfection. It may have been clumsy to fall from his
bike, but in dying beside the bollards on the
tarmac he'd done what I wanted to do: merged
with the space around him, sunk and flowed into
it until there was no distance between it and him
– and merged, too, with his actions, merged to
the extent of having no more consciousness of
them. He'd stopped being separate, removed,
imperfect. Cut out the detour. Then both mind
and actions had resolved themselves into pure
stasis. The spot that this had happened on was
the ground zero of perfection – all perfection: the
one he'd achieved, the one I wanted, the one
everyone else wanted but just didn't know they
wanted and in any case didn't have eight and a
half million pounds to help them pursue even if
they had known. It was sacred ground, blessed
ground – and anyone who occupied it in the way
he'd occupied it would become blessed too. And

so I had to re-enact his death: for myself, certainly, but for the world in general as well. No one who understands this could accuse me of not being generous.

In the part of the night where it's quietest, around three or four o'clock, I started wondering where this black man's soul had disappeared to as it left his body. His thoughts, impressions, memories, whatever: the background noise we all have in our head that stops us from forgetting we're alive. It had to go somewhere: it couldn't just vaporize – it must have gushed, trickled or dripped onto some surface, stained it somehow. Everything must leave some kind of mark. I scoured the thin card surfaces of Roger's model. They were so white, so blank. I decided to mark them, and went to the kitchen to find something to stain the white card with.

In the cupboard above the kitchen unit that I'd practised turning sideways round, I found vinegar, Worcestershire Sauce and blue peppermint essence. I got a blank piece of paper and experiemented with each of these. Worcestershire Sauce made the best stain, by far. I found a half-drunk bottle of wine and tried staining the paper with that too. The consistency was thinner but the colour was fantastic. It looked like blood.

'Blood!' I said aloud to my empty apartment. 'I should have used blood in the first place.'

I took a small knife from a drawer, pricked my finger with its point and squeezed the flesh and skin until a small bauble of blood grew on it. Holding my finger upright so as not to lose the bauble, I went back to the living room and pressed it to the card, stamping my print across the middle of the road in blood. Then I sat back and looked at it till morning.

It was a giant print, spanning the pavement on both sides, its contours swirling round bollards, cars and shop fronts, doubling back around the phone box, gathering the killers and their victim together in the same large, undulating sweep. They were too small to make it out, of course, or even to know that it was there. No: it was legible only from above, a landing field for elevated, more enlightened beings.

CHAPTER 12

The actual surfaces, when I saw them later that day, were sensational. If the diagrams had been like abstract paintings, then the road itself was like an old grand master – one of those Dutch ones thick with rippling layers of oil paint. Its tarmac was old, fissured and cracked. And its markings! They were faded, worn by time and light into faint echoes of the instructions that they'd once pronounced so boldly. The road was cambered, like most roads. It had rained recently and its central area was dry, but had wet tyre tracks running over it. Its edges were still wet. Around the seams where road met kerb and kerb-stone pavement, water and dirt had been skilfully mixed to form muddy, pockmarked ridges. In places these ran into puddles in whose centres hung large clouds of mud hemmed in by borders that turned rusty and then clear, as though the artist had used them to clean his brush.

Chewing gum, cigarette butts and bottle tops had been distributed randomly across the area and sunk into its outer membrane, become one with tarmac, stone, dirt, water, mud. If you were to cut out ten square centimetres of it like you do with fields on school geography trips – ten centimetres by ten centimetres wide and ten more deep – you'd find so much to analyse, so many layers, just so much *matter* – that your study of it would branch out and become endless until, finally, you threw your hands up in despair and announced to whatever authority it was you were reporting to: *There's too much here, too much to process, just too much.*

I arrived at the re-enactment area from the south. Police tape had been unwound across the street where Shakespeare Road ran into Coldharbour Lane, beneath a bridge that crossed the road perpendicular to the bridge I'd been stopped by on the day of the actual shooting. A policeman had been posted there to turn traffic away. I showed him the pass Naz had biked over to me one hour earlier; he let me through. Naz came over to greet me, but I paused beside the policeman and asked him:

'Were you here on the day the shooting happened?'

'No,' he said.

'I mean, not *here* here, but just on the other side of the cordoned-off area?'

'I wasn't there that day,' he said.

I stared at him intently for a few more seconds, then walked on with Naz.

'Slept well?' Naz asked.

I hadn't slept at all. My tiredness made the dappled pattern of wet and dry patches on the pavement stand out more intensely. The air was bright but not bright-blue: the sun was beaming from behind a thin layer of white cloud. Its light cast shadows and reflections: from the bollards and the phone box and on the surfaces of puddles.

'Whatever,' I said. 'How long do we have?'

'We've got until six o'clock this evening,' he said.

'Get it extended,' I told him.

'They won't let us have more time,' he said.

'Pay them,' I said. 'Offer them double what we've paid already, and if they say no, then double that again. Is all the area between the lines of tape ours?'

'Yes,' said Naz.

The cordoned-off stretch ran between the bridge and the traffic lights I'd been stopped by on the first day – but of this area only about a third was primary re-enactment space. The other two thirds were given over to back-up: cars and boxes, tables, a big van from whose back doors two women were handing out coffee. The vehicles were all parked unusually: not flat against the kerb but willy-nilly, right across the road, irregular.

'When you see that, it's usually because there's been an accident,' I told Naz.

'Sorry?' he said.

'Or the fair,' I said. 'If it's on grass.'

He looked at me intently for a while. Then his eyes lit up and he said:

'Oh yes, I see. I always liked the fair.'

'Me too,' I said.

We smiled at one another, then I looked across our area. One of Frank's people who I recognized from the building was lifting replica sub-machine guns from a box and carrying them with another man towards the van the two women were serving coffee from. Another man was stepping from a dull red BMW he'd parked in the middle of the road beside the traffic lights. Another, shortish man I hadn't seen before was standing two feet behind him, watching the goings-on. I looked back at the ground. Besides being layered and cracked, it was also plumbed: dotted with holes and outlets that had been placed there strategically when the street had first been laid. There was a small cover set into the tarmac that had 'water' written on it and another almost identical one that said 'London Transport'. A larger, rounder one set into a hydrant carried two strings of figures, *EM124* and *B125*; another simply bore the letter *C*. All these openings to tubes and pipelines, outlets and supply points, connections feeding back to who knew where. I saw we had a lot of work to do.

'Where are the re-enactors?' I asked.

'Over there,' said Naz.

He pointed to the van. Three black men were standing around behind it, drinking coffee. Two of them were the same ones I'd pointed out to Naz the day we'd hired the Soho Theatre; the third I'd not seen before. He was riding around in small circles on a red sports bicycle, trying to keep going without putting his feet down.

'Is that the victim?' I asked.

'Yes,' replied Naz.

'Stand him down,' I said. 'I'll take his place. Send the other two over to me. And Naz?'

'Yes?'

'I want to pay the people who've done all the organizing bits more.'

'Which ones do you mean?' he asked.

'The people who've worked with you to get all the elements of this coordinated. Not the ones who actually do stuff, but the ones who make the other people's stuff all fit together. You understand?'

'I do,' said Naz. 'But you're already paying them generously.'

'Pay them more generously, then,' I said.

I pressed my thumb to my finger just where I'd stuck the knife in a few hours earlier as I said this. Money was like blood, I figured. I'd barely pricked myself; I had plenty more to give.

Naz walked across to the three black men by the van. I saw him take the man who'd been riding the bicycle in circles to one side and talk to him. The man got off the bike, talked to Naz some more, then strode back to the van, reached in, took out a bag and walked off towards the police tape. The other two, meanwhile, came sauntering over to me. I briefed them.

'What I want you to do,' I said, 'is drive that BMW from over there beside the lights to just up there beside the Green Man.'

'Your man talked us through the sequence,' one of them said. He had a London accent and an affable, smiley face.

'Yes,' I told him, 'but you must park it just there, see? Exactly there. Its bonnet, front, its nose, should be exactly there, no further forward than the end of the Green Man's second window. You park it there, then get out – you take your guns with you – and walk across the street firing at me.'

'At you?' the same man asked me.

'Yes,' I said. 'I'll be re-enacting the victim's role. You must walk across the street quite slowly, almost casually, firing at me. But don't fire until – here, come with me.'

I walked them over to the phone box.

'I'll start here,' I continued. 'I'll have just left this phone box when you pull up. Or I'll just be leaving it. I'll get on my bike and start pedalling, riding in this direction, over here. That's when you should start shooting: as I come up to just here, where Movement Cars starts.'

'Where should we stand?' the man asked again.

'There,' I said. I walked them back across the street to a spot just in the middle where the cracks branched out into a cell-like pattern of repeating hexagons. 'Walk from the car up to here. No further than here, though. You can keep firing, but just stop advancing once you reach this spot. I'll try to turn into this road here, Belinda Road, and my bike's handlebars will twist under me, and I'll fall off, then get up again, and you shoot again and I'll go down again. You guys should stand here while I do that. Stand here for a while, then go back to the car. Yes, do it like that. Do it just like that.'

The other man spoke now. Unlike his friend he had a strong West Indian accent:

'You're the boss,' he said.

I signalled over to Naz, who had been talking on his mobile. He came over to us.

'Ready to go?' he asked.

'Yes,' I said. 'What news on the time front?'

'Working on it,' he said.

He called Frank and Annie over. They had Frank's man in tow, plus the man I'd seen handling the submachine guns with him a few minutes earlier. They carried one gun each.

'Sid,' Frank told me by way of introduction. 'He's an effects man I've worked with on several films. He'll show our friends here how the guns work. You can take up your position if you like.'

'Okay,' I said – but I stayed to watch this Sid explain the working of the guns.

'Basically,' said Sid, 'they're like real ten-millimetre Uzis with the chamber taken out. They'll make a nice bang. You've got two magazines,' he went on, pointing to two metallic blocks Frank's man was holding, 'which clip in under here. Look, try it.'

He handed the guns to the two black men. Frank's man handed them the magazines. They held both awkwardly. Neither could get their magazine to clip in properly. Sid showed them how to wedge the Uzis' butts against their stomachs just below the ribs and guide the magazines in upwards with their left hand from below, feeling for the slot and catch. They tried it a few times, nodding in satisfaction when they got it right. I envied them. I thought of asking to try too, but didn't want to get all self-indulgent. Besides, things were moving on. The coffee van was being shifted and the re-enactment area cleared of all personnel. The two black men were being led towards the BMW and handed its keys. The bicycle was being brought to me. I took it, wheeled it over to the phone box, balanced it against the railings just beside this, then opened the phone box's door and stepped inside.

The street's sounds drained away and I was back in a cocoon – the same cocoon I'd been placed in when my phone connection had been ripped out of the wall the day the Settlement came through. The cabin had a little shelf in it. Perhaps this black man whose last moments I was re-enacting had rested his address book on this shelf as he made his final phone call. Had the book been shabby, fat and bulging? Yellow? I pictured it as yellow, tattered but not fat. Then it went blue and thin, like those vocabulary books you get in school.

On the window above the shelf the figure of a messenger blowing a horn was stencilled in silhouette. Beyond it was the caged façade of Movement

Cars, with the words *Airports, Stations, Light, Removals, Any Distance* painted on the window. The letters were painted on in white and with a blue outline that had been extended outwards on each letter's right so they seemed to be casting shadows. What did *Light* mean? I picked up the phone's receiver. I didn't call anyone or put any money in the slot: I just stood there holding the receiver in my hand. When my phone socket had been ripped out of the wall it had lain across my floor looking disgusting, like something that's come out of something.

Inside the cabin it was quiet. There was no traffic passing by. My staff's vehicles, drawn across the road, formed an insulating wall between the re-enactment zone and the outside. In front of and between the vehicles people stood quite still – all mine, a lot of people – looking straight in my direction, at the phone box. Then I heard the BMW's motor start up: the sound of a spark plug firing a charge of compressed gasoline and of expanded gas shooting a piston off again and again and again – slowly at first, then faster, then after a few seconds so fast that the individual shots merged into a hum of infinite self-repetition without origin or end. It had begun.

I saw the BMW pass the phone box on the far side of the street from the corner of my eye, and again in the metal of the cabin's wall, reflected. I set the receiver back onto its cradle and opened the phone box's door. I stepped out, turned my bicycle around and swung my right leg across its bar. The two men had backed the car into the space I'd shown them and were getting out. They'd parked it just right, exactly where I'd told them to. It was very good. The tingling started in my spine again.

I pushed off the pavement with my foot and let the bike roll forwards, its handlebars wobbling. As its front wheel passed a white foam cup lying on the ground, I looked up and to my left at the two men. They'd taken out their sub-machine guns and were pointing them at me. The man with the West Indian accent opened fire. His gun made a tremendous noise. The other man opened fire too, not half a second after the first one. The noise of the two guns together was quite deafening. The affable man with the London accent grimaced as he shot. The other man's face was expressionless, indifferent, the face of an assassin.

The tingling grew more intense as I raised my buttocks from the bike's seat and started pedalling furiously, past the grilled windows of Movement Cars, down the dip into Belinda Road. The two men kept marching on me across Coldharbour Lane, firing as they advanced. Just in front of the brush-cleaning puddle at the edge of Belinda Road I turned the bike's wheel sharply to the right and went over the handlebars. As I fell to the ground a whole tumult of images came at me: the edge of the black bar with no name, a streak of gold, some sky, a lamppost, tarmac and the coloured patterns

241

floating on the puddle's surface. After I'd stopped tumbling and become still, the patterns took the form of Greek or Russian letters. I looked away from the puddle, up towards the men: they had stopped firing and were standing still, exactly where I'd told them to stand, by the hexagon-cell patterns in the road. It was all good.

The men were waiting for me to get up again. I pushed myself up with my hands and noticed they were numb. This was good – very, very good. I stood up and felt the tingling rush to my head. The two men fired again. I turned from them, dropped to my knees, then let my upper body sink back down towards the ground until my face lay on the tarmac. I lay there for a few seconds, quite still. Then I rolled over onto my back and stood up again. The two men were getting back into their car.

'Wait!' I shouted at them.

They stopped.

'Wait!' I shouted again. 'You shouldn't drive off. You shouldn't even walk back to the car. When you've stopped shooting at me for the last time, just turn your backs on me and stop.'

'What shall we do when we've stopped?' the man with the London accent asked.

'Nothing,' I told him. 'Just stop, and stand there with your backs to me. We'll stop the whole scene there, but hold it for a while in that position. Okay?'

He nodded. I looked at his friend. He nodded too, slowly.

'Good,' I said. 'Let's do it again.'

We resumed our positions. Back in the phone box, I looked through the window. The BMW was turning round by the traffic lights, beside the shortish man I'd noticed earlier. Just over half the crew and back-up people had chosen that end of the area to stand at and watch from; eight or so more were gathered at the far end, the end I'd entered from, beneath the bridge. The cabin's glass was clear, not wrinkled like the windows of my building. All the same, I looked instinctively across to the roof of the building on the far side of the road, scanning it for cats, then realized my mistake and turned the other way.

The grill across Movement Cars' façade was, now I looked at it more closely, actually four panels of grill, each panel being made up of three sections of criss-crossing metal lines. It looked like graph paper, with large square areas containing smaller ones that framed, positioned and related every mark or object lying behind them – a ready-made forensic grid. Most of the grid's squares were pretty blank. The lower left-hand-side one, though, the one closest to the pavement at the corner of Belinda Road, had two bunches of flowers stuffed behind it. They were hanging upside down, wrapped in plastic. Two grid-columns across were the painted words: *Movement Cars, Airports, Stations, Light, Removals, Any Distance.* They ran over all three of the column's larger squares; the *n* and *t* of *Movement* ran into the next column, the column to the right. It was *Light Removals*, not *Light* then *Removals*: I knew that already, but had just forgotten that I knew.

The dull red BMW passed the phone box again. Again I saw it twice: once from the corner of my eye and once reflected in the metal of the cabin's wall – only it seemed flatter and more elongated this time. When the driver turned the engine off, for a half-second or so I could make out the individual firings of the piston as these slowed down and died off. I opened the phone box's door, stepped out and got onto my bicycle. Again the tingling kicked in as I passed the white foam cup. Again the two men took their guns out and I pedalled furiously. This time when the bike dipped from the pavement to the road I felt my altitude drop, like you do on aeroplanes when they make their descent. The same tumult of images came to me as I went over the handle-bars: a portion of the black bar with no name, a streak of gold, some sky, a lamppost, tarmac and the puddle with the Greek or Russian letters floating on its surface. I got up, let them shoot me a second time, went down again and lay with my face on the tarmac looking at the under-carriage of a parked van, at the patterned markings on one of its hubcaps.

I lay there for longer this time than I had the last. There was no noise behind me, no footsteps: the two killers had remembered what I'd told them and were standing there quite still. I lay there on the tarmac for a long time tingling, looking at the hubcap.

Then I got up and we did it again, and again, and again.

After running through the shooting for the fifth time I was satisfied we'd got the actions right: the movement, the positions. Now we could begin working on what lay beneath the surfaces of these – on what was inside, intimate.

'Let's do it at half speed,' I said.

The black man with the London accent frowned.

'You mean we should drive slower?' he asked.

'Drive, walk, everything,' I said.

One of Naz's men was striding over to us with a clipboard in his hand. I waved him away and continued:

'Everything. The same as before, but at half speed.'

'Like in an action replay on TV?' he asked.

'Well,' I said, 'sort of. Only don't do all your movements in slow motion. Do them normally, but at half the normal speed. Or at the normal speed, but take twice as long doing them.'

They both stood there for a few seconds, taking in what I'd said. Then the taller man, the one with the West Indian accent, started nodding. I saw that his lips were curled into a smile.

'You're the boss,' he said again.

We took up our positions once more. Inside the phone box this time I examined every surface it had to present. My man, the victim, would have taken all these in – but then his brain would have edited most of them back out again, dismissed them as mundane, irrelevant. A mistake: perhaps if he'd paid more attention to the environment around him some association might have warned him of what was about to happen, even saved his life. He must have done something wrong, crossed someone, broken some code of the underworld. So if he'd looked more carefully at the cabin's metal wall and taken in the fact that the dull red BMW was passing slowly by, too slowly perhaps, and connected this with the last time he'd seen that car or its reflection, who he'd been with then . . . who knows? The stencilled figure on the window, the messenger, knew something was up and was trying to announce this with his horn – to blare it out, a warning; his free hand, the one not holding the instrument, was raised in alarm. And then the silence, like the silence in a forest when a predator is on the prowl and every other creature's gone to ground except his prey, too tied up in his own concerns, in sniffing roots or chewing grass or daydreaming to read the glaring signs . . .

I stood with the receiver in my hand. The digital display strip said *Insert Coins*. Outside, from beneath their grid, the windows of Movement Cars promised wide-open spaces opening to even wider distances – airports, stations and removals, light. An empty green beer bottle sat directly beneath the hanging plastic-wrapped flowers; it seemed to be offering itself to them as a vase if only they'd abandon their position in the grid, come down and turn the right way round again. The pavement, when I stepped out onto it this time, seemed even more richly patterned than it had before. Its stained flagstones ran past the phone cabin and Movement Cars to three or so feet before Belinda Road, then gave over to short, staccato brickwork before melting, as the pavement dipped onto the road itself, into poured tarmac. It was like a quilt, a handmade, patterned quilt laid out for this man to take his final steps across and then lie down and die on: a quilted deathbed. It struck me that the world, or chance, or maybe death itself if you can speak of such a thing, must have loved this man in some way to prepare for him such a richly textured fabric to gather and wrap him up in.

The killers had parked and were leaving their car. Behind them the windows of the Green Man rose up, impassive. When my man, the dead man, saw the two men heading for him with their guns out, just as his first apprehension that there was malice in the air – finally gleaned from the arrangement of bodies and objects, from the grimace on the face of one man and the cold, neutral expression of the other – developed into full-blown understanding that they'd come to kill him: in this instant, this sub-instant, he would have searched the space around him for an exit, for somewhere to go, to hide. He would have pictured the space behind the windows, a space he'd seen before: the pub's lounge with its stools and pool table, the toilets behind this with their window leading to the yard beyond. His mind would have asked this space to take him in, to shelter him – and been told: *No, you can't get there without being shot; it's just not possible.* It would have asked the same question of Movement Cars' window, and been told: *No, there's a grill here, and you couldn't pass through glass even if there weren't.* It might even have looked to the holes plumbed into the street's surface: the water outlet and the London Transport one and the ones with strings of letters and even the one with just the C – and been told, by each one: *No, you can't enter here; you'll have to find another exit.*

The two men had brought their guns out again and were raising them to point at me. I was swinging my right leg over the saddle of my bicycle, looking at them and the space around us. There was only one way out: the strip of pavement on the far side of Belinda Road. It led past the black bar with no name to the bridge and then away along Coldharbour Lane. Separated from the road by a line of bollards, it looked like a sluice, a ramp, a runnel – one that opened to another place where there were no men with guns pointing at me. That's why my man had chosen that direction. By the time he'd reached the dip into Belinda Road, passing the puddle into which his blood would soon flow, he'd have realized that he'd never make it out that way. That's why he changed direction. I went over the bike's handle-bars this time serenely, calmly, taking time to greet the now familiar moments of landscape that came at me.

The sky, this time round, had become totally consistent, clouds running together into an unbunched white continuum. The black bar's outer wall was detailed with reliefs and ridges and long lines of painted gold. The grill over the window of Movement Cars, reflected in the puddle and viewed from this angle, looked like the gridded ceiling of a dodgem ring. The letters were behind it. They weren't Greek or Russian at all: they were the *A* and *r* of *Airports* reversed by the water's surface. To the puddle's left two bottle tops lay on the ground. I lay there looking at them. My man would have seen these too. They were beer bottle tops. He would have looked at them and thought about the men who'd drunk the beers and wondered why it couldn't be him drinking them right now, these beers, off in some other place, around a table with friends perhaps, or at home with his family, instead of lying here being killed. Beyond these was a plastic shopping bag. On the bag's side were printed the words *Got yours?* Just before I stood up for the last time I murmured, to the puddle, the white sky, the black bar and the pockmarked, littered road surface around me:

'Yes, I got mine.'

My two assassins took their time in killing me.

The slowed-down pace at which they raised and fired their guns, the lack of concern or interest this seemed to imply, the total absence on my part of any attempt to escape although I had plenty of time to do so – all these made our actions passive. We weren't doing them: they were being done. The guns were being fired, I was being hit, being returned to the ground. The ground's surface was neutral – neither warm nor cold. Lying on it once more, I looked over at the phone box. It was horizontal now; the stencilled messenger was on his side, his arms spread out, a forensic outline just like I would be within an hour or so. I turned my head the other way. Everything was tilted: bollards leant away from me as they rose like plinths, like columns of temples or Acropolises. The black bar's exterior ran diagonally down the street, the golden markings on it forming dots and dashes. Its fire doors were closed; two blue-and-white signs on them bore the words *Fire Escape Keep Clear* – two times, repeated. When I let my head roll slightly back, a bollard hid all these words except for one of the two *Escapes*. Would my man have seen this, just before the life dribbled out of him towards the puddle? *Escape?*

Above the word *Escape*, cloud, white and unbroken. There was no movement anywhere. I lay there doing nothing, staring. I lay there for so long that I wasn't even staring any more – just lying there with my eyes open while nothing happened. Shadows became longer, deeper; the sky grew slightly darker, more entrenched. There was no noise anywhere, no noise at all – just the massed silence of whole scores of people waiting, like me, infinitely patient.

I never left. Not actively, at least. I have vague memories of being lifted, held above a bed of some sort, handled tenderly and delicately, but I can't really trust these. All I can report with any degree of authority is that I found myself back in my living room some time later, and that that same doctor, or perhaps another one, was shining his little torch into my eyes.

CHAPTER 13

I spent the next three days drifting into and out of trances. They were like waking comas: I wouldn't move for long stretches of time, or register any stimuli around me – sound, light, anything – and yet I'd be fully conscious: my eyes would be wide open and I'd seem to be engrossed in something. I'd remain in this state for several hours on end.

I know about these trances because Naz and Doctor Trevellian described them to me. Trevellian was the name of the doctor with the leather suitcase and the little torch – one of them at least. Perhaps they've run together, all these doctors, in my mind. At any rate, a Doctor Trevellian, who had a little torch and various other accessories which he kept in a battered leather suitcase, was often in my flat, observing me. I couldn't do much about it: I was too weak to throw him out and so prone to lapses back into my trance that I couldn't even issue orders properly. The funny thing is, though, that I didn't mind his presence. He kept very still. He didn't flap around, pace up and down or even move his arms much when examining me. He stood still observing me from a few feet away, as passive as a statue – or closer, frozen above me with his torch held steady in his right hand, casting down a beam of yellow light. He would talk about me to Naz, describing my condition:

'He's manifesting,' I heard him explain, 'the autonomic symptoms of trauma: masked facies, decreased eye blink, cogwheel rigidity, postural flexion, mydriasis . . .'

'Mydriasis?' Naz asked.

'Dilation of the pupil. All these suggest cat-echolamine depletion in the central nervous system. Plus a high level of opioids.'

'Opioids?' Naz repeated. 'He's certainly not taking drugs. I'd know if he were.'

'I'm not suggesting he's been taking drugs,' Trevellian answered. 'But response to trauma is often mediated by endogenous opioids. That is to say, the body administers its own painkillers – hefty ones. The problem is, these can be rather pleasant – so pleasant, in fact, that the system goes looking for more of them. The stronger the trauma, the stronger the dose, and hence the stronger the compulsion to trigger new releases. Reasonably intelligent laboratory animals will return again and again to the source of their trauma, the electrified button or whatever it is, although they know they'll get the shock again. They do it just to get that fix: the buzzing, the serenity . . .'

'You think he's doing the same?' Naz asked.

'He wasn't shot, was he?' I heard Trevellian counter. 'In real life, I mean?'

'I don't think so,' Naz replied.

I sat there without speaking or moving, listening to them discussing me. I liked being discussed: not because it made me seem interesting or important, but because it made me passive. I listened to them for a while; then their conversation faded as I drifted back into a trance.

Things carried on like that for three days, as I mentioned earlier – although it didn't seem like three days then. It didn't seem like any period. Each time I passed the edges of a new trance time became irrelevant, suspended, each instant widening right out into a huge warm yellow pool I could just lie in, passive, without end. What happened further in, towards the trance's centre, I can't say. I know I experienced it, but I have no memory of it: no imprint, nothing.

On the fourth day, when I was strong enough to move around my flat again, I had the papers brought to me. Two of them carried reports of another shooting. It had taken place in Brixton on the day we'd done our re-enactment, not half a mile away. Two men on foot had shot another in a car. They'd walked up to the window, raised their guns and shot him through the glass while he waited in traffic. He'd died instantly, his head all blown across the seats and dashboard. It was connected to the first shooting, apparently: revenge, a countermove, something like that.

I phoned Naz:

'Have you heard about the second shooting?' I asked him.

'Yes,' he said. 'Strange, huh?'

'I should like you to repeat the procedure you went through last week and set up a re-enactment of this one, too.'

'I thought you might,' Naz said. 'I'll get on to it.'

I walked out to the corner shop to buy more papers. It was mid-afternoon. The evening paper, stacked up on the counter, carried the headline:

Brixton: Third Man Shot as Turf Wars Escalate.

I was confused. As far as I knew only two men had been shot: my guy on his red bicycle and then this other man in his car. Perhaps there'd been two men in the car and both had been shot. But then why say 'third man'? Surely 'second and third men' would make more sense. Besides, it was today's paper. Feeling a tinge of dizziness, I bought it.

All soon became clear: it turned out that yet another shooting had happened, just off Brixton Hill. The killers had used a motorbike this time. The victim had been returning to his flat, and they'd ridden up to him and shot him without taking off their helmets or dismounting, then sped off again. I liked that: a motorbike, its weaving movements as it cut past cars and posts onto the pavement where the man would have been fumbling with his keys outside his building. Then the way he'd have seen his own face reflected fish-eye in the visors of his killers, like a funfair's hall of mirrors. The attack had been revenge for the revenge, another countermove. *Turf Wars*. I thought of those patches in garden centres, piled up in squares, then of squares of a chessboard, then of a forensic grid. I walked back to my flat and phoned Naz again:

'Did you know there's been another one?' I said.

'I do,' said Naz. 'We just spoke. You've asked me to set up a re-enactment of it.'

'No,' I said. 'I know that – but there's been another other one.'

There was a silence at Naz's end.

'Hello?' I said.

'Yes,' said Naz. 'Well, shall we . . .'

'Absolutely,' I told him. 'We'll re-enact it too. And Naz?'

'Yes?'

'Could you get Roger to . . .'

'Of course,' said Naz. 'I'd thought of that already. He's delivering the second one to me tonight. I'll get him to model the third one too.'

An hour later I switched my building into *on* mode. Before we started, I held a meeting in the lobby. All the re-enactors were there – plus Frank, Annie and their people, and these people's back-up with their radios and clipboards. I stood on the second step, addressing them.

'I want to slow it down,' I told them. 'Everything slower – much, much slower. As slow as it can be. In fact, you should hardly move at all. That doesn't mean you shouldn't do your things, perform your actions. I want you to be performing them, but to be performing them so slowly that each instant . . . that each instant . . . as though it could expand – you understand? – and be . . . if each instant was – well, that bit doesn't matter; you don't have to know that. But the point is that you have to be doing your actions very slowly, but still doing them. Is that clear?'

People looked around at one another and then back towards me, vaguely nodding.

'So with you, for example,' I continued, pointing at my pianist, 'you need to hold each note, each chord, for as long as possible. You have a pedal for that, right?'

The bald pate of my pianist's head went white and he raised his eyes from the floor to my feet.

'A pedal?' he repeated glumly.

'Yes, a pedal,' I said. 'You have two: one that muffles the sound and another that extends it, don't you?'

He thought about this for a while; then his head went even whiter as he nodded sadly.

'Good,' I said. 'Start out at normal – no, at half speed – and when you slow down, when you're in the most slowed-down bit of all, just hold the chord for as long as you can. Hit the keys again if you need to. Understood?'

My pianist looked down at the floor and nodded again. Then he started shuffling back towards the staircase.

'Wait!' I said.

He stopped, still staring down. I looked at his bald pate for a few more seconds and then told him:

'Okay, you can go.'

I turned now to the concierge.

'Now, you,' I told her, 'are already static. I mean, you just stand there in the lobby doing nothing. Which is good. But now I want you to do nothing even slower.'

She looked confused, my concierge. She had her mask off and was holding it in her hand, but her face was kind of mask-like – like those theatre masks they had in ancient times: worried, haggard, filled with a low-level kind of dread.

'What I mean,' I told her, 'is that you should think more slowly. Not just think more slowly, but relate to everything around you slower. So if you move your eyes inside your mask, then move them slowly and think to yourself: *Now I'm seeing this bit of wall, and still this bit, and now, so slowly, inch by inch, the section next to it, and now an edge of door, but I don't know it's door because I haven't had time to work it out yet* – and think all this really slowly too. You see what I mean now?'

The dread on her face seemed to heighten slightly as she nodded back at me.

'It's important,' I told her. 'I'll know if you're doing it right. Do it right and I'll make sure you get a bonus. I'll give you all bonuses if you get it right.'

I broke the meeting up and told people to go to their positions. I went up to my flat and looked at the crack in the bathroom while I waited. I hadn't gone through this in quite a while. A smell was hanging in the air: the smell of congealed fat. I poked my head out of the window and looked down at the liver lady's out-vent. It had clogged up again. The fat caking its slats was turning black. New vapour was starting to squeeze its way out, accompanied by the sound of liver starting to sizzle. Within a few seconds the new liver's smell had reached me. It still had that sharp and acrid edge, like cordite. We'd tried and tried to get rid of it, and failed – besides which, no one else but me smelt cordite. I did, though, beyond question: cordite.

The phone rang in my living room. It was Naz, telling me that everything was ready.

'Slowed right down, right?' I asked him.

'Slowed right down, just as you requested,' he replied.

I left my flat and walked down the first flight of stairs. I started walking down them really slowly; but then after a few steps I got bored, so I went back to normal speed. I wasn't bound by the rules – everyone else was, but not me.

The pianist, playing at half speed as I'd asked him, made his first mistake and repeated the passage, then again, then again, more and more slowly each time. I stopped beside the window at the stairs' first turning and looked out. I held my eyes level with a kink in the glass pane, then moved my head several millimetres down so that the kink enveloped a cat who was slinking along the facing rooftop. I let my head slide very slowly to the side so that the cat stayed in the centre of the kink, as though the kink were a gun's viewfinder and the cat a target. By jolting my head slightly to one side and back again I found that I could make the cat move back to where it had been a second earlier. I did this for a while: the more the cat moved forwards, the more I kinked it back to where it had been before, minutely moving and jolting my head as I looped it. Eventually it disappeared from view and I moved on.

My liver lady was emerging from her flat. I slowed down on the staircase as her eyes caught mine. I looked at her and breathed in and out slowly. Moving at half speed, she lowered her rubbish bag to the floor, released her hold on it and turned her head to face me. I slowed down further and she slowed down too, so much that she was almost static – stooped, her right hand hovering half a foot above the rubbish bag. She didn't say anything. Neither did I. The pianist's notes had merged into a single chord which he was holding just as I'd instructed him. I stared at her and felt the edges of my vision widening. The walls around her door, the mosaicked floor that emanated from its base, the ceiling – all these seemed to both expand and brighten. I felt myself beginning to drift into them, these surfaces – and to drift once more close to the edges of a trance.

We were both moving so slowly by now that we were, technically speaking, not moving. We stayed that way for a long time; then, still holding the liver lady's eyes with mine, I very slowly, very carefully moved my right foot backwards, up one step. My liver lady moved her right hand slowly back towards her rubbish bag. Still moving so slowly it was almost imperceptible, I changed direction again and brought my right foot back down. She moved her right hand away from the bag again, at the same speed. I repeated the sequence, kinking the fragment of the episode that we were lingering on back to just before it had begun; she came back with me. We did this several times – then became completely still, the two of us suspended in the midst of our two separate ongoing actions.

We stayed there for a very long time, facing one another. The pianist's chords stretched out, elastic, like elastic when you stretch it and it opens up its flesh to you, shows you its cracks, its pores. The chords stretched and became softer, richer, wider; then they kinked back, reinstating themselves as he hit the keys again. I and my liver lady stood there. We were standing, and still standing – then I was back in my bath, watching hot steam swirl around the crack. Then I was being lifted, held, laid down. Then nothing.

The next day I went and watched the sunlight falling from the windows onto the patterned floor of the staircase. I lay on the small landing where the stairs turned between the second and third floors and stared. The sunlight filled the corridors of white between the pattern's straight black lines like water flooding a maze in slow motion, like it had the first time I'd observed it some weeks back – but this time the light seemed somehow higher, sharper, more acute. It also seemed to flood it more quickly than it had before, not slower.

I didn't slip into a trance this time – quite the opposite. I sat back up and wondered why it should seem faster when I'd made the whole building run slower. I decided to time it, went to borrow Annie's watch – then realized I'd have to wait until tomorrow for the sunlight to flood across then leave that patch again. I stood the building down again, got some rest and staked out the spot at the same time the next day, Annie's watch – with precision sports timer that measured down to tenths and hundredths of seconds – at hand.

When I'd timed it before, the whole process had taken three hours and fourteen minutes. I remembered. Today, when the light's front edge arrived, I started the watch, then watched the edge trickle furtively across the landing like the advance guard of an army, the first scouts and snipers. In its wake the bolder, broader block, the light's main column, moved in and occupied the floor making no secret of its presence, covering the whole plain with its dazzling brilliance, its trumpets and flags and cannons. I lay there watching and timing, letting the watch run right through to the moment, several minutes after the main column's eventual departure, when the sunlight's rearguard, its last stragglers, took one final look back over the deserted camp and, becoming frightened of the massing troops of darkness, scurried on.

When I'd timed this before it had taken three hours and fourteen minutes. This time it all took place within three hours. Within two hours, forty-three minutes and twenty-seven point four-five seconds, to be precise. I didn't like this. Something had gone wrong. I called in Frank and Annie.

'The sunlight's not doing it right,' I said.

Neither of them answered at first. Then Annie asked:

'What do you mean, not doing it right?'

'I mean,' I said, 'that it's running over the floor too quickly. I measured the time the shaft falls from these windows onto the floor, from the first moment that it hits it to the time it leaves. I measured it when we first started doing these re-enactments, and I measured it today, and I can tell you without a doubt that it's going faster now than it was then.'

There was another pause, then Annie ventured, in a quiet, nervous voice:

'It's later in the year.'

'What's later in the year?' I asked.

'It's later now than it was when you first measured it,' Annie explained. 'Later in the year, further from midsummer. The sun's at a different angle to us than it was.'

I thought about that for a while until I understood it.

'Right,' I said. 'Of course. I mean . . . of course. I mean, I knew that, but I hadn't . . . I hadn't, I mean . . . Thank you. You may go now, both.'

Frank and Annie slunk back to their posts. I stayed there in the dull light of the stairwell, looking up. I thought of the sun up in space, a small star no bigger in comparison with other stars than those tiny specks of dust I'd seen suspended at the stairwell's top some weeks ago, when the real sun was closer to us. It struck me that the specks would be there now, right up above me, hanging from nothing, just floating in the neutral, neither warm nor cold air, and that when the sun disappeared completely they might fall.

The models arrived the next day: Roger's models of the second and third shootings. They were beautiful, even more detailed than the first one. A shoe shop next to where the man was shot in his car had tiny shoes in its window, and there were trees lining the street where the third man had gone down. The forensic reports arrived later that day, and I read them carefully. Naz had everything ready for the first new re-enactment, of the second shooting, two days later. I'd rested plenty so as to be strong and hadn't lapsed back into a trance for almost one week – but when we did the re-enactment, as soon as we slowed it down to half speed, I became totally weak and vacant and had to be carried home again.

A day of intermittent trances followed. Naz had scheduled the third re-enactment for the day after the second, but had to delay it for two days until I got my strength back. When we did it the same thing happened: I just drifted off. There was that widening-out of the space around me, and of the moment too: the suspension, the becoming passive, endless – then losing the motorbike, the trees, the pavement as I drifted further in, towards the core that left no imprint.

Two or three more days of trances followed this one. I'd surface like an underwater swimmer coming up for air, filling his lungs just so that he can dive again, plunge back towards his deep-sea caves and waving strands of seaweed and outlandish fish or whatever it was that has so captivated him. Sometimes I'd be hooked out, plucked and hauled right up into the daylight where I'd find Trevellian shining his torch into me, its shaft falling across my mind's patterned surfaces but managing to occupy them only briefly before it retreated and the inner darkness massed again.

Odd things were unearthed, bits of memory that must have been floating around like the fragment of bone inside my knee. I heard ambulance drivers discussing their experiences of treating people who'd been hit by different falling objects, and the varying chances of survival in each instance.

'Scaffolding's not that bad,' one of them was saying. 'Masonry, on the other hand . . .'

'Masonry's lethal,' his colleague concurred. 'But for my money helicopters are the worst. I arrived at a helicopter crash site once. The people on the ground don't only risk being crushed; there's also the rotating blade to think about. Cut you in two, it will. And the explosion . . .'

'Ah yes, the explosion,' the first one repeated. I could hear their voices clearly for a while, then they faded out.

Another bit of memory that got churned up was of some earth that had got onto my sleeve. It seemed to have come from plants, like the lush green ones the Portuguese woman had delivered to my building – only the earth from her plants hadn't got onto my sleeve. This earth that I remembered in my trance had spilled all over me in all its inconvenient bittiness, a hundred bits all rolling around and staining things and generally being in the wrong place. This image gave over to a vision of the weird man from the Dogstar, asking, again and again: *Where does it all go?* as he stood by my table, glaring. Greg was there, explaining to this man:

'He wants to be authentic, is all. That's the reason.'

The weird man repeated his line again but, although the words were the same ones, they somehow came out as *Harder and harder to lift up.* There was a gush of blue goop, then the two ambulance men were back, sifting through wreckage.

'History,' said one. 'It's lethal, all this debris. Look: propeller, head.'

'Flotsam,' said the other. 'Jetsam. All these little bits, repeating. The real event he can't even discuss.'

Their voices and the image of the wreckage faded out again, and I found myself fully conscious, staring at the model Roger had made of the first shooting. The model had been demoted from the coffee table to the carpet on which I also turned out to be lying, so it was level with my head – only its vertical plane was my horizontal one and vice versa. Right in front of my eyes was the patch of road the two men had stood on as they fired, the spot where the cracks branched out into a cell-like pattern of repeating hexagons. Roger's model hadn't reproduced this pattern, but I had a clear memory of it. As the imprint of the hexagons grew stronger in my mind, so did my memory of the moment, the particular moment, when the two black men and I had stood there just prior to the re-enactment: when I'd walked them over to the spot and told them to fire from there. I'd told them to stop there, to keep firing, but not to advance any further. The one with a strong West Indian accent, the taller one, had told me *You're the boss* and then I'd asked Naz if he'd managed to buy us more time. Now, as I lay on the floor beside Roger's model remembering this moment of instruction, the moment assumed an intense significance.

I sat up, reached for my phone and called Naz.

'Are you back with us?' he asked.

'I'd like you to organize another re-enactment,' I said.

'I wasn't aware there'd been another shooting,' he said.

'I should like one,' I explained, 'of that moment just before we re-enacted the first shooting, when we stood in the road, me and them, and I told them where to stand. I want to re-enact that moment.'

There was a pause while the thing behind Naz's eyes whirred. Then he said:

'Excellent. In the same space?'

'Possibly,' I told him. 'Let me ponder that one.'

'Fine,' said Naz. 'I'll contact the two re-enactors, and we'll get the . . .'

'No!' I said. 'Not the same ones. We need other people to re-enact their roles.'

'You're right,' said Naz. 'Completely right. I should have seen that. I'll get straight on to it.'

An hour later he phoned me back:

'I've found two people. And people to play the backup people. You should have them re-enacted too.'

'My God!' I said. 'You're right! I'll need new re-enactors to re-enact standing around in the background. We can't have the same people doing that either.'

'There's more,' said Naz. 'I've instructed our back-up people not to tell them why they're to go through the sequence that they'll re-enact. It makes it more complex, more interesting.'

'Yes, you're right again,' I said. 'It does.'

I realized as I hung up that Naz was changing. He'd always been dedicated to my projects, ever since that first day that I'd met him in the Blueprint Café – but back then his dedication had been purely professional. Now, though, his in-built genius for logistics was mixed with something else: a kind of measured zeal, a quiet passion. He defended my work with a fierceness that was muted but unshakable. One afternoon, or morning, or evening perhaps, as I hovered round the edges of a trance, I heard him arguing with Doctor Trevellian.

'The re-enactments have to stop,' Trevellian was saying, keeping his voice beneath his breath.

'Out of the question,' Naz was answering in the same tone.

'But they're clearly exacerbating his condition!' Trevellian insisted, his voice rising.

'Still out of the question,' I heard Naz say. His voice was still level, calm. 'Besides, that's beyond your remit.'

'Curing him's beyond my remit?' Trevellian's voice was a snarl now.

'Telling him what to do and what not to do is,' Naz said, calm as ever. 'He decides that. You, like me, have been hired to ensure he can continue to pursue his projects.'

'If he's dead he won't be able to,' Trevellian snarled again.

'Is there a danger of that?' Naz asked.

Trevellian said nothing, but after a few seconds I heard him snort and throw an instrument into his case.

'We shall expect you here,' Naz said, 'at the same time tomorrow.'

Despite the state that I was in, I knew then that Naz was completely onside. More than onside: he was as involved in the whole game as I was – but for entirely different reasons. I understood this more fully two days later, during a lucid patch. Naz was sitting with me in my living room, going over the logistics for the re-enactment of the moment during the shooting re-enactment, the moment when I'd told the two men where to stand. He was fine-tuning the details – who needed to do what, when, the varying amounts of infor-mation different participants needed to know, where the real back-up people should stand as their original places were taken by the back-up re-enactors and so on. He had these notes and lists and diagrams laid out in front of him across the coffee table – but for the last five minutes he hadn't been looking at these at all. He'd just been staring straight ahead, into space. He looked vague, kind of drunk; for a moment I thought that *he* was about to slip off into a trance.

'Naz?' I asked him.

He didn't answer at first. His eyes had glazed over while the thing behind them processed. I'd seen them do that before, several times; only now the processing seemed to have stepped up a gear – several gears, gone into overdrive, become almost unbearably intense. It amazed me that his head didn't explode from the sheer fury of it all. I could almost *hear* the whirring: the whirring of his computations and of all his ancestry, of rows and rows of clerks and scribes and actuaries, their typewriters and ledgers and adding machines all converging inside his skull into giant systems hungry to execute ever larger commands. Eventually the whirring slowed down, the eyes became alive again, Naz turned his face to me and told me:

'Thank you.'

'Thank you?' I repeated. 'For what?'

'For the . . .' he began, then paused. 'Just for the . . .' He stopped again.

'For the what?' I asked.

'I've never managed so much information before,' he eventually replied.

His eyes were sparkling now. Yes, Naz *was* a zealot – but his zealotry wasn't religious: it was bureaucratic. And he *was* drunk: infected, driven onwards, on towards a kind of ecstasy just by the possibilities of information management my projects were opening up for him, each one more complex, more extreme. My executor.

One day I came out of a trance to find myself lying on my sofa. At the same moment that I became aware of where I was I also understood that there was someone else in the room. I looked up and thought I saw Doctor Trevellian. Doctor

271

Trevellian was a short man, as I mentioned earlier, with a moustache and a battered leather briefcase which was always by his side. This short man was standing in my living room, but this time there was no briefcase, and no moustache either. He was short, but he wasn't Doctor Trevellian, or anyone else I knew – although I thought I recognized him vaguely. He had a notebook in his hand, with the top page flipped open. He was looking at the notebook, then at me, then at the notebook again. He stood like that for some time; then, eventually, he spoke.

'So,' he said. 'This is the man who is re-staging the deaths of local gangsters who have met with violent ends.'

I could place him now: he'd been at the re-enactment of the first shooting – the man I'd seen standing behind the waiting BMW when I'd first arrived. He looked semi-official: smartish but a little ragged round the edges. Off-smart. He had a graphite-coloured jacket on and grey streaks in his hair. He must have been forty-odd.

'Are you a policeman?' I asked him.

'No,' he said. He glanced at his notebook again, then continued: 'This is also the man who has had set up a building in which certain mundane and, on the surface, meaningless moments are repeated and prolonged until they assume an almost sacred aspect.'

His voice had a slightly Scottish edge. It was quite dry. He spoke in the kind of tone a lawyer might use to address a jury, or a serious professor of history his students. I lay there, listening to him.

'He has, moreover, had the most trivial of incidents – a spillage that occurred during a visit to a tyre repair shop – played and replayed like a stuck record for the last three weeks, residual.'

'I'd forgotten about that,' I said.

'Forgotten about that, he says?' His tone rose slightly as he uttered this rhetorical question, then dipped again as he ploughed on. 'No less than one hundred and twenty actors have been used. Five hundred and eleven props – tyres, signs, tins, tools, all in working condition – have been assembled and deployed. And that's just for the tyre shop scene. The number of people who have been employed in some capacity or other over the course of all five re-enactments must be closer to one thousand.' He paused again and let the figure sink in, then continued: 'All these actions, into which so much energy has been invested, so many man-hours, so much money – all, taken as a whole, confront us with the question: for what purpose?'

He paused and looked at me intently.

'Does he, perhaps,' he started again suddenly, 'consider himself to be some kind of artist?'

He was still looking intently at me, as though calling on me to give an answer.

'Who, me?' I said.

His eyes mockingly scoured the empty room, then came to rest on me again.

'No,' I told him. 'I was never any good at art. In school.'

'In school, he wasn't any good at art,' he repeated, then struck off on another tack: 'In that case, could it rather be that he sees these acts as a kind of voodoo? Magic? As shamanic performances?'

'What's shamanic?' I asked.

Naz walked in just then. He seemed to know this man: he nodded at him, then started tapping at his mobile.

'Who is this?' I asked him.

'A borough councillor,' Naz said. 'He kept us posted on the shooting and found us our police mole. Don't worry: he's sound.'

I wasn't worried. I felt quite at ease just lying there, passive, being talked about. The piano music spilled up from downstairs.

'He's listening to Shostakovich,' the short councillor said.

'It's Rachmaninov,' Naz told him.

'Ah, Rachmaninov. And there's a smell, a kind of . . . is it cordite?'

'Yes!' I tried to shout to him, but my voice came out weak. 'Yes: finally! It is cordite! I knew it!'

Naz's phone beeped. He read from its screen:

'Of or pertaining to a priest-doctor of the Ural-Altaic peoples of Siberia. From the Tungusian *saman.*'

'Cordite! Didn't I say, right from the beginning . . .' I began, but then slipped off into a trance again.

I saw this councillor again, the next afternoon, or perhaps the one after that. I was feeling a lot stronger and had ventured out of my building to take some air beside the sports track. I was leaning by the knitted green wire fence watching a football team train. They were practising shooting: their coach placed ball after ball on the green asphalt surface among all the intersecting lines and circles and they ran up, one after the other, and kicked the balls into the goal, or tried to. Some of the balls missed, ricocheted back off the fence and got in the next shooter's way. The coach was shouting at his players to encourage them:

'Project!' he told them. 'Will it in the goal. Take your time. Slow each second down.'

This was good advice. You could see the ones who got the balls in breaking their movements into segments, really concentrating on each one. It wasn't that they took more time than the ones who missed – rather that they made the same amount of time expand. That's what all good sportsmen do: fill time up with space. That's what sprinters are doing when they run a hundred metres in less than ten seconds: they're expanding every second, every half-second, as though the moment were a cylinder around them and they were pushing its edges outwards so it takes in more track, more for them to run down before they reach the second's edge. A boxer who can duck, feint, twist and lunge before his opponent even sees him move, or a batsman who can calmly read, decode and play the swing and bounce of the hurtling ball: they're filling time up with space too. So are men who can catch bullets: it's easy enough if you just give yourself enough room to manoeuvre in. Watching these football players shoot now, I felt a huge wave of sadness for the three men who'd been killed, and an even greater one at not having managed, in my re-enactments, to fill the instant of their death with so much space that it retrieved them, kinked them back to life. Impossible, I know, but I still felt responsible, and sad.

The coach had introduced a new rule: if a player missed, he had to run around the track that hemmed the football pitch in. Three or four of them were jogging round it sluggishly, beneath the broken loudspeakers.

'In his coma,' a voice beside me said, 'he had to give a commentary.'

It was the short councillor again. He was standing by the fence beside me with his fingers poking through the diamond-shaped green holes. He must have been standing there for some time without me noticing him.

'Yes,' I said. 'It's true.' I didn't remember telling him that bit, about the sports dreams in my coma as I lay unconscious in the weeks after the accident. 'There was a format,' I said, 'and I had to fill it, or I'd die.'

'And ever since that time he's felt unreal. Inauthentic.'

'Yes,' I replied. I didn't remember telling him that bit either, but I must have done and then forgotten that I'd told him as I slipped into my trance.

'So when, recently, has he felt most real?' the short councillor asked. 'When has he felt least inauthentic?'

It was a very good question. I'd been so busy, so driven over the last few months, moving from project to project, from the building re-enactments to the tyre shop ones and then on to the shootings, that I hadn't paused to take stock of them all, to compare and contrast them, to ponder the question: *Which one has worked best?* They'd all had the same goal, their only goal: to allow me to be fluent, natural, to merge with actions and with objects until there was nothing separating us – and nothing separating me from the experience that I was having: no understanding, no learning first and emulating second-hand, no self-reflection, nothing: no detour. I'd gone to these extraordinary lengths in order to be real. And yet I'd never stopped and asked myself if it had worked. Naz had kind of asked me after the first building re-enactment – and the question had struck me as odd. The realness I was after wasn't something you could just 'do' once and then have 'got': it was a state, a mode – one that I needed to return to again and again and again. Opioids, Trevellian had said: endogenous opioids. A drug addict doesn't stop to ask himself: *Did it work?* He just wants more – bigger doses, more often: more.

And yet it was a good question, coming as it did: here, in front of this caged-in sports pitch, from the short councillor. Venturing outside after days of trances I felt lucid, fresh, refreshed. The clang of footballs hitting the caged goal was sharp; his question sharpened my whole mind, turned me into a sportsman, made me slow time down, expand it, push its edges out and move around inside it. I thought back over the last months, and beyond: right back to Paris, to the feeling that I'd had with Catherine of getting away with something. I thought back over the serenity, the floating sensation that I'd felt when walking past my liver lady as she put the bin bag out; over my elation when the blue goop had seemed to have dematerialized and become sky; the intense and overwhelming tingling that had fulgurated when I'd opened myself up and become passive lying on the tarmac by the phone box and had stayed with me for days; I let my thoughts run right up to that same morning. And yet to the simple question *When had I felt least unreal?* the answer was not any of these times.

It was, it slowly dawned on me, another time: a moment that had come about not through an orchestrated re-enactment, but by chance – without back-up people, two-way radios, architects, police moles and forensic reports, without piano loops and licences and demarcated zones.

I'd been alone: alone and yet surrounded by people. They'd been streaming past me, on the concourse outside Victoria Station. Commuters. I'd been going to see Matthew Younger: I'd come out of the tube just as rush hour was beginning, and commuters – men and women dressed in suits – had hurried past me. I'd stood still, facing the other way, feeling them hurrying, streaming. I'd turned the palms of my hands outwards, felt the tingling begin – and been struck by the thought that my posture was like the posture of a beggar, holding his hands out, asking passers-by for change. The tingling had grown; after a while I'd decided that I *would* ask them for change. I'd started murmuring:

'Spare change . . . spare change . . . spare change . . .'

I'd stood like this, gazing vaguely in front of me and murmuring *spare change*, for several minutes. Nobody had given me any; I didn't need or want their change: I'd just received eight and half million pounds. But being in that particular space, right then, in that particular relation to the others, to the world, had made me so serene, so intense that I'd felt almost real. I remembered, standing next to the short councillor now, having felt exactly that way: almost real. I turned to him and said:

'It was when I was outside Victoria Station, looking for my stockbroker's office, asking passers-by for change.'

The short councillor smiled – the type of smile

279

that implied he'd known what my answer would be before I'd even given it.

'Demanding money of which he most certainly had no need,' he said. 'That's what's made him feel most real.'

'Demanding money, yes,' I told him, 'but also the sense of . . .'

'Of what?' he asked.

'Of being on the other side of something. A veil, a screen, the law – I don't know . . .'

My voice petered out. The short councillor looked at me for a while, then said:

'Demanding money, having passed onto the other side, he says. The question follows: What will he do next?'

What would I do next? Another good question. It should be something like the scene outside Victoria that day. Perhaps I could just re-enact exactly that: hire the concourse and get my staff to be streaming commuters while I stood with my hands out facing them, asking them for change. I pictured it, but it didn't really catch my imagination. Re-enacting it wouldn't be enough: there'd be something missing, something fundamental.

I closed my eyes and straight away an image came to me: of a gun, then of several guns – a whole parade of them, laid out like in Dr Jauhari's diagrams, with their sleek finishes, curved handles and thick hammers. The image widened: I was with my staff, all in formation just like in my dream, an aeroplane-shaped phalanx. We

280

were on a demarcated surface, an interior concourse divided into areas, cut up by screens which we were penetrating, getting to the other side of. We were standing in a phalanx and demanding money, standing on the other side of something, holding guns – and the whole scene was intense, beautiful and real.

On the asphalt pitch a football hitting a caged goal slammed me back into the present. I turned to the short councillor and said:

'What I'd like to re-enact next is a bank heist.'

CHAPTER 14

One week later Naz and I found ourselves stepping back into the Blueprint Café. We were there to meet a man named Edward Samuels. In his heyday Samuels had been one of the UK's most prolific and audacious armed robbers. Besides holding up countless banks, he'd also stolen artworks, clothes, tobacco, televisions: whole shipments of all these. He'd always stolen in bulk. He'd hijacked lorries and raided warehouses. He'd been so adept at making large things disappear that he'd earned himself the name, among the underworld, of Elephant Thief – a moniker which, apparently, those who knew him well were permitted to abbreviate to Elephant.

Samuels's criminal career hadn't gone completely without hitch. He'd been imprisoned twice – the second time for an eleven-year stretch, of which he'd served seven. While in prison he'd started studying. He'd done some O levels, and then some A levels, then a degree in Criminal Psychology. He'd written an autobiography, *Elephant*, which he'd managed to get published shortly after leaving prison. That's how Naz had hooked up with him and set up our meeting: he'd read his book, then contacted his agent.

Naz told me all this stuff about Samuels while we took a taxi to the restaurant. As he did I pictured him. I pictured him as tall and quite athletic. I was more or less right. I picked Samuels out as soon as we walked in. He was burly and fiftyish, with straight white hair. He had high cheekbones and was sort of handsome. He'd brought a copy of his book with him – or so it seemed: a book which I assumed was his was lying on the table just in front of him, but when I sat down and glanced at it, it turned out to be called *The Psychopathology of Crime.*

'Still studying?' I asked him.

'Halfway through my MA,' Samuels said. His voice was husky and working class, but had a middle-class kind of assurance to it. 'I got the bug. In prison you go mad if you don't put your mind to something. The weights are okay for your murderers and psychos, but if you've got half a brain you want to use your time to educate your-self.'

'Why criminal psychology?' I asked.

'There were psychologists in prison, studying us,' Samuels said, picking at a breadstick. 'So I asked one of them to lend me some books. At first he lent me ones geared to the patient: how to manage anger, how to cope with this and that. Within a week I'd asked him to show me the ones he read. Books for psychologists.'

'Like textbooks?' I asked.

'Exactly,' he said. 'Reading these was like suddenly being given the key to my own past. Understanding it. If you don't want to repeat things, you have to understand them.'

I thought hard about what Samuels had just said, then told him:

'But I do want to repeat things.'

'So Nazrul's informed me,' Samuels answered. 'He says . . .'

'And I don't want to understand them. That's the . . .'

My voice trailed off. The waiter turned up. Naz and I ordered fish soup, kedgeree and sparkling water; Samuels ordered venison sausages and red wine.

'Did you serve us here before?' I asked the waiter.

He stepped back and looked at me.

'Possibly, sir,' he said. 'I'll remember you next time.'

When he'd gone I told Naz:

'Get his details when we leave. I might use him for something in the future.'

'Absolutely,' Naz said. He knew exactly what I meant.

I turned to Samuels again.

'So,' I said. 'Naz has filled you in on what we want?'

'He has indeed,' said Samuels. 'You want to pay me an enormous amount of money for advice on how to restage a bank heist.'

'Re-enact,' I said, 'yes. You think you can help out?'

'I'm certain I can,' he answered. 'I acted as a consultant on a crime film recently. But it's not a film you're making, is it?'

'No,' I said. 'Most definitely not. There'll be no cameras: just the re-enactors, doing it.'

'The principle's the same, though, isn't it?' said Samuels. 'You want to re-stage . . .'

'Re-enact,' I corrected him.

'Re-enact,' he continued, 'a bank heist.'

'Yes,' I said, 'that's correct. But down to the last details, ones you wouldn't bother putting in a film. In films you just have stuff to show the cameras: just fronts, enough to make it look right on the outside. I want it to *be* right. Intimately right, inside.'

'For the audience?' he asked.

'No,' I told him. 'For me.'

Samuels sat back in his chair and furrowed his brow. He was silent for a few seconds; then he asked:

'Where?'

'In a warehouse near Heathrow,' I said. 'We'll recreate the bank there, physically. Duplicate it.'

The waiter arrived with our drinks. I watched him set them down. I decided that I'd definitely have something re-enacted around him one day, when I got round to it. He walked away again. I sat back in my chair, drew my arms out wide and said to Samuels:

'Well!'

'Well . . .' he repeated, waiting for more.

'Well: tell me about bank robberies.'

'Oh!' he said. 'Yes, well – where to start?' He picked another breadstick up, then laid it out in front of him and said: 'I suppose that, for your purposes, I should tell you about their choreography.'

'Choreography?' I said. 'Like ballet?'

'More or less, yes,' Samuels answered. 'Who stands where, who does what, when, how they move: it's all very orchestrated.'

'Choreography,' I said. 'That's good, very good.'

'Yes, it is,' said Naz. 'It's very good.'

'And,' Samuels went on, gesturing first to the breadstick's right then to its left, 'this is not just from the robbers' side. It's from the bank's side too.'

'How come?' I asked. 'They don't know that the robbery's going to happen.'

'Aha!' said Samuels. 'Wrong. They don't know *when* it's going to happen. But it's pretty much a certainty that if you have banks you'll have robberies. All bank staff are highly drilled in preparation for these. Their actions are strictly programmed. The seven rules are even posted in every branch where all the staff can see them.'

'Seven?' I asked him.

'One: stay calm and don't provoke the robbers. Two: activate the alarm as soon as there's no risk in doing so. Three: only give the amount demanded, always including the bait money. Four: don't answer . . .'

'What's bait money?' I asked.

'It's surplus money that they always keep aside to hand over to robbers,' Samuels said. 'It's usually marked, and sometimes has a canister of ink in it that's set to explode in an hour or so. Anyway: four: don't answer phones – unless they tell you to, of course. Five: don't handle the demand note if they've used one, or touch anything they've touched. Six: observe the robbers – voices, height, faces if they're not wearing masks. Seven: remember which way they ran off.'

He took a sip of his wine before continuing:

'Now, the important ones from the robbers' point of view are the first three. The staff are programmed to behave a certain way, the robbers know this and the staff know they know, and the robbers know they know they know. So a robbery, ideally, follows a strict action-reaction pattern: A does X, B does Y in response, A then does Z and the whole interaction's run its course.'

He'd snapped the breadstick in two and, as he explained this, made one half be A and one half B, reacting to one another by changing their positions on the tablecloth. Naz and I watched them, listening.

'I say "ideally",' Samuels continued, 'because this pattern is to both sides' great advantage. The robbers get their money and the bank staff don't get killed. What messes it all up is when a factor no one has anticipated and built into the pattern breaks in.' He placed the salt shaker between the breadstick's two halves to illustrate this. 'A have-a-go hero jumping one of the robbers, a hysterical woman who won't obey commands, someone who tries to run out of the door . . .'

'Like with the carrot!' I said.

'Sorry?' Samuels asked, furrowing his brow again.

'It's . . . whatever. Carry on.'

Samuels hesitated, then resumed:

'This preset pattern, when it works, which it does most of the time to both sides' great relief, is heavily weighted in the bank's favour – but only from the moment that they activate the alarm. Their aim isn't to stop you robbing them: it's to set in motion the chain that will lead to your being nabbed by the police after you've left. You can't prevent this chain being set in motion – and the time from their hitting the alarm button to the police arriving is a matter of minutes: five, seven, maybe only two. Your goal is not to stop them doing this, but to carve out enough time for yourself to get in, out and away again before they do.'

'How do you do that?' I asked.

'With shock,' he answered. 'Psychology again, see? You rush in, fire a frightener, point guns around – and the staff are too scared to push alarms, or to do anything!'

His tone had changed now. He'd dropped the breadstick props; his eyes were kind of sparkling, as though lit up by memories of rushing into banks and pointing guns. He sipped his wine again, wiped his lip and continued:

'They're like bunnies in headlights: frozen. You step in and move them gently away from the counters, get them to lie down. You use their shock to create a . . . bridge, a . . . a suspension in which you can operate. A little enclave, a defile.'

I looked across at Naz and raised my eyebrow. He nodded, took his mobile out and tapped its keys. The waiter arrived with our food. He set the venison sausages Samuels had ordered in front of me by mistake. They were grey and wrinkled, like an elephant's trunk. I imagined trying to steal an elephant and then fence it, get rid of it, just spirit it away.

'Where does it all go?' I mumbled.

'Sorry?' Samuels asked.

'I . . . nothing,' I said. 'Whatever.'

We ate in silence for a while; then Samuels asked:

'So: this bank robbery you want to re-enact. Is it a particular one? One I did?'

I set my knife and fork down and thought about this for a moment. The other two looked at me while I thought. Eventually I told them:

'No, not a particular one. A mix of several ones, real and imaginary. Ones that could happen, ones that have, and ones that might at some time in the future.'

Naz's phone beeped just then. He scrolled through the display and read aloud:

'In military parlance, a narrow way along which troops can march only by files or with a narrow front, especially a mountain gorge or pass. The act of defiling, a march by files. 1835. Also a verb: to bruise, corrupt. From the French *défiler* and the Middle English *defoul*.'

'Very good,' I said. 'Very good indeed.'

'Yes,' Naz said. 'It's an excellent term. Marching in files.'

'A defile in time,' I said. 'A kink.'

'That too,' said Naz.

'What's that?' asked Samuels.

I turned to him and said:

'You're hired.'

Over the next few days we sent people round town looking for banks for us to model our re-enactment on. They were told to pay particular attention to access and escape routes. Corners were considered good spots. Main roads tend to be trafficky, which will slow police cars down. Side roads are small enough to be blocked to prevent your being pursued, and often lead off into mazy streets of residential areas, giving you lots of options. Proximity to police stations is, obviously, undesirable. I had double the number of people search for banks as had searched for my building some months back. Their reports were gathered back at Naz's headquarters in the blue-and-white building near mine, their findings pinned up on maps and laid out in charts and tables which, needless to say, I entirely ignored.

I found the bank myself, of course. It was in Chiswick, not far from the river. I opened an account there. I put a quarter of a million pounds in it, and was immediately invited to a meeting with the manager. I found reasons to drop in – making deposits and withdrawals, picking up cards, returning forms and so on – almost daily for a week. I had Samuels, Annie and Frank open accounts and had them visit frequently as well, to allow them to familiarize themselves with the bank's layout. Naz had someone look up the firm of architects that had converted the building and procure a copy of the plans so that we'd get the measurements and dimensions right when we reconstructed the interior. It had a partially carpeted stone floor: I told Frank to memorize not only the floor's pattern, but also any stains or cracks this and the carpet had on them. Annie bought a hidden camera from a spying-equipment shop in Mayfair and photographed the walls – their notices and posters, where these had been stuck, the little tears or dog-ears they had in them – so that these, just like the space itself, could be replicated accurately.

Constructing the duplicate bank inside the Heathrow warehouse took two weeks. I'd had the tyre and cascading blue-goop loop closed down and the replicated shop and café stripped out soon after I'd decided to do the re-enactment of my giving instructions to my killers, which I'd then abandoned as soon as I'd decided on the bank heist one; but we kept two of the drivers who'd taken my role in the blue-goop tyre re-enactment – one to re-enact the driver of the vehicles in which we, the robber re-enactors, would approach and exit the scene and one to drive the security van that would arrive to collect the money we'd be stealing.

Annie had photographed the street immediately outside the bank: the kerb, its markings. There was a tiny dead-end road beside the building, just large enough for one van to park in. The security van would pull in here; we'd watched the real one do this several times. A yellow line ran all along this tiny road. When the line reached the stump where the road stopped, it curved round with the same gradient as the running track outside my building. The Council's street painters had painted it originally at a right angle – you could still see the old, half-washed-away first layer of paint extending further towards the stump's corners – but then they, or maybe the next ones a few years later, had changed their minds and made it curved. Someone must have decided: the painters themselves, or maybe the Chiswick Council Road Markings Committee, in closed session debate in the Town Hall. Anyway, Annie photographed this and we replicated it faithfully: the same curve, the same half-washed-away layer extending from beneath.

Samuels spent a lot of time watching the bank from outside, logging the times of the van's visits.

They vary these, he explained – but if you watch for long enough you work out the variation's sequence and how often it repeats itself. It always did eventually, he told me. It was just a matter of patience, of waiting it out until the pattern became visible.

'I like patience,' I said. 'But I noticed you haven't been writing the times down.'

'I log it all up here,' he said, tapping his head. 'That's why they called me Elephant: because of my retentive memory.'

'I thought it was because . . .'

'That too,' he said. 'It's all in my book. I'll give you a copy.'

He did, but I didn't read it. I was too busy watching everything come together. Three weeks after our first meeting with Samuels in the Blueprint Café we were ready to start practising the re-enactment. This one needed a lot of practice. There was so much choreography involved, as Samuels had warned us. There were re-enactors for the robbers, re-enactors for the staff, for the security-van men and members of the public both inside and outside the bank: thirty-four primary re-enactors in all. This one was by far the most ambitious I'd attempted. The most complex, too, in terms of information management: the walls of Naz's office became caked with charts: planning charts, flow charts and Venn diagrams, lists and indexes and keys to charts and indexes to lists. If I visited him there in the evenings after the practices I'd find him busy drawing up another one, or annotating one already there, or simply sitting at his desk between them all, silent, his eyes glazed-over while the whole room silently echoed with his manic whirring.

The procedure we came up with went like this: the security van would pull into the tiny stump-road beside the bank in order to deliver new cash – which was no good for stealing because it's easily traceable – and to pick up bags of old notes, which were what we wanted. This van carried four re-enactors. Two of these men would carry the new money into the bank; a third would accompany them to the door but remain just outside, while the fourth stayed in the van. Security men do this to create linked lines of sight, from inside the bank back to the truck via the man at the door – like the way buzzards hover in long lines, each one a mile apart, so that if one sees food and goes down the ones on either side of him in the chain go down to join him and the whole chain will soon know about it.

Once inside the bank, Security Guard Re-enactors One and Two would be checked in at the far end of the counter, through a set of double doors known to employees as the 'airlock' because one couldn't be opened till the other one was closed, to an area protected by armour-plated glass. Once safely inside this area, they would hand over the new sacks to a cashier re-enactor, who'd then prepare a receipt for them while they waited for the bags of old notes, stored in vaults down-stairs, to be brought to ground level in a small electric lift.

This whole transaction would take place out of view of the bank's public area. There was one spot, though, just in front of the enquiry desk, from which it could be seen. We had an accomplice re-enactor stand in the enquiry desk queue and walk out of the bank as soon as he saw the lift carrying the old money arrive. That was what Samuels called the 'showout': the sign for the robber re-enactors to spring into action.

We'd be waiting in two cars parked one on each side of the street. The first would drive over and pull up across the entrance to the stump-road, blocking the security van in. Simultaneously three of us would run out of this and three more from the other car towards the bank. Robber Re-enactor One would throw Security Guard Re-enactor Three to the floor and take his place, holding the door ajar and setting up our own buzzard-like sight chain. Robber Re-enactors Two, Three and Four would run into the bank's lobby and form a phalanx, Two firing the 'fright-ener' from his shotgun at the ceiling before bringing the gun down to point at the bank staff re-enactors and telling them to move back from their counters, while Three also pointed a gun at them. Robber Re-enactors Four and Five, mean-while, would move forward and smash the airlock's doors with sledgehammers. Once inside the armour-glass enclosure, they'd be joined by Three, who, while Two kept his gun trained on the staff and customer re-enactors, would help them carry the bags out of the bank – three large bags, one each, held with both hands in front of the stomach – with Four eventually joining One at the door to exit behind them and escape in the two cars. The whole robbery sequence had to take no more than ninety seconds.

We ran through it countless times. In the early run-throughs we had everyone wear labels on their back: R1, R2 and so on for the robbers, C1 and so on for the clerks, P numbers for members of the public. We all looked like marathon runners, or entrants in a ballroom dancing contest. We added things and took things away. The first time Robber Five carried his bag across the lobby, for example, he tripped on a wrinkle in the carpet and fell over. Everyone laughed, but I said: 'Do that each time.'

'What, fall over?' he said.

'No, just trip, but don't quite fall over.'

I calculated that if he slightly tripped on purpose, this would prevent his tripping by mistake – forestall that event, as it were. After we'd run through it a few more times the wrinkle had been flattened. I got Frank to stick a piece of wood beneath it, so that it would kink and Robber Five could semi-trip each time. Another thing I tweaked was the departure from the bank of the accomplice in the enquiry desk line – the show-out. During the first few days' practices he'd just step out, turn around and walk away. It looked awkward. I felt there must be a better way for him to do this, but I didn't quite know how. After a week it struck me:

'Do it like a tight end,' I said.

'A what?' the re-enactor asked me.

'A tight end in American football,' I said.

I'd watched lots of American football on TV after the accident, in hospital late at night when I couldn't sleep. I'd found it hypnotic: how the endlessly repeated static line-ups sprung into moving set pieces which the coaches signalled in from the touchlines by semaphore. Sometimes there'd even be two people semaphoring, one of them sending fake signals to confuse the other team's code-breakers.

'Is he the guy that throws the ball?' the accomplice re-enactor asked me.

'No,' I said. 'That's the quarterback. The tight end's the guy that's in the line but is also eligible to receive the ball. So often he's set with the others, crouching down; then just before the play begins, before the snap, he peels out and runs behind the other crouchers, parallel to them. I want you to leave the line like that. Not running, obviously – but peeling the same way.'

'Okay,' he said.

We tried it. It looked beautiful.

After almost two more weeks, when we'd got most of the movements right, we had Robber Re-enactors Five and Six actually smash down the airlock's doors. They took some breaking. Watching them smash down the first, then move into the space between the two, then smash the second one and move on, I thought of explorers moving over polar ice, or mountaineers – how they have to secure each new position, no matter how small an advance it represents, before they progress to the next. We also used real guns. Naz got some shotguns – the type used for shooting pheasants. We needed the guns to be real for when Robber Re-enactor Two fired off the frightener. He fired it at the ceiling, and small bits of plaster fell down. The first time I saw him do this I thought of Matthew Younger, how plaster flakes had fallen onto him when he'd visited me in my building when it was all being set up. Strangely enough, when I got home that evening I found a message from him on my answering machine.

'Please contact me,' he said. 'Your stocks are rocketing, but the level of exposure has become almost unbearable, and I have qualms about the sectors' overall stability. You can call me at the office, or out of office hours on either of the following numbers . . .'

As I listened to his voice, I thought of what my short councillor had said: that I was wreaking magic, like a shaman. Maybe Matthew Younger had called me and left his message at the same instant that the plaster was falling. I'd never know. I did see the short councillor, though: he turned up the next day at the replica bank.

'Just as he said beside the football pitch,' he said. 'A hold-up. He will simulate the robbing of a bank.'

'Yes,' I said. 'Re-enact.'

'And re-enact and re-enact again, one presumes,' he continued. 'His ultimate goal, of course, being to – how shall we put it? To attain – no, to *accede to* – a kind of authenticity through this strange, pointless residual.'

Just then I had to take up my position – I was Robber Re-enactor Three – but after we'd rehearsed the procedure again, I went looking for him so that I could ask him what he meant by 'residual'. He'd used the word twice now. I couldn't find him, though.

I decided to sit out the next couple of run-throughs. I put a marker, one of the spare re-enactors, in for me, stood to one side and watched. It was all working very well. The way Robber One's leg held the door open, slightly bent; the movement of Robber Two's gun as it described an arc across the lobby from inside the main door while Robber Three did the same but faster and from the floor's centre, like the second and third hands of a clock set slightly apart; the way the tight end-accomplice turned as he peeled out of the line, his shoulders inclining so the left was slightly lower than the right, then straightening again; the sight of the clerks, customers and security men lying horizontal on the floor, static and abject – all these movements and positions carried an intensity that emanated way beyond them. As I stood watching them I felt that tingling start up at my spine's base again.

Samuels came over and stood beside me for a while, watching the re-enactors running through their inter-locking sequences.

'We used to do this too,' he said after a while.

'Do what?' I asked.

'Dry runs. Simulations. Before any major robbery. We didn't just go through it on paper: we rehearsed it too, like this.'

I turned and looked at him.

'You mean you'd re-enact the robberies in advance?' I asked, incredulous.

'Well, yes, that's what I'm saying. Not re-enact: pre-enact, I suppose. But yes, of course.'

I thought about that, hard. It started to make me feel dizzy. I walked over to Naz and told him that I wanted to go home.

'What?' he said, staring intently into space.

'I need to go home,' I said again.

He stared straight ahead for a few more seconds; then, eventually, he turned to me and said: 'Oh, right. I'll have you driven back.'

An hour later I was lying in my bath looking at the crack on the wall again. Piano music was wafting up from downstairs. The steam rising off the bath water seemed to be swirling in the patterns of the bank raid: the arcs of the guns, the half-trip on the kink. I was still thinking about what Samuels had said. I tried to map it all out on the surface of the water: I let one cluster of foam-bubbles be the duplicated bank at Heathrow and our exercises there; I moved another to the left and let it be the bank in Chiswick, the real bank on which we'd modelled our replica; I sculpted a third cluster together, moved it to the right and let it be the places in which Samuels and his gang used to practise their turning and pointing and exiting before they raided banks – their pre-enactments. I lay and watched the three foam clusters for a long time, comparing them. After a while I cupped my hands around the clusters to the right and to the left of the first one and dragged these back towards the centre of the bath, compacting all three together.

As I did this I had a revelation. The revelation sent a jolt through me – almost a shock, as though the water had become electric. I jumped out of the bath, ran naked to the living room, snatched the phone from its cradle and dialled Naz's number.

'I'm back at the office,' he said. 'I've started notating where second-string objects and people are. The ones not directly involved in the re-enactment: things like the coffee table and the ladder. For if you decide to re-enact the pre-parations at a later date. We could . . .'

'Naz!' I told him. 'Listen to me! Naz!'

'What?' he asked.

'I've had an idea,' I said. I gulped, and tasted soap. I was so excited that I could hardly speak.

'I should like,' I continued, 'to transfer the re-enactment of the bank heist to the actual bank.'

There was a pause, then Naz said:

'That's good. Yes: very good. I'll go about making arrangements with the bank.'

'Arrangements?' I said. 'What arrangements?'

'To procure it,' he said. 'We'll have to do it on a Sunday, obviously. Or a bank holiday.'

'No!' I said. 'Don't get their permission.'

'I don't understand,' he said. 'I thought you just said you wanted to do it in the bank. The bank we modelled our bank on, in Chiswick, right?'

'Right!' I said. 'But I don't want them to know we'll do it. We'll just do it there, our re-enactment, right there in the bank!'

'But what about the staff? We'll have to replace the real staff with re-enactors.'

'No we won't!' I told him. 'We'll just stand our staff re-enactors down and use the real staff.'

'But how will they know that it's a re-enactment and not an actual hold-up?'

'They won't!' I said. 'But it doesn't matter: they've been trained to do exactly what the re-enactors have been trained to do. Both should re-enact the same movements identically. Naz? Are you there?'

There was a long, long pause. When Naz eventually spoke, his voice was very deep and very slow.

'That's brilliant,' he said. 'Just brilliant.'

CHAPTER 15

Naz went along with it. Of course he did. It seems strange, thinking of it now, with the advantage – as they say – of hindsight, that he didn't try to talk me out of it or bring our professional liaison to an end – just walk out, quit, have done. Going along with my decision put everything he had in jeopardy: his job, his future, even his freedom. In law, we'd be robbing a bank. There were no two ways about it. In the eyes of the staff, the customers and bystanders and police it wouldn't be a performance, a simulation, a re-staging: it would be a heist – pure and simple, straight up. A bank robbery.

Yes, looking at it from the outside, now, it does seem strange – but thinking back to when we were inside that time, intimately inside it, it doesn't seem strange at all. Even before he acquiesced with that decision, Naz's talent for logistics had become inflamed, blown up into an obsession that was edging into a delirium. If I woke up in the small hours of the morning and looked over from my building towards his, I'd see a dim light on and know that he was working there, alone, poring over his data like some Gnostic monk toiling away by oil lamp copying scripture. He looked unhealthy, sick through lack of sleep. His cheeks were pale and jaundiced. Like me, he'd become an addict – although to a different drug. This latest scheme, with its intricate complexities, its massively raised stakes, offered him a hit more perfect, more refined than before. No: I hadn't stopped to calculate the chances of his accepting or rejecting my order before I issued it; it hadn't even occurred to me – but if it had, if I'd been capable of stopping and calculating, I'd have thought it through and realized that there was no question but that he would go along with it.

And me? Why had I decided to transfer the robbery re-enactment to the bank itself? For the same reason I'd done everything I'd done since David Simpson's party: to be real – to become fluent, natural, to cut out the detour that sweeps us around what's fundamental to events, preventing us from touching their core: the detour that makes us all second-hand and second-rate. I felt that, by this stage, I'd got so close to doing this. Watching the re-enactors' movements as they practised that day, their guns' arcs, the turning of their shoulders, the postures of the prone customers and clerks – watching all these, feeling the tingling moving up my spine again, I'd had the feeling that I was closing in on this core. After stalking it for months, just like I'd stalked my building – stalking it with my small arsenal of craft and money, violence and passivity and patience, through a host of downwind trails and patterns, re-enactments that had honed and sharpened my skills – after all this, I could smell blood. Now I needed to move in for the kill.

But to do this required a leap of genius: a leap to another level, one that contained and swallowed all the levels I'd been operating on up to now. Samuels's offhand comment about dry-runs had opened the gateway to that other level for me; pushing the three bath-foam clusters together, and the revelation this had brought on, had propelled me up there. Yes: lifting the re-enactment out of its demarcated zone and slotting it back into the world, into an actual bank whose staff didn't know it was a re-enactment: that would return my motions and my gestures to ground zero and hour zero, to the point at which the re-enactment merged with the event. It would let me penetrate and live inside the core, be seamless, perfect, real.

And so our goals aligned, mine and Naz's. He needed me as much as I needed him. And need him I did, more than ever. In order for the re-enactment to pay off – to produce the defile Samuels had talked about, that sportsmanlike expansion in which we could move around and do our thing – we had to get everything co-ordinated absolutely perfectly. We'd have no chance to repeat it; there could be no slight mistimings, no slipping bin bags, leakage onto floors or falling cats – and certainly no skiving off and substituting

tapes. And then not only was total control of movement and of matter necessary – every surface,
every gesture, every last half-trip on a carpet's kink
– but so, too, was control of information. We had
to treat information *as* matter: stop it spilling,
seeping, trickling, dribbling, whatever: getting in
the wrong place and becoming mess. That's how
bank robbers who get clean away from the scene
of the robbery itself get tripped up, Samuels had
told us earlier: someone speaks to someone who
tells someone else who tells their girlfriend who
tells three of her friends, and then soon it's
common knowledge and only a matter of time
before the police get to hear about it.

'If our heist were a real one,' Naz explained to
me as we sat alone in his office one evening,
surrounded by his flow charts, 'a normal one I
mean, there'd be eight people involved: the five
robbers, the two drivers and the show-out man.'

'The tight-end accomplice,' I said.

'Right,' said Naz. 'But in our operation there are
thirty-four primary re-enactors, plus six imme-
diate back-up people, ones that need to be there
all the time, although these ones will stop being
necessary from the moment that the location
transfers to the real bank – as, of course, will
twenty-seven of the primary re-enactors –
although to call them "unnecessary" is misleading,
as it's necessary they continue to believe that
they'll be necessary right up until the last minute.
So with thirty-four, plus six, plus eleven secondary

back-up people and a further twenty-eight (at a conservative guess) tertiary ones – caterers, builders, taxi drivers, basically anyone who's visited the warehouse more than once – you can appreciate that the probability of information leakage, were we to put even a handful of these people in the picture over the next few days, is pretty much one hundred per cent.'

'Well, then we just don't tell them,' I said. 'Any of them.'

'*A*: that doesn't work,' Naz answered. 'The drivers will need to have learnt escape routes – and secondary routes in case the first routes are blocked up, and tertiary ones and so on. *B*: that in itself is only half the problem – no, one third. Beside outward leakage both before and after the event, there's the need to safeguard against inward leakage – re-enactors learning of your change of plan. And then there's sideways leakage. Look: I've marked it here.'

He pointed to a flow chart in which arrows clustered round three circles. I thought of the foam clusters in the bath again, how I'd moved them apart and then together.

'By sideways leakage I mean leakage between different staff groups: re-enactor-re-enactor, re-enactor-back-up, back-up-secondary-back-up and so on. The permutations are multiple.'

'So what do we do?' I asked him.

'Well,' he said. 'I've stratified all the participants into five NTK, or Need to Know, categories.

Within each category there's a twofold decision to be made: how much they need to know, and when they need to know it . . .'

He went on for ages like this. I zoned out and lost myself among the curves and arrows of the charts, tracing in them arcs and pirouettes, entrances and escape routes, defiles. It was light when Naz's lecture stopped. The outcome seemed to be that his NTK structure was like a pyramid: at the top, in the first category, me and Naz; below us, in the second, the two driver re-enactors, in the next the five other robber re-enactors and so on, widening with each layer. Layer Two would have to be informed of the change of venue before other layers. Layer Three could be told at the final minute, and even then wouldn't be told that the real bank staff wouldn't know that this was a re-enactment, or even be told that they were real bank staff. We'd just say we'd brought in new staff, public and security guard re-enactors to make it all seem fresher and more realistic. As for Layer Four . . .

'Fine,' I said. 'Whatever. Let's go back up to the warehouse.'

I was impatient to get back to it all – back to the movement, the swinging arcs, the peeling shoulders. When we got there I announced:

'We're going to add a bit to the whole sequence now. We're going to practise getting into cars and driving off.'

'Oh yes?' said Samuels.

'Yes,' I told him. 'Widen it out a bit.'

He choreographed this over the next two days: who ran to which car, which pulled out first, how one, turning, paused for a moment in the middle of the road to block the traffic so the other could cut off into a side street. We marked these roads' beginnings out in paint, extending the carefully copied markings we'd done earlier out of the warehouse's wide hangar-door entrance onto the concrete of the airport ground outside. I wanted the markings done as accurately as possible: the white Give Way dashes, the yellow lines. There was this one big, dark patch on the concrete where some engine oil or tar must have been spilt before we moved there; it was semi-solid, like black mould or a small growth or birth mark sprouting from the surface of the ground. I told Annie's people to remove it, scrub it off. There wasn't an oil patch on the road in Chiswick. They went at it with brushes, then with trowels, then with all types of chemicals, but it was unshiftable. On the third day of running through the get-away sequence, after I'd put a marker in for myself so that I could watch it from the outside – the cars turning, stopping, cutting, looping back – this dark patch kept snagging my attention as the cars cut past it. It was annoying me. I thought of something that the short councillor had said to me a few days earlier, and called Naz over.

'What?' he asked.

'I'd like you to have the word "residual" looked up.'

'Residual?'

'R-e-s-i-d-u-a-l'

Naz tapped a message into his mobile, then stood with me watching the cars turn and cut. His eyes, still sunk, glowed darkly. After a while he said:

'We'll need to disappear afterwards.'

'Disappear?' I said. I looked up at the sky. It was blue. It was a bright, clear early autumn day. 'How can we disappear?'

'Get out. Cover our tracks. We should remove all traces of our activities here, and get ourselves and all the re-enactors well out of the picture.'

'Where can we all go?' I asked.

'It's very complicated,' Naz said. 'There are several . . .'

Just then, his phone beeped. He scrolled through his menu and read:

'Of or pertaining to that which is left – e.g. in mathematics.'

'Left over like the half,' I said. 'A shard.'

'In physics,' Naz continued, 'of what remains after a process of evaporation; in law, that which – again – remains of an estate after all charges, debts, etc. have been paid. Residuary legatee: one to whom the residue of an estate is paid. Resid . . .'

'Accrued,' I said.

'What?' Naz asked.

'Go on,' I said.

'Residual analysis: calculus substituting method of fluxions, 1801. Residual heat of a cooling globe,

1896. Residual error in a set of observations, 1871.'

'It's because the time of year had changed. But that's not how he used it.'

'Who?' asked Naz.

'The short councillor,' I said. 'He used it like a . . . you know, like a thing. A residual.'

'A noun,' said Naz. 'What short councillor?'

'Yes, that's right: a noun. This strange, pointless residual. And he pronounced the s as an s, not as a z. Re-c-idual. Have it looked up with that spelling.'

'What spelling?' Naz asked.

'R-e-c-i-d-u-a-l.'

Naz tapped at his mobile again. I looked away, back up at the sky. A mile or so away, on the main runways, aeroplanes were taxying, turning and taking off, these huge steel crates all packed with people and their clutter moaning and tingling as they stretched their arms out, palms up, rising. Planes that had taken off earlier were dwindling to specks that hung suspended in the air's outer reaches for a while, then disappeared. I thought back to my stairwell, then to the tyre and cascading sticky liquid re-enactment that we'd done in this same warehouse. I'd told Annie and Frank to come up with something, some device, that would stop the blue goop from falling on me – make all its particles go up instead, become sky, disappear. Frank had thought of feeding it up through a tube towards the ceiling and then through the roof, transforming it into a mist.

'We could do that,' I said.

'What's that?' Naz asked.

'All vaporize and be sprayed upwards. When we have to disappear, like you said. Remove traces, all that stuff.'

Naz's eyes went vacant while the thing behind them whirred. Another plane passed overhead, moaning and tingling.

'Or just take planes,' I said. 'They'll take us out of the picture.'

Naz's whole body tensed. He was completely static for a while, his musculature suspended while the calculating part of him took all the system's energy. After a while the body part switched back on and he said:

'Planes are a very good idea.' He thought for a while more, then added: 'Two planes. No, three. We'll have to separate the re-enactors who'll have been at the bank from the others. They can't mix before they board their flights.'

'Fine,' I said. 'Whatever.'

'And then . . .' Naz began; his phone beeped. He looked at it, then slipped it back into his pocket and continued: 'And then we'd also have to separate . . .'

'Is that the dictionary people?' I asked him. 'What do they say?'

'Word not found,' he said.

'What do they mean, not found?'

'"Recidual": word not found,' he repeated.

I started to feel dizzy.

'It must be there,' I said. 'A noun: r-e-c-i . . .'

'I spelt it that way,' Naz said; 'just as you told me. They say there's no "recidual" in the dictionary.'

'Well tell them to go and find a bigger dictionary, then!' I said. I was really feeling bad now. 'And if you see that short councillor here . . .'

'What short councillor?' Naz asked.

I leant against the replicated bank's exterior, against a white stone slab. The stone was neither warm nor cold; it had an outer layer of grit that kind of slid against the solid stone beneath it. Nearby, the cars turned and cut.

'I should like . . .' I started. 'Naz . . .'

Naz wasn't paying attention to me. He was standing quite still, looking out across the runways. Luckily Samuels turned up just then, put his arm around my waist and held me upright.

'You should go home,' someone said.

I was driven back to my building. Naz came by a few hours later, in the middle of the night. He looked dreadful: sallow-cheeked and gaunt.

'What have you found?' I asked him.

'There's just one way . . .' he began.

'One way to what?' I said. 'What's this got to do . . .'

'Just one way to stop information leakage. To be absolutely certain.'

'Yes, but what about "recidual"?' I asked.

'No: this is more important,' Naz said. 'Listen.'

'No!' I said. I sat up on my sofa. 'You listen,

313

Naz: *I* say what's important. Tell me what they found.'

Naz's eyes rested on a spot vaguely near my head for a few seconds. I could see him running what I'd just said past his data-checkers, and deciding I was right: I *did* say what was important. Without me, no plans, no Need to Know charts, nothing. He turned his head sideways, reached into his pocket, took his mobile out and said:

'They found similar words, but not that one. They looked in the complete twelve-volume dictionary. Do you want me to read you what they found?'

'Of course I do!' I told him.

'Recision,' he read; 'the act of rescinding, taking away (limb, act of parliament, etc.). Recidivate: to fall back, relapse – into sickness, sin, debt . . .'

'Matthew Younger thinks I'm too exposed,' I said. 'But exposure is good. How could it all have happened in the first place if I hadn't been exposed?'

'Recidivist: one who recidivates; recidivous, of or pertaining to a . . . and so on. But that's all,' Naz said. 'No recidual.' He put his mobile back into his pocket and continued: 'I have to discuss a matter of the utmost . . .'

'I think it might be something to do with music,' I said. 'A recidual. Hey! Call my pianist up. He'll know.'

'I'll do that after we've been through this matter I have to discuss with you,' he said. 'It's absolutely

314

vital. I've realized there's only one way to ensure that . . .'

'No. Call him up now!' I said.

Naz paused again, then realized he had no choice but to comply, stood up and made the necessary call. Five minutes later my pianist was in my living room. One of his two tufts of hair was flattened, while the other sprouted outwards from his temple. His eyes were puffy; one of them was caked with sleep. He shuffled slowly forwards, then stopped three or so yards from me.

'What's a recidual?' I asked him.

He stared glumly at my carpet and said nothing. I could tell he'd heard my question, though, because the top of his bald pate whitened.

'A recidual,' I said again. 'It must be something to do with music.'

He still didn't say anything.

'Like *capriccioso*,' I continued, '*con allegro* – all those things that they write in the margins. The composers. Or a type of piece, its name, like a concerto, a sonata: a recidual.'

'Therz a rosotatof,' my pianist mumbled sadly.

'What?' I said.

'There's a recitative,' he said in his dull mono-tone. 'In opera. *Recitatif. Recitativo.* Half singing, half speaking.'

'That's good,' I said, 'but . . .'

'Or a recital,' he continued, his pate whitening still more.

'A recital,' I said. 'Yes.'

I thought about that for a while. Eventually my pianist asked:

'Can I go now?'

'No,' I said. 'Stay there.'

I stared at his bald pate more, letting my vision blur into its whiteness. I stared for a long time. I don't know how long; I lost track. Eventually he was gone, and Naz was trying to grab hold of my attention.

'What?' I said. 'Where's my pianist?'

'Listen,' said Naz. 'There's only one way.'

'One way to what?' I asked,

'One way to guarantee there'll be no information leakage.'

'Oh, that again,' I said.

'The only way,' Naz went on, his voice quiet and softly shaking, 'is to eliminate the channels it could leak through.'

'What do you mean, "eliminate"?' I asked him.

'Eliminate,' he said again. His voice was shaking so much it reminded me of spoons in egg-and-spoon races, the way they shake and rattle – as though the task of carrying what it had to say were too much. It still shook as Naz continued: 'Remove, take out, vaporize.'

'Oh, vaporize,' I said. 'A fine mist, yes. I like that.'

Naz stared straight at me now. His eyes looked as though they were about to burst.

'I could organize that,' he said, his voice a croak now.

'Oh, yes, fine, go ahead,' I told him.

'Do you understand?' he asked.

I looked at him, trying to understand. He could organize for channels to be vaporized. Channels meant people. He spoke again, more slowly:

'I . . . could . . . *organize* . . . that . . .' he croaked again.

Beads of sweat were growing on his temples. *Vaporize*, I thought: Naz wants to vaporize these people. I pictured them again being fed through a tube and propelled upwards, turned into a mist, becoming sky. I thought first of the re-enactors who'd be with me in the bank, pictured them dematerializing, going blue, invisible, not there. They'd be the first ones to be vaporized. But then the other ones, the ones who'd been stood down: they'd have to be vaporized as well. And then –

'How many channels would you need to vaporize?' I asked.

He looked back at me, sallow, manic, ill, and croaked:

'All of them. The whole pyramid.'

I looked at him again, and tried to understand that too. The whole pyramid meant not just the re-enactors: it meant all the back-up people – Annie, Frank, their people and the people that liaised between their people and the other people's people. The sub-back-up people too: the electricians, carpenters and caterers.

'The whole lot of them!' I said. 'Everyone! How would you . . .'

'When they're in the air,' Naz said, his voice still croaking. 'We get them all up in the air – all of them, every last member of your staff – and then . . .'

'Every last member! That means my liver lady and my pianist! And my motorbike enthusiast and my boring couple and my concierge as well!'

'It's the only way,' Naz repeated. 'We get them all up in an aeroplane, and then . . .'

He stopped speaking, but his eyes still stared straight at me, making sure I understood what he was telling me. I looked away from them and saw in my mind's eye a plane bursting open and transforming itself into cloud.

'Wow!' I said. 'That's beautiful.'

I saw it in my mind again: the plane became a pillow ripping open, its stuffing of feathers rushing outwards, merging with the air.

'Wow!' I whispered.

I saw it a third time – this time as a puff, a dehiscence, a flower erupting through its outer membrane and exploding into millions of tiny pollen specks, becoming light. I'd never seen something so wonderful before.

'Wow! That is *really* beautiful,' I said.

We sat in silence for a while, Naz sweating and bulging, I running this picture through my mind again and again and again. Eventually I turned to him and told him:

'Yes, fine. Go ahead.'

Naz stood up and walked towards the door. I

told him to put the building into *on* mode; he left; then I got into my bath.

I lay there for the rest of the night, picturing planes bursting, flowers dehiscing. I felt happy – happy to have seen such a beautiful image. I listened to the pianist's notes run, snag and loop, to liver sizzling and the vague electric hum of televisions, Hoovers and extractor fans. I listened to these fondly: this would be one of the last times. My pyramid was like a Pharaoh's pyramid. I was the Pharaoh. They were my loyal servants, all the others; my reward to them was to allow them to accompany me on the first segment of my final voyage. As I watched steam drifting off the water and up past the crack, I pictured all my people lifted up, abstracted, framed like saints in churches' stained-glass windows, each eternally performing their own action. I pictured the liver lady bright-coloured and two-dimensional, bending slightly forward lowering her rubbish bag, her left hand on her hip, the pianist sitting in profile at his piano practising, the motorbike enthusiast flat, kneeling, fiddling with his engine. I pictured the back-up people framed holding bright walkie-talkies and bright clipboards in bright, colourful Staff Heaven, the cat putter-outers reunited with the cats they'd posted there before them while extras hovered round the edges like cherubic choruses. I pictured this all night, lying in my bath, watching steam rising, vaporizing.

Naz chartered planes: a huge one for all the

others and a tiny private jet for us. He told them whatever he told them: one thing to Layer Two, another to Layer Three and yet another to Layer Four and so on, each of his stories calculated to slot in with the others so that the behaviour of group *B*, seen from the viewpoint of group *D*, wouldn't seem inconsistent with Story Four, nor the knowledge-pool of *C*, grounded in Story Two, spill over into that of *A* and short-circuit that group's behaviour towards – and so on and so on, every angle forecast and anticipated so as to get them all onto their plane before the cracks in the story (the overarching yarn involved a trip to North Africa, some project there, another re-enactment, sums of money so vast no one could refuse) showed, up into the air so they could vaporize, dehisce. He sneaked away for furtive meetings with airport staff and with Irish Republicans or Muslim Fundamentalists or who knows what, and came back looking, as always these days, sallow, manic, driven.

I didn't follow all that – I didn't need to, didn't want to: I was totally absorbed by our rehearsals, by the routes and movements, the arcs, phalanxes and lines, the peeling out, cutting, stopping, turning back. We'd rehearsed the get-away so many times that the cars' tyres had scored marks across the tarmac, just like the Fiesta's tyres had in the other re-enactment, the cascading blue-goop one. The black patch was still there next to them: the big, dark, semi-solid growth of engine oil or tar. I stopped finding it annoying and started wondering what had made it: something must have happened there, some event, to have left this mark. After we'd finished practising one day I went over to it, crouched beside it, poked it with my finger. It was hard, but not brash or unfriendly. Its surface, viewed from just an inch away, was full of little pores – cracked, open, showing paths leading to the growth's interior.

'It's like a sponge,' I said.

'What's that?' asked Samuels, who'd appeared beside me.

'Like a sponge. Flesh. Bits.'

Samuels looked down at the patch, then told me:

'Nazrul wants you to go with him somewhere.'

This was the day, Naz reminded me as we sat in the car being driven back to Chiswick, on which we were to tell the driver re-enactors that we'd switched the re-enactment's scene back to the actual bank.

'They're Layer Two, remember?' Naz said. 'They have to practise driving through the streets. The story they've been given is Story Three, Version One – which it is vital not to mix with Version Two.'

'Fine,' I told him. 'Whatever.'

We practised driving through the streets around the real bank. We only did the turning, cutting and stopping bit immediately outside the bank one time, and even then in a subdued way so as not to attract attention – but all the other streets we wove through time and again. It was autumn; trees were turning brown, yellow and red. If I let my eyes glaze over and unfocus the colours merged into a smooth, continual flow. In a few weeks, I thought to myself, the leaves would fall, then lie around in piles until someone carted them away.

'Like artichokes,' I said.

'This is Route Seven,' Naz was telling Driver Re-enactor One. 'Route Seven, Version. *A*. Remember that.'

'Or they might just decompose. Merge with each other and the tarmac.'

'At this point,' Naz said, 'you can switch over to Route Eight, depending on the variables. There are three . . .'

'Leaves leave marks too, sometimes,' I said. 'Outlines on the tarmac, their own skeletons. Like photos. Or Hiroshima. When they fall.'

Later, as we were driven back towards the warehouse, Naz said to me:

'Two days to go. The mechanism is being set in place this evening.'

The image of the plane dehiscing played across my mind again. I watched it, smiled, then looked back out of the car's window. The West London traffic was slow. I turned my head forward and stared through the sound-proof glass at the chauffeur's shoulders. He'd soon be dematerialized as well. I felt very affectionate towards this man. I stared hard at his jacket, letting its blue curves and wrinkles sink into my mind so that I'd remember them afterwards, when he was gone. We passed Shepherd's Bush, then broke out onto the motorway and speeded up. As we did, Naz turned to me and asked:

'When was it that you came into contact with cordite, then?'

'Cordite?' I said. 'I don't think I've ever been near cordite.'

CHAPTER 16

The day came, finally. Then again, perhaps it didn't.

In one sense, the actions we'd decided to perform had all happened already. They'd happened countless times: in our rehearsals at the warehouse, in the robbery training drills the real bank staff and real security guards had been through, and in the thousands, tens of thousands, maybe even millions of robberies that had taken place ever since mankind first started circulating currency. They'd never stopped happening, intermittently, everywhere, and our repetition of them here in Chiswick on this sunny autumn afternoon was no more than an echo – an echo of an echo of an echo, like the vague memory of a football being kicked against a wall somewhere by some boy, once, long after the original boy has been forgotten, faded, gone, replaced by countless boys kicking footballs against walls in every street of every city.

In another sense, though, it had never happened – and, this being not a real event but a staged one, albeit one staged in a real venue, it never would. It would always be to come, held in a future hovering just beyond our reach. I and the other re-enactors were like a set of devotees to a religion not yet founded: patient, waiting for our deity to appear, to manifest himself to us, redeem us; and our gestures were all votive ones, acts of anticipation.

I don't know. But I know one thing for sure: it was a fuck-up. It went wrong. Matter, for all my intricate preparations, all my bluffs and sleights of hand, played a blinder. Double-bluffed me. Tripped me up again. I know two things: one, it was a fuck-up; two, it was a very happy day.

To start, then, from the moment – the long, stretched-out moment – during which we waited, set in our positions, for it to begin, to start again: we sat, seven of us, six robber re-enactors and two drivers, in two cars, one parked on each side of the street outside the bank. We sat in silence, waiting. The other re-enactors in my car looked through the windows fascinated, watching shoppers, businessmen, mothers with pushchairs and traffic wardens walking up and down the pavement, entering and leaving shops, crossing the road, milling around at bus stops. They watched them intently, looking for cracks in their personas – inconsistencies in their dress, the way they moved and so on – that might show them up as the re-enactors they'd been told they were. Their eyes followed these people round corners, trying to spot the re-enactment zone's edge. They'd been told that the zone would be wide and not demarcated as clearly as the shooting ones had been; that its edges would be blurred, buffered by side and back streets as they merged gradually, almost imperceptibly, with real space. They'd been told this – but they still looked for some kind of boundary.

I watched too, with the same fascination. I stared amazed at the passers-by: their postures, their joints' articulation as they moved. They were all doing it just right: standing, moving, everything – and this without even knowing they were doing it. The pavement's very surface seemed as charged, as fired up as my staircase had been when I'd moved down it on the day of the first building re-enactment. The markings on the surface of the road – perfect reproductions of the ones outside my warehouse, lines whose pigmentation, texture and layout I knew so well – seemed infused with the same toxic level of significance. The whole area seemed to be silently zinging, zinging enough to make detectors, if there'd been detectors for this type of thing, croak so much that their needles went right off the register and broke their springs.

Occasionally I'd let my eyes run out to corners, looking, like the other re-enactors, for an edge, although I knew there was no edge, that the re-enactment zone was non-existent, or that it was infinite, which amounted in this case to the same thing. Mostly I'd make my head move slowly forwards past the door frame where the metal gave over to glass, advancing it so there was more window in which more street was revealed. It kept on coming, rolling in, expanding, more and more of it: people, trees, lampposts, cars and buses, shop fronts with reflective windows in which more cars, buses, people and trees flowed and luxuriated, all rolling in slowly, coming to me, here.

'It's arriving,' one of the re-enactors said; 'the van's arriving.'

I'd listened to him speak those same words countless times already, in rehearsals. I'd scripted them myself; I'd told him to say exactly those ones, to repeat the word 'arriving' and replace 'it's' with 'the van's' in the second half, although the 'it' already was the van. I'd heard them over and over, spoken in exactly the same tone, at the same speed, volume and pitch – but now the words were different. During our rehearsals, they'd been accurate – accurate in that we'd had the replica van turn up and park in the replica road as the re-enactor practised speaking them. Now, though, they were more than accurate: they were *true*. The van – the real van with real guards inside – was arriving, pulling into the real stump-road and parking. It had turned up of its own accord, and turned the words into the truest ever spoken. The van did more than turn up: it emerged – emerged into the scene, like a creature emerging from a cave or like a stain, a mark, an image emerging across photographic paper when it's dunked in liquid. It emerged: started out small, then grew,

327

and then was big and there – right there, where it was meant to be.

I watched it, utterly fixated. It was a perfect likeness of the van we'd used up at the warehouse. More than perfect: it was identical in make and size and registration, in the faded finish on its sides, the way its edges turned – but then it was more, more even than the sum of all its likenesses. Sitting above the rubbed-out and rerouted yellow line, resting on its bulging rubber tyres, its dull, pobbled steps waiting to be trodden on, its dirty indicators and exhaust protruding from its rear – sitting there, it seemed bigger, its sides more faded, its tyres more bulging, its edges more turning, its steps more pobbled, more ready to take weight and relinquish it again, its indicators and exhaust more dirty, more protruding. There was something excessive about its sheer presence, something overwhelming. It made me breathe in sharply, suddenly; it made my cheeks flush and my eyes sting.

'Wow,' I whispered. 'That's just . . . wow.'

The van emerged into the scene; men emerged from it and the whole event emerged, like a photo emerging. I didn't even need to see it. I closed my eyes and let it all develop in my mind. I pictured the scene inside the bank: Guards One and Two were being checked in at the far end of the counter; they were passing through the airlock, through the first and now the second set of doors, into the inner area. They were handing the sacks of new notes to the cashier; the cashier, in perfect imitation of our stood-down cashier re-enactor, was preparing a receipt for them and calling up the bags of old notes from the vaults downstairs, the ones we wanted. They were waiting; we were waiting; the guard in the van was waiting, and so were its pobbled steps, its indicators and exhaust; the street was waiting: yellow and white lines, kerbs and pavements were all waiting, waiting while the lift emitted its little electric whine, its cables taut with the strain of bearing these lumps up from the building's insides, shoving them out into the world.

My eyes still closed, I watched the bags emerging now, being lifted from their tray. A lifting feeling moved up through my body; I felt my organs lift inside me. I watched the tight-end-accomplice re-enactor peel out of the line by the enquiry desk and, watching this, felt weightless, light and dense at the same time. As he peeled out his shoulders inclined so that the left was slightly lower than the right; they inclined, cut a banked semicircle through the air above the carpet and then straightened again as he glided just behind the other people queuing, parallel to them, and headed to the door.

I pushed my breath out in a sigh, a rush, opening my mouth like someone who's come up from underwater to emerge into the daylight – and as this breath rushed out of me I opened my eyes and unpacked the whole scene, breathed it all out into the daylight too. It all came out just right, everything in position, where it should be, doing what it should: the bank, the street, its lines, the van. The tight-end-accomplice re-enactor was emerging from the door. Then I was emerging too, emerging from the car and gliding across the street towards the bank door as I slipped my ice-hockey mask on, my gliding and slipping mirrored by the four other robber re-enactors gliding from four different positions – two sides of two cars – towards the same point, the same door, like synchronized swimmers gliding from the corners of a pool to fall into formation in the middle.

I knew the formation – knew it intimately. I knew which bit moved where and how the whole thing changed shape as it flowed across the ground. I'd created it; I'd dreamt it up. I'd watched it from the outside, sketched and measured it from sideways on and from behind. I'd projected its components and its angles onto Naz's tables, pyramids and flow charts, seen them gather and disperse in wisps of steam rising off my bath's surface. I'd taken my position in it time and time again, moved through it, stepping, turning, swinging till each part of me knew where to go, instinctively, at every point on its trajectory. But none of that compared to now. As I and the others swept in through the door to take up our positions in the phalanx, I knew I was somewhere different – that I'd reached an intimate cell, a chamber far beneath the surface of the movements and positions. I was right inside the pattern, merging, part of it as it changed and, duplicating itself yet again, here, now, transformed itself and started to become real.

The defile yawned open. All edges – of objects and surfaces, the counters and the screens, the carpet, the edges of seconds too – seemed to draw back while remaining where they were; normal distances and measures became huge. I could have done anything: before another person's eyes had completed a single blink, I could have run about all over, gone and moved cars around in the street outside, swapped babies in their pushchairs, climbed the bank's walls and walked across its ceiling or just stood there upside down. As it was, I stayed inside the moment at which I was passing Robber Re-enactor One as he stood over Guard Three just inside the doorway. I lingered in that moment, in the instant I was sweeping past him, for a long time, taking in the posture of his leg, the angle of its knee, the straight line of his left arm as it held the guard below him while the right arm, lifted so its hand was at head level, held a gun to the guard's head. I drank it all up, absorbing it like blotting paper or like ultrasensitive film, letting it cut right through me, into me till I became the surface on which it emerged.

Then sound came in: the sound of the shotgun firing off the frightener. The sound was elongated, stretched out so much that it became soft and porous, so it seemed to have slowed down, right down into a hum, gentle and reassuring. Plaster crumbled from the ceiling and fell gently, bitty powder snow. Robber Re-enactor Two was delivering his line:

'Everybody lie down.'

He didn't shout the line, but rather spoke it in a voice without inflection – deadpan, neutral, just like the voice in which I'd made the tyre-boy re-enactors speak their lines during the blue-goop re-enactment. This line, too, was elongated; it seemed to stretch out on both sides of itself, to build itself an inner chamber in which it could be spoken almost imperceptibly within the longer speaking of it – spoken intimately, a tender echo.

Then it was quiet. The customers and clerks, the real ones who'd replaced the customer and clerk re-enactors we'd stood down, were lying on the floor like babies being put to sleep. Above them, like a mobile hanging from a cot, Robber Re-enactor Two's shotgun swung. I swung mine too, made it describe an arc across the lobby, an arc like a clock's pendulum transported to a horizontal plane – a grandfather clock's pendulum, slow, steady and repetitive.

Another sound came now: the tinkle of glass splintering as Four re-enacted the smashing of the airlock's first door; then, growing out of that sound, a second as Five re-enacted the smashing of the next door. The glass was high-tech modern glass that crumbles into bits and falls rather than breaking into jagged segments; it fell softly, tinkling like a music box – an old, antique one tinkling out a slow and high-pitched tune, a lullaby.

I started on the sequence that I had to re-enact at this point: moving across the floor and through the broken airlock to join Four and Five, pick up one of the bags and carry it back over to the door and out into the street. This, too, I'd practised endlessly – but it was different now. The bag, just like the van, was more imposing than the bags we'd used before – its weave more regular and repetitive, its thread more fibrous, the small, isolated clusters of letters and numbers dotted about its surface more cryptic than those on the ones I'd carried in rehearsals. It was baggier. It bulged just like the liver lady's rubbish bag had – bulged irregularly, in a slightly awkward way. It was hard to lift up: I felt it stretching, felt its weight being dispersed around my upper body, the way it acted on each muscle. All my muscles were articulated now, working together, merging as I carried it, merging without my having to tell them how to merge.

'A system,' I said to the cashier. 'And I don't have to learn it first. I'm getting away with it.'

I was getting away with it. For me, the bag held something priceless. Its money was like rubbish to me: rubbish, dead weight, matter – and for that reason it was valuable, invaluable, as precious as a golden fleece or lost ark or Rosetta Stone. I glided across the floor with it towards the door. Four and Five glided in front of me. Two was still standing static, moving his gun from one corner of the bank towards the other and then back again, slow and regular as a lawn-sprinkler. I raised my bag slightly as it and I cleared the airlock's stump, then lowered it again and let it glide above the carpet like a crop-spraying aircraft gliding over fields of wheat. I let my eyes follow the carpet's surface as we glided, let them run along its perfectly reproduced gold on red, its turns and cut-backs, the way these repeated themselves regularly for several yards then quickened, shortening as the carpet crinkled in the rise up to the kink on which Five, gliding two feet in front of me, was about to re-enact his half-trip. My eyes moved forward to his foot and lingered there, watching it anticipate the kink; I saw the foot surge forwards, its toes pointing downwards, backwards, turning over like a ballet dancer's toes . . .

But there was no kink in this carpet. Why should there have been? There had been one at the warehouse, but that had just appeared there. In the rehearsals, after Five had tripped on it that one time, I'd told him to half-trip each time he passed it. I'd even had Frank slip a small piece of wood under the carpet, to make sure the wrinkle stayed there. Five had got so used to half-tripping on it over the weeks of rehearsals – ten, twenty times each day, over and over – that the half-trip had become instinctive, second nature. Now, as we did the re-enactment itself, he applied the same force, gave it the same forward thrust, the same turn of the toes – only there was no kink. The carpet was flat. I saw his foot feel for the kink, and feel more, staying behind while the rest of him moved on. The rest of him moved so far on that eventually it yanked the foot up into the air behind it. His whole back leg rose behind him until it was horizontal, then continued rising until it was so high that his shoulders went down and he toppled over.

He toppled – but before he did, his upper body flew forwards above the carpet unsupported, carried by its own momentum. His arms were pulled back like the arms of a free-falling parachutist; his chest was pushed out like a swan's chest. It reminded me of a ship's figurehead I'd once seen – an old ship's figurehead with lifted head and body thrust out to the waves. I could see that he was about to crash straight into Two. I thought of carrots, and of air traffic controllers, and watched the collision unfold.

It was his head that made first contact. It went into Two's stomach, which gave in the same way the buffer on the end of a segment of train gives as a new segment is coupled with it. Five's head drove into Two's stomach, but his neck seemed to move the other way – to contraflow, its flesh wrinkling back in waves towards his shoulders. It looked like the crumple zones they build into the fronts of modern cars. Two let out a grunt as his own shoulders hunched forwards; his left hand released the barrel of the shotgun, rose into the air, then fell onto Five's back, where it stayed, tenderly, holding Five's body in place as the two of them started to go down.

Their fall was long and slow. Two's left leg had risen from the ground as soon as Five crashed into him; his right leg, though, stayed planted, and for a while held up the whole tangled composition of two heads and torsos, four arms, three legs, a bag and a gun. It seemed to be willing itself to believe it could support the knotted constellation, all this levitated matter, keep it buoyant, carry it on into some imaginary future. It couldn't, of course: gravity was against it. I watched it buckle like a giraffe's legs do in old films when the giraffe has been shot by hunters, then give up, resigning itself to its inevitable impact on the ground.

Not all of Two gave up, though: as the rest of him, all his parts and the new parts he'd acquired, Five's parts, landed over a large area of carpet – twisting and folding as they hit; compressing further in some cases and in others unlocking, breaking apart – his right hand remained raised. The gun was still held in it, the palm wrapped around the butt, the index finger hooked across the trigger. It must have been an instinct to tug back against the last solid thing there was that made him pull this. The gun went off. Four, just in front of me, crumpled and toppled too.

Now the whole scene went static, like it had been on my staircase when the liver lady and I had slowed down so much that we'd come to a standstill. Two and Five lay static on the floor, half joined and half unjoined, like acrobats frozen in mid-manoeuvre. Four lay fetal, curled up, still. I stood still on the floor behind him. The only thing that moved was a deep red flow coming from Four's chest. It emerged from his chest and advanced onto the carpet.

'Beautiful!' I whispered.

Whines spread across the lobby, running in ripples from the staff and customers, a collective murmur in their sleep as the dream they were all dreaming hit this patch of turbulence. Robber Re-enactor One walked over from the doorway, slid his mask off, looked at Four and said:

'Oh my God!'

His face was white. He slipped Four's mask off. Four's face was white too. His eyes were empty. He was pretty dead. One looked up from him and announced in a loud voice:

'Stop the re-enactment!'

No one answered. One looked around him at the whining people. He took three steps in the direction of a corner where two customers were lying. Sensing him approach, they whined more, wriggling, burrowing into the ground. One leant down, placed his hand on one of their shoulders and said:

'He's hurt. We've got to stop the re-enactment now!'

The customer let out a squeal and bucked with fear. One turned away from him and shouted to the staff behind the counters:

'It's stopped! The re-enactment's stopped! We have to stop it now!'

Nobody moved. Of course nobody moved. Stop what? This re-enactment was unstoppable. Even I couldn't have stopped it. Not that I wanted to. Something miraculous was happening. I looked at Two and Five lying on the floor. They seemed now less like acrobats than sculptures. The bag that had slipped from Five's hand and the gun that now lay beside Two's looked to me like wedges of surplus matter stripped away to reveal them. Something else was being revealed too, something that had been there all along, present but hidden, now emerging, everywhere. It was palpable: I could sense this new emergence in the very air. The others could sense it too: Five, One and Two were looking around the bank, at the customers and staff and at each other, their eyes widening, their bodies growing more and more alert, inquisitive, aroused. Then One, his voice quivering with slow terror, said, so quietly it was almost to himself:

'They don't know.'

'What?' said Five.

'They don't know,' One repeated. 'These people don't know that it's a re-enactment.'

There was silence for a moment while Five and Two digested what One had just said. One turned to me and, voice still quivering, whispered:

'It's real!'

The tingling really burst its banks now; it flowed

outwards from my spine's base and flowed all around my body. Once more I was weightless; once again the moment spread its edges out, became a still, clear pool swallowing everything else up in its contentedness. I let my head fall back; my arms started rising outwards from my sides, the palms of my hands turning upwards. I felt I was being elevated, that my body had become unbearably light and unbearably dense at the same time. The intensity augmented until all my senses were going off at once. There was noise all around me, a chorus: screaming, shouting, banging, alarms ringing, people running around bumping into things and each other. I knelt down beside Four. The blood was advancing from his chest in a steady, broad column, marching on across the carpet's plain, making its gold lines crinkle like flags in a breeze. His bag had slouched into the floor just like the liver lady's bag had; its contents, no longer suspended in space by his arm, had rearranged themselves into a state of rest. The blood was flowing round it, dampening one of its edges, eddying into a pool behind a crinkle, as though the bag and not he had leaked.

Further on, the blood column had pulled to a halt and pitched camp in the formation of an elongated oval, a deep red patch. On its surface I could see the wall reflected – and the broken glass doors of the airlock, the counter's edge, part of a poster on the wall, the ceiling. Four had opened himself up, become a diagram, a sketch, an imprint. I lay down flat so that my head was right beside this pool and followed the reflections. The objects – the doors' stump, the edge, the poster's corner – had become abstracted, separated from the space around them, freed from distances to float around together in this pool of reproductions, like my staff in their stained-glass window heaven.

'Speculation,' I said; 'contemplation of the heavens. Money, blood and light. Removals. Any Distance.'

I moved my head over to Four's body and poked my finger into the wound in his chest. The wound was raised, not sunk; parts of his flesh had broken through the skin and risen, like rising dough. The flesh was both firm and soft; it gave to the touch but kept its shape. When I brought my eyes right up to it, I saw that it was riddled with tiny holes – natural, pin-prick holes, like breathing holes. Much bigger, irregular cracks had opened among these where bits of shot had entered him. I could see some way into the tunnels that the cracks' insides formed, but then they turned and narrowed as they disappeared deeper inside him.

'Yes, really like a sponge,' I said.

Then I was walking from the bank. I walked quite calmly. No one tried to stop me. They all ran and screamed and bumped and fell – but I had a cylinder around me, an airlock. I was walking calmly through the bank's door, out into the daylight again. I was walking across the street, passing the yellow and white lines, the spot where the raised patch wasn't. Then I was in the car again and it was pulling out, cutting an arc across the middle of the street, pausing, then gliding on. The street was rotating slowly round: the mothers with pushchairs and the traffic and the traffic wardens and the people at the bus stops and the other windows full of their reflections – rotating around me. I was an astronaut suspended, slowly turning, among galaxies of coloured matter. I closed my eyes and felt the movement, the rotation – then opened them again and was overwhelmed by sunlight. It was streaming from the sun's chest, gushing out, cascading, splashing off cars' wheels, bonnets and windscreens and off shop fronts, trickling along the road's lines and markings, pulsing past people's legs and along gutters, dribbling from roofs and trees. It was spilling everywhere, overflowing, just too much, too much to absorb.

'So maybe it's okay for it to fall,' I said.

'Where are the others?' asked the driver re-enactor.

'They have the same texture,' I told him.

'They have what?' he asked. 'What was the second gunshot?'

'The same texture,' I said. 'Light and blood.'

Two of the other robber re-enactors had joined us in the car now: Five and Two I think, or maybe Five and One. Not Four, in any case. We turned and bumped into another car, paused for a moment and then glided on.

'He dented me and just drove off,' I told them. 'The guy in Peckham. I was angry at the time, but that's fine now, though. Everything's fine – even the shard in my knee. The half.'

It was fine – all of it. I felt very happy. We'd left the main road and were weaving through side streets, the same ones we'd practised weaving through two days ago. The same trees lined the road on both sides – oaks, ashes and plane trees whose red, brown and yellow leaves were merging again into a flow of colour; some leaves were falling, flickering in the sunlight as they drifted downwards. There was one fir tree too, that wasn't molting.

'A reciduous tree,' I told the others, pointing it out as we passed it.

They weren't listening to me. They seemed very unhappy. They were shouting at the driver re-enactor, screaming at him, telling him the whole thing had been real and not a re-enactment, over and over again. I turned to them and told them:

'But it was a re-enactment. That's the beauty of it. It became real while it was going on. Thanks to the ghost kink, mainly – the kink the other kink left when we took it away.'

This didn't seem to calm them down at all. They shouted, yelped and whimpered as we drove on through the falling coloured leaves. One of them kept asking what they should all do now.

'Oh, just carry on,' I told him. 'Carry right on. It will all be fine.'

I remembered saying this to the boy on the staircase. I recalled his worried face, his satchel and his shoes. I looked straight at the re-enactor who'd asked me the question, smiled at him reassuringly and said:

'You can't go back there. They won't understand. Come on with me and everything will be resolved.'

I think he understood that I was right. Of course he couldn't go back to the bank. What would he do? Explain that it had all been a performance? Throw in the stuff about fridge doors and cigarettes and carrots and De Niro for good measure? He didn't even know about all that, and didn't look as though he could have articulated it very coherently even if I'd briefed him on it. He was pretty agitated. They all were. They moaned and wept and yelped and shrieked. I listened to them for a while, trying to work out the rhythm of the various sounds, the moans and wails and yelps – which followed what, how long it took for the whole sequence to repeat itself – but gave up after a while. It was too complex to pin down right now; I'd have to get it re-enacted later. I looked back out of the window at the merging, falling leaves. These faded into concrete, into bridges, stilts and overpasses as we merged with the motorway past Shepherd's Bush. The concrete, too, was merging, flowing all around us, tilting and swivelling above us, inclining away below, dwindling and disappearing, then emerging again a little later to flow back, converge – these flowing blocks, these columns, all this matter.

Naz met us at the warehouse. He was standing outside it, just inside the compound gates. He opened the car door and looked at me.

'You've got blood on you!' he said.

'Money, blood and light,' I told him, beaming as I stepped out of the car. 'Naz, it was brilliant!'

Naz stuck his head inside the car where the wailing, yelping re-enactors were still sitting. When they started wailing at him, telling him what had happened, a strange change came over him. It wasn't dramatic or hysterical: it was more like a computer crashing – the way the screen, rather than explode or send its figures dancing higgledy-piggledy around, simply freezes. He pulled his head out of the car; his body stiffened and his eyes went into suspension while the thing behind them tried to whir. I watched him, fascinated, and saw straight away that it couldn't whir any more: it had frozen. The others were haranguing him, shouting at him that he'd known, he'd set them up, Four's dead, they're murderers, this, that, the other. He just stood there on the tarmac, all locked up. The sunlight streamed around him, falling and cascading everywhere. When his eyes switched on again – half-on, as though in shut-down mode already – he asked where the other re-enactors were.

'Who knows?' I said, stepping into the ware-house. '*En route*, caught, still at the bank. I don't know. Hey, nice work!'

The duplicate bank had been razed. You could still see where counters and walls had risen from the ground: their stumps were still there – those and a few bits of rubble, a few splinters, a few tears and holes. It was like a smashed-up and rubbed-over ground plan, a ghost replica. I ran my eyes slowly across its surface. I let them linger on the spot from which the tight-end-accomplice re-enactor had peeled out, then on the spot where I'd stood, planted, as my gun had described an arc above the floor. I still had my gun now. I was standing in the spot where Robber Re-enactor Two had stood, facing the counters and the airlock. I raised the gun's barrel with my left hand and made it describe an arc again, slowly sweeping it from side to side. I ran my eyes on to where the lift had borne up the three bags for us to carry; then I ran them back across the ground where the carpet had been, projecting back onto this bare concrete floor its golden lines, the way they turned and cut against the red, repeating.

I glided my eyes over it at a low altitude again – but this time in reverse, the way Two would have seen it as the three of us approached him with our bags. He, too, would have seen Five's foot feeling for the kink, then seen him topple, seen his torso hurtling towards him, borne by its own momentum. He also would have known that a collision was imminent, that nothing could be done to stop it. Two, the real Robber Re-enactor Two, had come into the warehouse. He'd entered, like I had, from the spot where the duplicate lift had been, the inner area. He was crying, lumbering forwards slowly, aimlessly. I'd got so into replaying the whole event from his perspective that I'd started to overbalance. I let my left leg come up and my left hand leave my shotgun's barrel; I sucked my stomach in and hunched my shoulders forwards; I let my right leg buckle, straighten and then keel over backwards, carrying the rest of me with it – carrying all of me except my right hand, which stayed raised, its palm still wrapped around the shotgun's butt, its index finger hooked across the trigger.

Two was as far from me as Four had been from him when he, Two, had shot him, Four, in the bank. He was still moving forwards, lumbering towards me. So I shot him. It was half instinctive, a reflex, as I'd first suspected: to tug against the last solid thing there was, which was the trigger – tug against it as though it were a fixed point that the body could be pulled back up from. But I'd be lying if I said it was only that that made me pull the trigger and shoot Two. I did it because I wanted to. Seeing him standing there in Four's position as I stood in his, replaying in first my mind and then my body his slow fall, I'd felt the same compulsion to shoot him as I'd felt outside Victoria Station that day to ask passers-by for change. Essentially, it was the movements, the positions and the tingling that made me do it – nothing more.

The new blast echoed round the warehouse. It made its walls tingle too – its walls, its ceiling and its floor. They tingled and hummed and sang and seemed to levitate. Sawdust took off from the floor and swirled around circling in the air; small lumps of rubble jumped. Two levitated too: he took off from the spot where he was standing – took off like a helicopter rising straight up, only he rose up and slightly backwards at the same time. He hovered for a while in the air and then crumpled back into the ground.

I got up, walked over to where he lay and looked down at him. He was lying on his back.

'He should be on his side,' I said, to no one in particular.

I knelt down beside him and pulled him into the same fetal position Four had ended up in. Two's eyes, too, were empty. He was pretty dead as well. His blood was also flowing – but it wasn't as clean as Four's blood. It had these bits in it, these grains and lumps. I poked at his exposed flesh with my finger. It was a lot like Four's flesh: it had that same sponge-like texture, soft and firm at the same time.

Naz had come into the warehouse. He was moving really slowly. Eventually he stopped a few feet from me, and his eyes tracked across the floor where Two's blood was gathering in a pool.

'Wow, look at it,' I said. 'It's just a . . . a thing. A patch. A little bit repeating.'

I prodded Two's exposed flesh again, felt it first slightly give and then resist.

'Isn't it beautiful?' I said to Naz. 'You could take everything away – vaporize, replicate, transubstantiate, whatever – and this would still be there. However many times.'

Naz didn't answer. He just stood there, locked up, closed down, vacant. He was pretty useless. I had to lead him back to the car and drive it myself the short distance to the airport terminal with the two remaining re-enactors moaning and quivering around me. We parked in a long-stay car park. I asked Naz to hand us all our tickets. He just turned his head halfway towards me and said nothing. I reached into his jacket, found the tickets, handed the re-enactors theirs and kept hold of mine and Naz's. I told everyone we'd enter the terminal together and then separate, the two re-enactors heading for their gate while Naz and I went to the special check-in desk for private planes.

'Will we have to pass through a metal detector?' I asked Naz.

Naz stared ahead of him in silence.

'Naz!' I said again. 'Do we have to . . .'

'No,' he answered. His voice had changed so it was somewhere between the same monotone my pianist spoke in and the one I'd instructed my various re-enactors to use.

'That's good!' I said. 'You're getting into it.'

I folded my shotgun and placed it inside a bag. I liked it now, wanted to keep it with me, carry it around like a king carries around his sceptre. I was feeling even more regal than normal: with Naz out of action I'd assumed direct executive command of everything – logistics, paperwork, the lot. I proclaimed to the car in general:

'There's nothing to be worried about. It's a very happy day. A beautiful day. And now we shall all go into the air.'

We left the car, processed across the car park and entered the terminal building, the others lumbering along behind me. I called a halt, mustered them all together and was about to send the two re-enactors off to where they had to go when something caught my eye. It was one of those coffee concessions, the Seattle-theme ones. We were in a different terminal to the one where I'd met Catherine, but this terminal had a concession too – although not in exactly the same spot. The counter, till and coffee machines were arranged differently as well, although they were all the same size and shape and colour as the ones in the first terminal's concession. It was the same, but slightly different. I approached the counter.

'I'd like nine small cappuccinos,' I said.

'Heyy! Nine short – nine?' he said.

'Yup,' I told him, showing him my loyalty card and handing him a twenty-pound note. 'I've got nine more to go. So: nine, plus one.'

He started lining the cups up, but a thought struck me and I told him:

'You can strip the other eight away. The other nine, I mean. It's only the remaining one I want. The extra one.'

He looked perplexed now.

'I can't really stamp the card and give you your extra one unless I make the other nine.'

'Oh, I'll pay for the nine,' I said. 'But it's just the tenth I want. You can keep the nine, or throw them out, or do whatever you want. I'll get nine more next time round.'

'Next time round?' he asked.

'Whatever,' I said.

I paid him; he stamped my card and handed me a new one with the first cup on it stamped, then gave me my extra coffee. I walked back over to where the others had been mustered. Only Naz was still there, standing all locked up and vacant.

'Where have the re-enactors gone?' I asked him.

He didn't answer, of course. I don't think he even understood the question.

'Oh, well,' I said. 'They can leak. That's good. So where's our check-in desk?'

I looked around the terminal. There was a newsagent's shop a few yards away. Outside it, a free-standing bill-board had the evening headline stuck to it. *Shares Tumble*, it announced.

'That's good too!' I said. 'No: that's brilliant! It all accrues, then tumbles. Like the sun.'

I found our desk. It was wider than normal desks, which is strange given that the planes people checked into from it were smaller. We checked in; the woman asked us if we had any luggage; I said no, just this little bag; I'd take it with me as hand luggage. We were led through a little door onto the concourse and driven in a strange electric car a bit like a golf buggy out across the airport towards a strip on which a bunch of little planes were lined up. Then we got out, walked a few feet across the tarmac and climbed some steps into a tiny private jet. A stewardess stood at the door to greet us.

'Is your friend alright?' she asked me as we passed her.

'Oh, he's had a shock,' I said. 'He had it coming, though. In all, it's a very happy day.'

The cockpit was only a few yards from where our seats were. It was separated from the cabin by a small partition door, which was ajar. As we walked past this door the pilot half-turned round and said:

'Welcome aboard, folks.'

I liked the way he half-turned, how he let his upper body swivel without fully revolving. The way he said his line as well. He said it just like pilots are supposed to say it. I'd have to get the whole thing re-enacted one day. We sat down. The stewardess said we'd been cleared to take off straight away, but would we like a drink once we were airborne? She had wine, spirits, tea, coffee, water . . .

'Coffee!' I said. 'I'll have coffee again.'

Naz didn't ask for anything. He just stared straight ahead, like a statue. The stewardess asked him to fasten his seatbelt; when he didn't react to her request, she leant over and fastened it herself. She checked mine too, then gasped and said:

'Oh! You've got blood on your wrist. There's a bit on your face, too. Let me bring you a cloth.'

'Don't worry,' I said, smiling at her. 'That's just fine. I'll take a bit of mess into the air with me. It's only fair.'

She smiled back at me a little awkwardly, then went and strapped herself into her own seat. We taxied across the ground; then we turned, paused, turned again and started accelerating into the long runway, the plane tingling, levitating. We took off, banked, rose, broke through a small, isolated bit of cloud, then stabilized. The stewardess brought coffee. She handed it to me on a tray, like Matthew Younger's secretary had – but it was in a straight cup, not the three-part type. I sipped it, then looked over at Naz. He was still staring straight ahead – but now he was sweating and mumbling nonsensical half-words beneath his breath. Poor Naz. He wanted everything perfect, neat, wanted all matter organized and filed away so that it wasn't mess. He had to learn too: matter's what makes us alive – the bitty flow, the scar tissue, signature of the world's very first disaster and promissory note guaranteeing its last. Try to iron it out at your peril. Naz had tried, and it had fucked him up. I tried to make out what it was that he was mumbling. It seemed to be data: figures, hours, appointments, places, all abandoning their posts and scrambling for the exits, sweating their way out of him, rats scurrying from a sinking ship.

The pilot's radio crackled in the cockpit. It made me think of Annie and her back-up people. They'd have taken off within the last hour; perhaps their plane had already exploded. I wondered if it would be over sea or land. If it was land, perhaps a bit of debris might even fall on someone and leave me an heir. I imagined a team of aviation accident investigators reconstructing the plane over a period of months, gathering each scrap of fuselage, piecing them all together like a jigsaw, reconstructing the positions of the passengers and baggage – who'd sat where, whose bag had contained what and so on. Back at the bank the police forensic team would already be running through their paces, the chief investigator choosing a search pattern, his subordinates making sketches and gathering prints while detectives interviewed the witnesses, interviewed eventually the two re-enactors someone would find gibbering insanely in the terminal toilets, making them go over the whole episode again and again and again. Reconstructions, everywhere. I looked down at the interlocking, hemmed-in fields, and had a vision of the whole world's surface cordoned off, demarcated, broken into grids in which self-duplicating patterns endlessly repeated.

The vision faded as the stewardess emerged from the cockpit. She looked out of sorts.

'The tower have asked if we'd mind turning back,' she said.

'Turning back?' I repeated. I thought about this for a while, then smiled at her and told her: 'I suppose not. It might be quite good.'

She smiled back awkwardly again and said:

'I'll go and tell the captain, then. That you said it's okay.'

With that, she disappeared into the cockpit. A few seconds later we banked and turned. My coffee cup slid to the side of the table top; coffee sloshed over the edge onto its surface. We righted again. The coffee trickled back into the middle of the table top, towards my sleeve. I didn't move my hand out of the way; I wanted it to stain it. It was tarry. Matthew Younger had apologized and handed me a handkerchief. *Shares Tumble*, the headline had said. Five had tumbled, Four had crumpled. Naz was sweating, mumbling. I called the stewardess over.

'A napkin?' she asked, eyeing the spilt coffee.

'It's not that,' I said. 'It's that I should like us to turn back out again.'

'Out again?' she repeated.

'Yes,' I said. 'I should like us to resume our original course now.'

She turned around and went back to the cockpit. After a few moments the plane banked again, but to the other side this time. I felt weight shifting in the cabin and my body, felt myself becoming weightless for an instant, a sensation of being held just above something. On the table top the coffee ran again. The plane turned and then straightened, heading back out. I smiled and looked out of the window. The sun was low on the horizon, making the few clouds in the sky glow blue and red and mauve. Higher up, lingering vapour trails had turned blood crimson. Our trail would be visible from the ground: an eight, plus that first bit where we'd first set off – fainter, drifted to the side by now, discarded, recidual, a remainder. In the cockpit the radio crackled again. The pilot called out to me:

'Now they're *ordering* us to turn back.'

'*Ordering*!' I repeated. 'That's pretty cool.'

We turned and started heading back. The stewardess stood still beside the cabin door, avoiding eye contact with me. After a couple of minutes I called to the pilot.

'I should like you to turn back out once more,' I said.

'We can't do that,' he called back. 'I'm afraid the Civil Aviation Authority's commands override yours.'

'That's annoying,' I said. 'Isn't there anything . . .'

My voice trailed off as I pondered what to do. I liked this turning back and forth in mid-air, this banking one way, straightening, then banking back another, the feeling of weightlessness, suspension. I didn't want it to stop. I looked around me – then I had a brilliant idea.

'Tell them I'm hijacking you,' I called back to the pilot.

I reached down into my bag, pulled out my shotgun and brought the barrel back up straight. The stewardess screamed. Naz did nothing. The pilot swivelled his upper body halfway round again, saw the gun pointing at the cockpit and shouted:

'Jesus! If you shoot that, we'll all die.'

'Don't worry,' I told him. 'Don't worry at all. I won't let us die. I just want to keep the sequence in place.'

The radio crackled more. The pilot spoke into it in a hushed, urgent voice, telling the tower what was happening. The tower crackled back to him; he half-turned to me again and asked:

'Where do you want to go?'

'Go?' I said. 'Nowhere. Just keep doing this.'

'Doing what?' he asked.

'Turning back, then turning out. Then turning back again. The way we're doing it right now.'

He spoke into his radio again; it crackled back to him; he half-turned towards me and asked:

'You want us to keep turning, out and back, like this?'

'Yup,' I said. 'Just keep on. The same pattern. It will all be fine.'

I looked out of the window again. I felt really happy. We passed through a small cloud. The cloud, seen from inside like this, was gritty, like spilled earth or dust flakes in a stairwell. Eventually the sun would set for ever – burn out, *pop*, extinguish – and the universe would run down like a Fisher Price toy whose spring has unwound to its very end. Then there'd be no more music, no more loops. Or maybe, before that, we'd just run out of fuel. For now, though, the clouds tilted and the weightlessness set in once more as we banked, turning, heading back, again.

ACKNOWLEDGEMENTS

Many thanks to:

Clémentine Deliss and Thomas Boutoux at Metronome Press, for first bringing *Remainder* into the public realm with the MP Paris edition of 2005; Alessandro Gallenzi, Elisabetta Minervini and Mike Stocks at Alma Books, for the dedication they have shown in the preparation of the first UK edition; Jonny Pegg and Mike Shaw at Curtis Brown, for their untiring support; and Johnny Rich and Tarquin Edwards, for generously sharing their experiences of (post-) trauma with me.